Praise for the Jaya Jones Trea

"Charming characters, a hint of romanti
amount of danger will garner more fans

...../.ers Weekly

"With a world-class puzzle to solve and riveting plot twists to unravel, *Quicksand* had me on the edge of my seat for the entire book...Don't miss one of the best new mystery series around!"
— Kate Carlisle,
New York Times Bestselling Author of the Bibliophile Mysteries

"A delicious tall tale about a treasure map, magicians, musicians, mysterious ancestors, and a few bad men."
— *Mystery Scene Magazine*

"A joy-filled ride of suspenseful action, elaborate scams, and witty dialogue. The villains are as wily as the heroes, and every twist is intelligent and unexpected, ensuring that this is a novel that will delight lovers of history, romance, and elaborate capers."
— *Kings River Life Magazine*

"Forget about Indiana Jones. Jaya Jones is swinging into action, using both her mind and wits to solve a mystery...Readers will be ensnared by this entertaining tale."
— *RT Book Reviews* (four stars)

"*Quicksand* has all the ingredients I love—intrigue, witty banter, and a twisty mystery that hopscotches across France!"
— Sara Rosett,
Author of the Ellie Avery Mystery Series

"Pandian's second entry sets a playful tone yet provides enough twists to keep mystery buffs engaged, too. The author streamlines an intricate plot....[and] brings a dynamic freshness to her cozy."
— *Library Journal*

"If Indiana Jones had a sister, it would definitely be historian Jaya Jones."

— *Suspense Magazine*

"Has everything a mystery lover could ask for: ghostly presences, Italian aristocrats, jewel thieves, failed actors, sitar players, and magic tricks, not to mention dabs of authentic history and academic skullduggery."

— *Publishers Weekly*

"Move over Vicky Bliss and Joan Wilder, historian Jaya Jones is here to stay! Mysterious maps, legendary pirates, and hidden treasure—Jaya's latest quest is a whirlwind of adventure."

— Chantelle Aimée Osman,
The Sirens of Suspense

"*Pirate Vishnu* is fast-paced and fascinating as Jaya's investigation leads her this time to India and back to her own family's secrets."

—Susan C. Shea,
Author of the Dani O'Rourke mysteries

"Pandian's new series may well captivate a generation of readers, combining the suspenseful, mysterious and romantic. Four stars."

— *RT Book Reviews*

"Witty, clever, and twisty... Do you like Agatha Christie? Elizabeth Peters? Then you're going to love Gigi Pandian."

— Aaron Elkins,
Edgar Award-Winning Author of the Gideon Oliver Mysteries

"Fans of Elizabeth Peters will adore following along with Jaya Jones and a cast of quirky characters as they pursue a fabled treasure."

—Juliet Blackwell,
New York Times Bestselling Author of the Art Lover's Mysteries

THE GLASS THIEF

**The Jaya Jones Treasure Hunt Mystery Series
by Gigi Pandian**

<u>Novels</u>

ARTIFACT (#1)
PIRATE VISHNU (#2)
QUICKSAND (#3)
MICHELANGELO'S GHOST (#4)
THE NINJA'S ILLUSION (#5)
THE GLASS THIEF (#6)

<u>Short Stories</u>

THE LIBRARY GHOST OF TANGLEWOOD INN
THE CAMBODIAN CURSE & OTHER STORIES

THE GLASS THIEF

A JAYA JONES TREASURE HUNT MYSTERY

GIGI PANDIAN

HENERY PRESS

Copyright

THE GLASS THIEF
A Jaya Jones Treasure Hunt Mystery Collection
Part of the Henery Press Mystery Collection

First Edition | November 2019

Henery Press
www.henerypress.com

Trade Paperback ISBN-13: 978-1-63511-555-0
Digital epub ISBN-13: 978-1-63511-556-7
Kindle ISBN-13: 978-1-63511-557-4
Hardcover ISBN-13: 978-1-63511-558-1

Printed in the United States of America

To the memory of Elizabeth Peters (Barbara Mertz),
whose intrepid heroines inspired Jaya Jones.

ACKNOWLEDGMENTS

I'm grateful for so many people who made this book possible. My critique partners Nancy Adams, Emberly Nesbitt, Sue Parman, Brian Selfon, and Diane Vallere. Additional early readers Ellen Byron, Joe Crawford, Nancy Tingley, and Stina Va. At Henery Press, my editor Maria Edwards for keen insights, and Kendel Lynn for believing in Jaya from the start. My agent Jill Marsal, for ten years of support and guidance (ten years!).

For research help, big thanks to Stina Va for pointing out what did and didn't ring true about Cambodia, Nancy Tingley for Southeast Asian art history expertise, and John Stucky at San Francisco's Asian Art Museum who searched for *nagas* with me. In Cambodia, my guides Mr. Ratha and Mr. Pel, tuk-tuk driver Mr. Visith, and countless others who generously answered my questions—and shared their recipes. Any mistakes in these pages are my own.

For inspiration, thanks to Shelly Dickson Carr for inspiring me to write a locked-room mystery into a full-length novel for the first time, and Beth Mertz for giving her blessing for how I pay homage to her mom Elizabeth Peters' character Vicky Bliss in *The Glass Thief*.

And for making all of this possible, my wonderful family, who've always believed in me, and my readers, without whom this wouldn't be nearly as fun. It's because of you that this series will be continuing. Thank you.

For additional goodies to express my thanks, you can sign up for my email newsletter: gigipandian.com/newsletter.

Prologue

Paris, France

As the clock struck midnight two nights before Christmas, and dim rays of moonlight shone through the stained-glass windows of the old mansion, the Delacroix family's prized Serpent King sculpture vanished and prodigal son Luc was murdered—for the second time that day.

Luc's strange death wasn't the first to have taken place in this haunted mansion. Nor was it the first time the Serpent King had caused a death in the family.

Perhaps we should start at the true beginning of the story.

The first suspicious death at the Parisian mansion took place nearly seventy years ago. It was two nights before Christmas in 1950 when an invisible assailant pushed Beauregard Delacroix down the stairs. Exactly one year later, Beauregard's widow Delphine suffered the same fate. Only this time, the unfortunate victim lived long enough to identify her killer—a ghost.

Thus, each year since 1951, on the night before Christmas Eve, the Delacroix family made it a point to leave their home before dusk, not returning until daybreak the next morning. There was no discussion of alternatives. They knew no mortal security could protect them.

Tragedy had followed the family across continents. The

family fortunes had come from Beauregard's grandfather Algernon, a high-ranking official in India with the French East India Company. Algernon had fallen victim to an early death from a tropical fever.

Algernon was outwardly a gentle man who helped those less fortunate. But if you were unfortunate enough to get a closer look, in private grandfather Algernon was a brutal tyrant. And his grandson Beauregard was his most apt pupil. One who would prove to be Algernon's worthy successor. By 1950, Beauregard Delacroix had turned around the fortunes of his once-great family's tea business, no small accomplishment in post-war France.

Yet one can't maintain an empire without making enemies. You must never show weakness. You must work your employees to the bone. You should proudly display the riches your noble ancestors rescued from heathen countries. And if your family demanded too much of you, they should be put in their place. They were not the ones rebuilding the family's stature. "Spend time with my children?" he was known to remark, aghast at the thought. "That's what a wife and the governess are for."

That was how it came to be that on the snowy winter's night in 1950, the women and children of the household were the ones who had decorated for Christmas. Yet all was not silent after they had gone to sleep. As the clock struck midnight, Beauregard Delacroix was pushed down the winding staircase of the palatial Parisian mansion so forcefully that he broke his neck. Nobody in the grand household admitted to seeing or hearing a thing.

During the year that followed Beauregard's death, his wife Delphine proved you could run a thriving tea company without exploiting your workers, and that you could be a good mother and run a business. But someone in the house was displeased with her methods. Strange occurrences began to take place. Always at night, when people were sleeping. Unexplained footsteps. Delphine found her possessions moved from room to room. The children were tired from sleepless nights, certain they felt the presence of someone watching them. *Surely it couldn't be Beauregard speaking to her from beyond the grave, could it?* *Delphine herself wouldn't admit this fanciful weakness, yet makeup didn't fool the governess or the housekeeper, who saw the dark circles under their employer's eyes.*

Delphine was hopeful that Christmas would cheer the worried household. Desperate, it could be said. On the first anniversary of her husband's death, she took her two children to visit Beauregard's grave, then returned to their home to prepare for the guests who would be arriving the next day for Christmas Eve. With the Christmas tree adorned, the staircase bannisters woven with ivy, and the mistletoe hung, the household went to bed contented at eleven o'clock.

They were all awakened an hour later, when a wail echoed through the walls. All the witnesses agreed it wasn't a scream. It was an otherworldly wail.

Tying dressing gowns around them, each crept out of their bedrooms. The daughter. The son. The governess. The cook. The housekeeper.

They found Delphine Delacroix lying at the bottom of the staircase.

"She's breathing!" the housekeeper cried.

"Beauregard." Delphine's voice was weak.

"Your husband has passed," the housekeeper murmured softly.

"No." Delphine's voice was firmer now, though still shaky. "He pushed me. Because of the Serpent."

With her last ounce of strength, she lifted her thin arm and pointed at the portrait that had hung over the staircase for as long as she'd lived in that cursed house.

"You see?" she hissed. "He's watching us."

All eyes followed Delphine's gaze to the painting of the family patriarch, Algernon Delacroix. Only now...it was no longer Algernon's face in the painting. The change was unmistakable. The face now looked like his son, the late Beauregard Delacroix.

"The master's ghost!" the governess cried. "His ghost did this to Madame Delacroix!"

Delphine Delacroix lost consciousness, never to wake again. Leaving her family and staff to wonder what exactly had happened that night. What had she meant about the Serpent? And could the ghost of her husband be real? Since that night, no member of the Delacroix family would sleep in the mansion on that fateful anniversary.

Yet memories fade. People try to forget the horrors that put a stain on a family. And the new generation questions the folly of their elders.

The family ghost was supernatural hogwash, Luc Delacroix had always said to himself. Thus it came to be that Beauregard's cocky grandson decided to disregard his mother and his young wife's pleas and thumb his nose at family superstition.

He should have listened. Perhaps then he could have avoided his own premature death, which was an even stranger story than being killed by the ghost of his angry ancestor.

Luc brushed off any sense of foreboding as he and his friend Tristan Rubens walked through the snowy path that led to the house where he'd grown up. Darkness was falling, and they'd brought two bottles of wine and a picnic basket with baguettes, cheese, and Christmas treats. There was no such thing as ghosts, the friends told themselves. Tonight, they would prove everyone wrong.

As the clouds parted and a bright moon shone through the windows of the old mansion on the frigid evening two days before Christmas, the serpent statue originally looted from the tea plantations of Munnar disappeared from the house, and Luc Delacroix met his end two ways.

First, strangled beyond locked glass doors as his friend looked on in horror until there was no life left in Luc Delacroix's body. Then, the ghost brought Luc back to life, only to kill him a second time, this time mirroring his grandfather Beauregard's death. The invisible hand that had raised Luc from the dead pushed him down the stairs.

The ghost's anger was growing. What would it do next?

CHAPTER 1

"I'm a patient man." Raj waved the phone in front of my face and scowled. "But the restaurant isn't your personal answering service. We need the line clear for reservations."

I dropped my messenger bag to the floor and took the phone. "This is Jaya."

"You weren't answering your phone."

The voice was that of Miles, my underemployed poet neighbor who was working as my assistant. He was also dating my friend Tamarind, so I saw him quite a bit these days. Frequently enough to know he hated using the phone.

"I was in my car," I said.

"Glad I found you. You'll be there for a while?" There was a nervous cadence in his voice as he spoke.

"Yeah, what's up?"

"I'll be there soon." The line went dead.

I blinked at the phone for a few seconds before handing it back to Raj.

"Everything okay?" His anger was gone, replaced by fatherly concern.

"I hope so."

I'd arrived at the Tandoori Palace only moments before, hoping to eat an early dinner before my first set of the evening. I play tabla as live background music at the restaurant twice a week, accompanying my best friend Sanjay, who plays the sitar. It's a hobby for both of us, nothing we take too seriously, but a good way to release the tension from our demanding careers, mine as a historian and his as a stage magician. Being a historian might sound like a low-key job, but my experience has been about as far from relaxing as is humanly possible. Besides playing the tabla to let off steam, I also go on long runs in Golden Gate Park with bhangra music on my headphones and read pulpy adventure novels like Rick Coronado thrillers, those deliciously cheesy adventure novels staring Gabriela Glass. Though between teaching, research, and tracking down missing pieces of history around the world, I didn't have much time for anything else these days.

What was so important it couldn't wait and that Miles wouldn't tell me over the phone?

Before I could go in search of food to distract me from wondering about Miles, the break room door burst open with such force that it smacked into the row of lockers. I expected it would be one of tonight's servers or cooks dropping off their bag after arriving late. But none of the three people who walked in worked at the restaurant.

"There she is," Tamarind said, pointing at me. "Thank God we made it in time."

I have a doctorate in history, not medicine, so those aren't generally words I hear directed at me.

"You don't have your first music set for half an hour, right?"

I nodded, a sinking feeling filling my empty stomach. "What's the emergency?"

Tamarind strode across the room and picked up the messenger bag at my feet. "Not here. Too many ears. Is your car nearby?"

"You know it's only got two seats, right? And now you've got me really worried."

"We're sorry to interrupt, Dr. Jones," the young woman next to Tamarind said. "And we didn't mean to worry you. It's nothing like that."

Becca Courtland was one of the students in my advanced history seminar. The older I got, the younger students looked to me. But in Becca's case, it was justified. She had a perpetually innocent expression, as if waiting to be astonished by the world. It made her look like she was attending her first day of college, though she was in fact in her junior year. I envied her optimism. I wished I could recapture that feeling.

I recognized the young man next to her, but he wasn't in a class with me this semester. I was fairly certain his name was Wesley Oh. His black hair stood on end at various angles, as if he'd been struck by lightning, and I couldn't for the life of me tell if the look was purposeful or not.

Wesley grinned shyly as he ran a hand through the messy mop of hair. "It's not an emergency. Not exactly. We need your help."

"These two," Tamarind said, ushering them into seats around the break room's round wooden table, "made the biggest discovery at the library this afternoon."

Tamarind Ortega was a librarian at my university's library, so the enthusiastic grin on her face was understandable. I knew her well enough that I should have guessed the urgency and secrecy involved a library discovery.

One of my best friends, the librarian was a few years younger than my thirty-one years, and we'd met at the library shortly after I started my job as an assistant professor of history. It was sisterhood at first sight. She was nearly a foot taller and twice as heavy as me, so we were never confused for each other, but people frequently underestimated both of us. We'd bonded over our love for academia in spite of the fact that neither of us looked or acted like traditional academics.

"You'd already left your office hours," Wesley said as he slid his backpack off his shoulders and under the table. "Tamarind thought we'd be able to catch you here. Sorry to interrupt your evening, Jaya, but we didn't want to wait until tomorrow."

I tried to cover my amused smile as I joined them at the table. I asked my underclassmen students to call me Professor Jones, but told my advanced seminar students they could call me Jaya. Wesley Oh had only taken an intro class with me but hadn't called me

Professor or Dr. Jones once, while my advanced seminar student Becca Courtland couldn't bring herself to use my first name.

The two couldn't have been more different. Becca, in a baby blue sundress, long blonde hair in a low pony tail, and her slim shoulders weighed down by a pristine pink shoulder bag stuffed with books. Her pink lip-gloss smile reflected the enthusiasm she showed in class. Wesley, his black hair askew, in frayed flip flops, a ratty T-shirt and skinny jeans, and an oversize black backpack encumbered only by a skateboard. The front wheels and the tip of its scuffed tangerine orange deck stuck out the top of the backpack and reached above his head like a crown.

My stomach rumbled, but I couldn't resist asking about their find. "What's the discovery?"

It was nearly the end of fall semester, and the final assignment I'd given my seminar students was to do original research into a forgotten piece of history, telling a story through original historical documents that wasn't told in history books or online encyclopedias. Becca was looking at forgotten aspects of the California Gold Rush, but Wesley?

Tamarind elbowed Wesley. "Go ahead and show her already. Oh wait! You aren't in her class with Becca. But you know about the notorious JAJ, right? Jaya Anand Jones, treasure hunter extraordinaire. One of the most brilliant minds in history on the planet. I'm sure you read about the treasures from India's colonial history that were hidden until she found them."

"Yeah, I had a class with Jaya last year," Wesley said.

"So you know not to let her small stature and boring hair fool you."

"What's the matter with my hair?" I ran my hand through my thick black hair.

"It's been the same since I met you." Tamarind's short hair was dyed lavender this week. Her natural hair color was black, but I'd rarely seen more than the roots that color. Last week it had been electric blue. "That's no way to live. Stop changing the subject. Check out what these two found."

Wesley handed me a faded document in a plastic sleeve. It was a handwritten letter. The paper was thick and expensive, and yellowed with age. The writing was cursive, written with a steady and educated hand. I couldn't read it, though. It was in French. The bottom section was missing, appearing to have been ripped at some point, so there was no signature.

"She gave us the acid-free plastic sleeve," Becca said. "The letter wasn't like that in the book."

She held up her cell phone. My first thought was that young people couldn't pay attention for more than a few seconds, until I realized she wasn't checking her social media feeds. She was holding up the screen for me to read.

"You're translating the French," I said, understanding dawning on me. I accepted the phone and read the translation.

Son,

> *My ship sank at port. Most of my possessions are buried at sea with the ship. But your inheritance is hidden safely. As for the fragile pieces, I will need to go back for them. I hope to return home soon.*

I'm not above admitting that my pulse quickened. I felt bad for the future historians of the world, who'd be sifting through sterile email files instead of handwritten letters. I looked up at them. "Where did you find this?"

"Here's where we found it." Becca handed me an old hardbound book with library markings. "Hidden between the pages of this book that was published in the late 1850s. That's when ships were being abandoned at the port and helping expand the city as landfill, right?"

Droves of sailors in the mid-nineteenth century abandoned their ships in the San Francisco Bay to go in search of their fortunes. While India's colonial history is my specialty, not San Francisco's, my town never stops surprising me. The ground we walk on in the city's Financial District was created out of landfill poured over a shallow part of the bay—much of it directly on top of the ships that had been abandoned during the Gold Rush when it was impossible to resist the lure of gold. If you walk through downtown San Francisco, you're literally walking on top of a graveyard of sunken ships.

Wesley grinned. "I can't believe they never taught us in high school how San Francisco is built on top of abandoned ships."

I looked back to the letter. Something was wrong. Not its age—it looked authentic, though we could test for that later. It was the words themselves. Again, it would be good to have a native French speaker translate it rather than a computer program, but even a slightly different wording wouldn't change what was nagging at me.

"What's up?" Tamarind asked. "We thought you'd be more excited that they found a buried Gold Rush treasure. Who do you think would own the gold today if they find it? This dude didn't sign his name."

"That's not what they found," I said. "Look at what the letter says. '*Son, My ship sank at port. Most of my possessions are buried at sea with the ship. But your inheritance is hidden safely. As for the fragile pieces, I will need to go back for them. I hope to return home soon.*' What's he telling his son?"

The three of them looked blankly at me.

"Why do you think he's writing home about sunken gold that he found in the California Gold Rush?" I asked.

"Because the letter—" Wesley began.

"What does the letter actually say?" I prompted.

"Socratic method," Tamarind murmured. "I love it."

"That there's some sort of treasure," Becca said, "buried with his sunken ship."

Wesley shook his head. "Most of his *possessions* were buried, but the inheritance is safely hidden. That doesn't mean his Gold Rush riches were on the ship. They might be safely hidden in the sunken ship, now covered by landfill. Or he might have gotten them off and hidden them elsewhere. The letter doesn't give us enough information to know."

"No," Becca said, comprehension lighting up her face. "I get it. The letter doesn't mention the Gold Rush at all. If he took the ship *to get here*, like all those men with adventurous spirits who were flocking to California and leaving their ships to sink, that means he already had whatever it was that he's talking about as his son's inheritance. Something fragile. Gold is sort of fragile, but it's not usually described that way."

"Exactly," I said. "From the contents of the letter and where you found it, we can speculate this was written by a person— probably a man, but not necessarily—from France or another French-speaking country, who came over on a ship that sank once it arrived. This person brought something with them."

"Some of which was hidden safely," Wesley said, "and some of which wasn't."

I rested my elbows on the table and looked from Wesley's excited grin to Becca's parted lips. I could almost see the gears whizzing in her mind. She was almost there. I leaned closer. "What does the *location* of the letter tell us?"

Becca gasped. "He never sent the letter. He stayed in San Francisco. So did his son's inheritance."

"Shut. Up." Tamarind smacked her palms onto the table. "Looks like we're off on a treasure hunt."

CHAPTER 2

"Midnight excursions underneath San Francisco!" Tamarind squealed.

"I'm sure the banks in the financial district have security cameras," I said.

"Buzz kill," Tamarind pouted.

"This starts with an armchair treasure hunt," I pointed out. "And it's not ours anyway. This is Becca and Wesley's project."

"Technically just Becca's," Wesley said. "At least she's the only one who'll be getting credit for it. I don't think it'll count for credit in my Historical Research Methods class. But I don't care. If I can help, I'm in."

Becca nodded. "This is going to be the coolest research project ever."

"Even if you don't find a treasure at the end?" I asked. "Beyond the fact that it could be *anywhere*, it's likely this unnamed man already retrieved his riches."

"But this is *real*." Becca grinned. "Not some boring account in a history book."

"Who cares if we find it," Wesley added. "It's the hunt, right?"

I smiled back. I love sharing my passion for history with my students. From the first day of the semester I could tell Becca was bright, but until today, I hadn't seen a spark of genuine interest in her. That was the most exciting thing about this discovery. There was the possibility that Becca and Wesley had stumbled across a missing piece of history that everyone else had overlooked, but, exciting though that was, the best discovery here was that the next generation of historians was being created before my eyes.

"The mystery letter is legit," Tamarind said. "The book Wesley found is an original edition from the 1850s, not a modern reprint, and nobody has checked it out in decades. Decades! Really, Jaya, your brethren need to step up their game. It's not like the internet can tell you everything."

"Or even be trusted," Wesley added.

"Don't even get me started," Tamarind said. "This kid gets it."

"Will you marry me?"

"I'd love to, but my boyfriend would kill me."

"But you can still help us at the library, right?" Becca cut in. "With whatever Dr. Jones recommends?"

Tamarind cracked her knuckles. "Damn straight."

I couldn't help feeling giddy that they were all so excited about this great project. An enticing find, but one that would require a lot of work. For the first decade I studied history, from my own undergrad years through graduate school and my first year as a professor, my most exciting archival finds were long-forgotten references in housekeeping ledgers of the staff of British East India Company merchants. I get a bigger rush from finding original documents that nobody has read in centuries than driving fast in my roadster. There's not much I love more than libraries and sifting through archives. In a world filled with so much uncertainty, it can ground us when we untangle the interwoven strands of the lives of those who came before.

When people think about history, they often think there are facts you can read in a book and accept as the truth. But in reality, it's a painstaking process to piece together what really happened at any given place and time. Painstaking, but also exhilarating. The remnants of history that have survived might not be dramatic in and of themselves, but the stories they tell when assembled can be miraculous. People who lived long before us had similar hopes and dreams, and their messages could reach us across the centuries and continents. In a world that can feel simultaneously connected and divided, history can show us our common humanity through the ages.

Like this letter. Was it written by someone who'd worked hard to save a few dollars over the course of his life that he considered a treasure? It was a possibility. It was also possible he was an adventurer who'd been on many ships and had accumulated items that could tell us more about missing gaps in history.

"This place smells like heaven," Tamarind said. "Since I'm here, I'm staying for dinner. I'll be back in a sec. Gonna call Miles."

"He's on his way already," I said.

Tamarind raised a pierced eyebrow.

"Don't ask," I said. "I don't have any answers. Apparently this was a bad day for me to leave my office earlier than usual."

"I'll get answers," she said, stepping out of the room with her phone to her ear.

My own boyfriend, Lane Peters, had been planning on coming to listen to tonight's set as well, but he'd had to cancel. His job as an art consultant didn't give him the most regular hours.

"What are our next steps?" Becca asked me.

"That's for you to figure out as your project," I said.

Becca groaned, but she did so with a smile on her face.

"I'll give you a hint to get started," I said. "Begin with the most obvious ideas, and narrow things down from there. For example, the letter certainly looks like it could be more than a century old. But there are all sorts of things that could make it look aged, like coffee stains or being wedged between the pages of a book made with poor quality, acidic paper."

"That's what I thought at first," Becca said. "I figured it was a joke some bored student had put into the book, which is why I ignored it—"

"Until she asked me to watch her stuff," Wesley said.

"He's doing a research project for Professor Veeran's class," Becca said, "so we were in the library together this afternoon. I had a big pile of books I hadn't finished with yet, so I asked him to watch my stuff while I went to get a snack, and when I came back he was upset that his own research wasn't as cool as mine. I asked him what he was talking about—"

"And I held up this letter she'd left on top of the book," Wesley said. "I was drowning in my own research, so I looked at what she was doing."

"I would never have taken it seriously," Becca said. "But when Wesley thought it looked real, we took it to Ms. Ortega."

Tamarind stepped back into the break room while Becca was speaking. "Ms. Ortega? What? You went to my mother? Not cool. Anyway, Miles wouldn't tell me anything either. Except that he'll be here soon. I'm telling you, strange things are afoot at the Circle K today." She shook her head. "We don't need a reservation or anything do we?"

I shook my head. "Not on a Wednesday."

"You want to eat here as well?" Becca asked Wesley.

"I can't afford this place," he murmured. It was soft enough I didn't think he expected anyone else to hear.

"My treat, you two," I said. "You made my day with this intriguing find."

After Becca and Wesley were seated I pulled their server aside to make sure she knew not to let the students pay for anything, that their table would be my treat, then went to sit with Tamarind.

"The dishy waiter said he'd bring out papadums right away," Tamarind said, "so you can at least have a few bites of food before your set."

It was five minutes before Sanjay and I were due to begin our first set of music, and Sanjay hadn't yet arrived. At least that was one thing that didn't worry me that night. It wasn't unusual for Sanjay to show up right before our set began, often in a dramatic flourish so his audience (even when it was the Tandoori Palace diners, not members of the audience of one of his magic shows) could witness a brief magic trick before the music began. I was the one who arrived early to eat at the restaurant, since head chef

Juan's secret menu items were off-the-charts spicy. Sanjay had been born and raised in the Silicon Valley, the child of parents who'd immigrated from India, and at an early age had rejected his mom's home cooking for being too spicy, begging for pizza instead. While he adored Indian desserts, he rejected even the mildest level of spice in a meal. Sometimes I really didn't understand my best friend.

A crispy papadum with imli chutney would have to do before I could eat a proper dinner after our first set. But as Miles walked in and I saw the look on his face, I forgot all about the steel thali platter that appeared at the same time.

Miles held a stack of papers clutched in his hands. He sat down at our table and rested his elbows on the oak table top. The owner, Raj, used to cover the tables with starchy white table cloths, but he was a businessman who changed with the times, so when exposed wood became *de rigueur*, he ditched the table cloths. Personally I thought his decision to start serving water out of mason jars had gone a bit too far, but the restaurant was always packed, so what did I know?

Miles usually had eyes only for Tamarind, but tonight he was laser-focused on me. He handed me the sheets of paper that had been stapled together. I glanced at the typed page and the first thing that caught my eye was the sketch of a cobra drawn on top of the page.

"Someone sent this to me?" I asked.

Miles had been screening emails and letters being sent to me ever since I'd uncovered a few historical treasures. Last year, a young reporter with more enthusiasm than accuracy had written that I was interested in having people contact me with their own historical mysteries. In spite of a retraction and my own efforts to inform people that I was actually a professor of history with a full-time teaching job, I'd been so inundated with correspondence that I'd had to change my personal email and get someone to help me sort through my inbox.

Miles nodded, reaching for Tamarind's hand but not taking his gaze from mine.

"I can't read your expression," I said. Which was odd. He didn't need to scribble fragments of poetry on his arms, as he was known to do, for people to guess he was a poet and have a clear sense of his feelings on any particular day.

"Something to be worried about?" I asked when he didn't respond. A couple of letter writers had given off a creepy vibe. Nothing that required a restraining order, but even Miles had felt it and been careful in his replies.

"I don't know where to begin," he finally said, "so I'll start with the reason I had to see you tonight. He said he needs to know today if you're willing to accept the challenge."

I sighed and popped a piece of the flaky papadum in my mouth. "Just because someone gives me an ultimatum with a ticking clock, doesn't mean we have to fall for it."

"What if that someone was Rick Coronado?" Miles looked expectantly at me.

"Shut. Up." Tamarind said.

"This request," he said, his eyes still locked on mine, "is like nothing you've received before. Rick Coronado is a fan of yours."

"He wrote her a fan letter?" Tamarind asked. "That's rad."

"Someone is playing a joke on me." I felt myself blushing. The thriller writer was one of my favorite authors, and thanks to a sly interviewer who'd seen a beaten-up copy of one of Coronado's novels sticking out of my messenger bag, the general public knew I liked reading his pulpy treasure hunt adventures.

I was trying to get taken seriously as a historian, not a treasure hunter, so I'd agreed to the interview with *History* magazine, assuming I would talk about the academic methods I'd used to solve historical mysteries. I hadn't realized the interviewer would also take liberties in describing me: *Historian Jaya Anand Jones, PhD, in her three-inch stilettos, head-to-toe black attire suitable for a heist film, and with a dog-eared Ricardo Coronado thriller sticking out of her red messenger bag, isn't your typical history professor.*

Didn't people realize how difficult it was to be short, or that it was possible to grow tired of brightly colored clothing when you'd been raised by a father who adored tie-dye? The heels and subdued colors helped me get taken seriously. At least when they weren't described like that.

And I was perfectly comfortable with my taste in pulpy adventure novels. I just would have been happier if the whole world wasn't privy to my personal reading habits.

"Well at least he can still write something," Tamarind said.

Rick Coronado hadn't written a new novel in seven years. Not since the mysterious occurrence that had caused him to stop writing. The incident he wouldn't speak of, that had caused him to become a recluse. He'd been eccentric to begin with, but whatever had happened all those years ago had pushed him over the edge.

"Rick Coronado," Miles said, "is back in the game. He's writing a novel in Jaya's honor."

"You're serious," Tamarind said. "Jaya, I know when Miles is dead serious."

"I'm serious," he said. "And so is Rick Coronado." He pressed the pages into my hands. "He'll only write the novel if you agree to read the pages and advise him on the story. He overnighted the package—and he wants your answer tonight."

CHAPTER 3

I opened my mouth to speak, even though I didn't know what I wanted to say.

I didn't have time to figure it out. Three paper butterflies drifted down to the table as gently as if they were flying. I looked up and saw Sanjay.

"We're on." He lifted his signature bowler hat from his head. His thick black hair never looked like he'd been wearing a hat, which was perhaps one of Sanjay's biggest feats of magic.

Miles plucked the pages out of my hands. "You can read them over your break."

"But—"

"We can start a few minutes late if you're in the middle of something," Sanjay said.

"Jaya needs more than a few minutes for this," Miles said.

I stood up and followed Sanjay to our makeshift stage in the corner, but glanced back at Miles. "I hate you."

"We love you too," Tamarind said, blowing me a kiss.

Was Rick Coronado really writing a novel in my honor? And he wanted my help? It had to be fake. The stack of papers looked more the length of a chapter or two than a whole novel. What was going on? And perhaps more importantly, what was up with my own reaction? If Rick Coronado was really writing a novel in my honor, I was more excited than I wanted to admit.

I kicked off my heels and settled into position, sitting cross-legged in front of my tabla, but my mind refused to focus on my drums.

Rick Coronado's books were more than they appeared on the surface. Yes, they were breezy adventures starring Gabriela Glass, a treasure-hunting hero who was impossibly brilliant, beautiful, and rich, and with a troubled past that gave her a soft spot for women in peril. Gabriela's journeys were quests in search of treasures, but she only accepted jobs from women who'd been wronged, as her own mother had been. Gabriela wasn't only after treasures—she sought justice for women.

The books had titles like *The Glass Fire, House of Glass, Shards of Glass, Broken Glass,* and occasionally place-name titles such as *Jaipur Glass, Mayan Glass.* And my personal favorite, *Empire of Glass,* about the impressive Angkorian Empire that once stretched across Cambodia into Thailand. I'd been interested in Cambodia's storied history since my first visit, when I backpacked through Asia in my twenties. I'd become even more intrigued after rescuing a Khmer bas relief that had been stolen from a small museum in San Francisco.

Rick Coronado used to publish a new Gabriela Glass novel every year. He hadn't killed her off when he stopped writing. He simply hadn't written a word of prose in seven years.

Until now.

Seven years ago, Coronado disappeared for six weeks. Afterwards, he'd sequestered himself in his home in upstate New York, leaving the house only to go walking a dog almost as big as himself. The mystery of what had caused him to hide away and reject the writing that had been his lifeblood was greater than anything he'd written into his adventure novels.

Nobody knew what had happened to Rick Coronado when he disappeared.

"Penny for your thoughts," Sanjay said, shaking me out of my reverie as he made a penny appear out of thin air. Or more likely, out of his bowler hat. I'd been stuck in my own thoughts longer than I realized, and he was already set up with his sitar.

After some unexpected distractions earlier that fall, Sanjay and I were back to our usual mid-week schedule of playing tabla and sitar for dinner guests. We were sporadic mid-week dinner entertainment at our friend Raj's Indian restaurant, but Raj paid professionals to play on the weekend.

"Two mysteries, and the evening is just getting started." I glanced over at Miles and Tamarind, but they were deep in conversation. Becca and Wesley were a few tables over, and Wesley waved when he saw me looking their way.

"A Gold Rush prospector who'd already found riches," I said, "and what might be an interesting proposal from Rick Coronado."

"That author who disappeared for several weeks a few years ago?" Sanjay asked.

"Seven years ago."

"Damn, where does the time go?" He shook his head.

"Yes, yes." Raj's bald head glistened as he stepped into our spotlight. "You've lost track of time. The tables are filled—I told you the mason jars were a good investment, Jaya."

"I'm pretty sure that has more to do with Juan's cooking," I said, running my fingertips across the surfaces of the two drums that formed the tabla. "But we're ready to go. You can turn on our mics."

The tabla, singular, refers to the two drums played with the fingertips and palms. The *daya* wooden drum, on the right for the main *raga* melody. The *baya*, on the left, is the more squat kettledrum that adds depth. Similar to how the left hand on a piano adds the deeper notes that anchor a song in place and can give steady underlying beats, the deeper sounding left drum balances the fast fingertip string of notes that can sound almost like a bell.

As we played our first set, I was sure I'd be too distracted to play well, but I'd been playing for so long that the music took over. Sanjay and I fell into our familiar rhythm.

I felt the vibrations under my fingertips as we ended a dramatic raga. The diners applauded. A whole hour had gone by.

I slipped my heels on and rushed back to the table where Miles and Tamarind were drinking mango lassis. Sanjay started to follow but spotted a couple of his fans waving him over to their table. The Hindi Houdini Heartbreakers were an online fan club, and several of the local members liked to see him even when he wasn't performing magic.

I'd once imagined the Hindi Houdini Heartbreakers as creepy stalkers, until I'd met some of them in person. The two who were in the audience tonight were sweet women who always spent lavishly at the restaurant, including leaving an extra big tip when they stayed longer to see both of our sets. I didn't know if they actually enjoyed our music. It didn't hurt that Sanjay was incredibly good looking (I wished my hair was half as gorgeous), funny (he'd killed it when he got a guest appearance on *The Late Show*), generous (he frequently did charity shows), and single.

"Damn," I said as soon as I sat down next to Tamarind. "Give me one second."

I paid Becca and Wesley's bill. They were having syrupy gulab jamun for dessert, and I stopped by their table to let them know the bill was taken care of.

"You guys are really good," Wesley said. "Want to join us on your break?"

"Dr. Jones has her friends to get back to," Becca said. "She said she had someone else meeting her too."

"Just a letter from someone who isn't here," I said, "but that I should read. If you'll excuse me."

"Of course," Becca said, but I caught the disappointment on her face.

Tamarind pushed a plate of food in front of me as I sat down, then rolled her eyes toward Miles. "He wanted to give you the chapters first, but I convinced him you need to know what you're getting into."

She handed me a handwritten letter. They say you shouldn't meet your heroes. Was reading a letter they wrote to you the same thing?

"Lucky this arrived on one of the days Miles is on campus sorting your mail," Tamarind said.

Lucky indeed. I shook off my sense of foreboding.

I pushed aside the food they'd ordered for me, took a deep breath, and tried to calm the butterflies rising in my stomach as I began to read the letter from Rick Coronado.

CHAPTER 4

Dear Dr. Jones,

I feel we're kindred spirits, you and I. You may know I haven't had occasion to leave my home much in several years. But I read avidly. I've read all about you and your travels. You're living the adventures I once wrote about.

I used to think writer's block wasn't real. Until I began suffering the affliction myself. Only when I read an article about you that mentioned you were reading one of my books did I realize I had more to say.

I've been working on a new Gabriela Glass novel, and the words are flowing out of me. I've written several chapters already. I've enclosed the first two. I don't know if I'm fooling myself or if they're any good. I need you to tell me—Is there a story here? Should I keep going?

I paused for a moment, realizing my hands were shaking. I didn't think it was lack of food, although I was vaguely aware my empty stomach was rumbling.

My overwhelming reaction was that this couldn't be real. Surely someone was attempting to play a joke on me. It wouldn't be the first time less than well-meaning people had attempted to reach me. At the same time, this felt like something the author would write. Although this was carrying an "eccentric" persona a bit far, even for him.

"Everything okay?" Tamarind asked. "Are you done reading the letter already?"

I shook my head and returned to the letter.

I'm nervous sending this to anyone. I haven't even shown these pages to my brother. You're the only person I'm sending this to. I already tore up the first letter I wrote...

I will wait until midnight on the day this arrives, and after that if I haven't heard from you I'll scrap the book. I can't bear to have the decision hanging over my head any longer.

Please show the enclosed pages to your inner circle to make your decision, but no one else. Call me at this number by midnight if you see promise in this story and are willing to help.

Sincerely, your humble fan,
Rick Coronado

His phone number and email address were included below his name. At least I was fairly confident it was his name. He'd signed the letter with a scrawling signature that looked like it belonged on the title page of one of his hardback thrillers.

I flipped the paper over. It was blank on the reverse side. The thick white bond bore no markings other than the black ink used to write the letter.

"He totally wants to be your writing buddy!" Tamarind squealed. A few heads from nearby tables turned our way.

"The correct term is 'critique partner,'" Miles said. He had a poetry critique group he met with at our local coffee shop.

"Oh, fine. You can call us whatever you want. The important thing is that he wants all our feedback." Tamarind leaned across the table and lowered her voice. "We're in your inner circle, right? I really hope so, 'cause we kinda already read the chapters."

"The time," I murmured. Was I already too late? "What time is it?"

"A little past seven thirty," Miles said.

"Rick Coronado lives in upstate New York. Midnight for him is nine o'clock here. That gives me less than an hour-and-a-half to get back to him." My heart thudded. That wasn't much time. Especially when I had another set to play in the meantime. "You said you already read the pages?"

"Of course." Miles sat up straighter as he sipped the last ounce of his lassi. "That's my job. His language is melodramatic, but that's his style, right?"

"Let me see it. Does it have to do with what he was working on when he disappeared?"

Tamarind's lips—purple to match her hair—parted in awe. "Do you mean, is he's telling you his own story, like you're his confessor? Wouldn't that be the best? But no, it doesn't look like it."

"It's more of an impossible crime story than a treasure hunt, like those cool mysteries from the Golden Age of detective fiction." Miles handed me the now-rumpled sheets of paper. It was a risk I assumed by hiring a poet with ink-stained fingers instead of someone who'd ever worked in an office. "That's when poetry was taken more seriously than it is today too." He shook his head sadly. "But there's an India connection. I assume that's why he thought you could help. Some bourgeois family from France who made their fortunes in India are now getting their comeuppance and being haunted by a ghost."

Tamarind smiled wickedly. "Gabriela Glass doesn't believe it's a ghost. She's helping a bereaved mom find out who killed her son and stole a family treasure. Check out the chapters to see for yourself—but don't forget your curry. I put in a request for Juan to make it extra spicy, so you've gotta eat it or it'll go to waste."

Juan's amazing curry was the last thing on my mind.

Courier, twelve-point font, double-spaced. This was Rick

Coronado's in-progress unpublished manuscript, *The Glass Thief.*

"Dr. Jones?"

I looked up from the first page and saw Becca and Wesley standing at the table.

"Thanks again for dinner," Wesley said. His backpack with the skateboard sticking out was slung over his shoulder and a baseball cap covered his wild black hair.

"You and your friend were really good," Becca added. "There's a line of people waiting for tables, so we won't linger for a second dessert."

"Come see me during my office hours tomorrow. I have some more ideas about that intriguing letter you found."

"Sorry to interrupt." Becca smiled shyly at Miles and Tamarind. "Thanks again."

"We should go," Wesley said. "See you tomorrow."

"O.M.G." Tamarind whispered as they walked away. "The clock is ticking." She flexed her arm and kissed her bicep. "Don't worry. I can keep Raj and Sanjay at bay for a while. I'll make sure you finish reading before they drag you back to the stage."

The Glass Thief
Chapter 1
Paris, France

As the clock struck midnight two nights before Christmas, and dim rays of moonlight shone through the stained-glass windows of the old mansion, the Delacroix family's prized Serpent King sculpture vanished and prodigal son Luc was murdered—for the second time that day.

Luc's strange death wasn't the first to have taken place in this haunted mansion. Nor was it the first time the Serpent King had caused a death in the family.

Perhaps we should start at the true beginning of the story.

CHAPTER 5

The Glass Thief
Chapter 2
Paris, France

Gabriela Glass stepped through the front gate of the mansion where the murder had taken place. Her gloved hand lingered on the wrought iron for a moment longer than necessary to click it back in place. The metal was forged with what at first glance looked like metal rose stems wrapping themselves around the solid beams of the gate, but a closer inspection revealed the barbed stems as the bodies of snakes, with their enigmatic serpentine faces visible in the center of the roses.

She thought of the snake-like man she was told had orchestrated the plot that had brought her here. Tristan Rubens. Tristan was the man who'd seen Luc murdered in the library as the twelve chimes echoed through the rooms adorned with portraits of Luc's ancestors, before Luc was raised from the dead only to be killed a second time. If Tristan was to be believed, it was either a case of a clever, cold-blooded murderer able to walk through walls and hover above pristine, freshly-fallen snow, or the work of a malicious ghost haunting the house. Or there was the simple answer: the man was lying.

Inside the grand entryway of the Art Nouveau

home, a doorman took her coat and gloves. Gabriela had walked through thick fog to get to the house, but felt barely warmer inside. This was not an inviting house. It was nearly Christmas, and a ten-foot Christmas tree stretched upward past the iron curves of the staircase railing toward the high ceiling. Pinpricks of white lights nestled in the fragrant pine needles and sparkles of red bulbs dangled from the branches, yet the overall impression was one of cold formality. No personal ornaments adorned the tree. This might as well have been a tree down the road in the window of Le Bon Marché department store.

Laura Delacroix stood in front of the tree. In the woman's rigid pose, black Chanel dress worn with a peacock blue Hermes scarf, and perfectly made up face, Gabriela caught only the faintest hint of the raw sadness of a mother losing a son. Red-rimmed eyes peered at Gabriela.

"I won't waste your time with pleasantries," Laura said in French.

"As you wish," Gabriela responded in kind.

Gabriela was fluent in the language, as she was in a dozen others, and she wished to put the grieving mother at ease. Gabriela's first languages were Spanish and English, but she'd been living and breathing other languages from soon after she could walk. French was one of her favorites.

"I already explained the private details of our family history." Laura's lip quivered, almost imperceptibly, but she pressed on. "In spite of the precautions we insisted on taking, leaving our home on the anniversary of our ancestors' strange deaths, two men were foolish enough to spend the night at the mansion on the most haunted night of the year. My son Luc and his friend Tristan Rubens. Tristan left the house

alive. My son did not."

"And you don't believe it was the ghost that killed him."

"I've lived in this house for so many years that I almost believe in the ghost. Almost." Her voice broke.

Gabriela turned away and traced her slender fingers over the wooden curves of an ornate grandfather clock, giving the woman time to compose herself. The French had a long history of building impressive clocks, and this one didn't disappoint. Gabriela was the most modern of women in many ways, but she cherished the pocket watch her grandfather had given her.

"I don't know what I think," Laura continued, "but I know what I feel. Tristan Rubens killed my son. I want you to prove it."

"Surely the police—"

"I have been wronged by this family I married into too many times," Laura interrupted. "The police aren't convinced of Tristan's guilt. Tristan was clever to use our ghost story to make witnesses believe they saw something they did not. I won't be so naïve as to suggest the police are imbeciles. Yet how can they conduct a proper investigation without all the facts? My husband will not reveal details of the valuable sculpture stolen at the time Luc was killed."

"He doesn't believe the sculpture is relevant?"

"No." Laura Delacroix's violet eyes blazed with anger. "Because his ancestor looted it from Munnar, India. This shocks you?"

"No. It angers me that a man would care more about his family's reputation than justice for them. For you."

"Gabriela Glass. I know your reputation well. You're equipped to trace the movements of a stolen antiquity. I have a proposition for you. If you can solve the supposedly impossible murder of my son, by following the movements of the stolen statue and proving how Tristan Rubens—not a ghost—is responsible, you will receive the Serpent King as your reward. You may do with it whatever you choose."

Gabriela considered the proposition. She usually helped women who were more downtrodden, but the crime intrigued her—as did the reward. "Tell me more about the Serpent King and how it disappeared from the house."

"I've shown you the photograph. The seven cobras, their teeth bared and hoods flared, looking almost human, carved out of a solid slab of sandstone rock." Laura shivered.

Gabriela didn't blame her. The fierce snakes were poised as if to strike. One cobra in particular inspired fear. And with its regal pose, devotion. "The Serpent King. He's the larger figure in the center? Why does the lower part of the carving lack detail? Was the sculpture unfinished?"

Laura shrugged. "There's no provenance to tell us. Algernon Delacroix brought it back from a trip to the tea plantations of Munnar. The story is he won the Serpent King from a Maharaja in a game of Chaturanga. But Algernon was a man of many secrets."

Laura's gaze left Gabriela's and turned to the tragic central staircase and up toward the portrait that loomed high above on the facing wall, watching them as they spoke. She pointed at the portrait.

Gabriela moved to the base of the grand staircase to get a better look at the huge, looming painting. The name carved into the frame was Algernon Delacroix, but the face! It so resembled the photograph she'd been shown of Luc, the man who had died here on these stairs only days before.

She felt a chill down to her bones. She was wearing a dress in emerald green, her signature color, and her silver silk scarf did little to warm her in the cold atmosphere.

"Each time a new patriarch in the family is killed in this house on the anniversary of the first suspicious death," Laura whispered, "the face in the portrait changes to his."

"Trickery, surely."

"Yes. Trickery enacted by the thief Tristan Rubens on the night he killed my son, in an attempt to blame the ghost. But—" Laura shuddered.

"But?"

"Is it trickery that no footsteps could be seen leaving the scene of the murder and theft, even though the snow stopped earlier in the evening? Yet somehow, the Serpent King disappeared from this house."

CHAPTER 6

I set the pages aside. Tamarind and Miles watched for my reaction.

I felt like I'd entered the *Twilight Zone* as soon as I stepped into the restaurant that evening. I was already feeling out of sorts because Raj had recently told us he was thinking of retiring soon, and the restaurant had become like a second home to me. I wished Lane hadn't canceled on me that night. It would be another day before I could tell him about all this. And I didn't have a day to make a decision.

"You need sustenance," Tamarind said, pushing the curry in front of me.

Raj caught my eye and tapped his watch.

Five minutes until our next set. There was time for me to make a phone call.

"Shut. Up." Tamarind said as I ignored the curry and tapped a number into my phone. "So you're in?"

"Was there ever a question?" I stood up.

"Touché."

I maneuvered my way through a group of people waiting to be seated and stepped outside. The light fog that so often fills the Inner Sunset neighborhood had descended, and though it wasn't raining, I felt light droplets of mist on my face. I called the number Rick Coronado had left. The phone rang three times. I pulled the phone away from my ear. The screen's clock assured me it was three minutes before eight. Over an hour before the deadline.

I pressed my ear back to the phone. Another ring sounded. Where was he?

After the fifth ring, a click sounded. My breath caught. A voicemail message kicked in. *This is Rick.* Followed by a beep.

"Hi, this is Jaya. I received the package you sent me. I'm honored you thought of me." And I had no idea what else to say. "It's an intriguing premise. I don't know how I can help you, but I hope you keep writing the book. I'll be up for several more hours if you want to call me back."

As I hung up, I became aware of laughter filling the sidewalk and the hum of cars in the street. Two giggling young couples stepped out of the Japanese restaurant two doors down. An antsy driver honked her horn at the electric car in front of hers as soon as the light at the corner changed to green. Half a dozen pedestrians filled the crosswalk at the busy intersection, including two who barely looked up from their cell phones. Life carried on as usual.

I glanced down at my phone. One minute before eight.

Back inside, Tamarind raised her eyebrows at me. I shook my head and proceeded to the stage. I took one last look at my phone before putting it away for an hour—and froze. Rick had texted me back.

I'm relieved you've accepted. More to follow soon.

I texted back, *Can you tell me more?* And added my home address and personal email, so he wouldn't have to go through Miles to reach me.

Tamarind was at my side five seconds later. "What? What is it? Are you having a stroke? Are you good about wearing compression socks on all those long flights you take? I know they're not sexy, but I read how they totally help with blood clots—"

"Why didn't he answer the phone?" As I showed the text to Tamarind, a terrible suspicion came to mind. I swore. "How do I know it's really him?"

In spite of the different set-up for Gabriela, the style was Rick Coronado's. My gut instinct told me it was him, but the rational part of my brain still wondered if this was a joke. I wished I hadn't just given out my home address. Maybe I could call his publisher to confirm. Though at eight o'clock in the evening in California, I doubted anyone in New York would answer the phone. That would have to wait until the next day.

"You think some *Misery* action is going on?" Tamarind asked.

That was something I hadn't considered. Now I *really* wished I hadn't just given out my address. "You think someone is holding him captive, so they can't risk him talking on the phone?"

"You're the one who suggested it."

I scowled at Tamarind. "I was thinking it might not be him at all. Maybe an unpublished writer who wants to get attention, or someone who doesn't like me and wants to get back at me."

"You're right." Tamarind pursed her purple lips. "That's more likely. What? You know it's true. There are a lot of people who aren't happy you've foiled their plans. But you know what they say. If you're not making some people love you and some people hate you, you're doing something wrong with your life."

The rumbles of my empty stomach were rivaling the volume of my drums by the time Sanjay and I finished our second set an hour later. Miles and Tamarind had left after slipping a note onto the stage to make sure I'd call her if I heard more from Rick. I hadn't.

As I packed my drums into their cushioned black case, the whiff of extra spicy curry hit my nostrils. Sanjay began coughing, which told me it wasn't my imagination. A second later, Juan appeared with a steaming bowl.

"You want to try my latest," he said, "or do you want something off the menu with less spice?"

"Never." I hopped down from the stage and took a bite. The curry was off-the-charts spicy. Just the way I liked it.

Sanjay coughed harder as he snapped his sitar case shut. "You two are crazy. See you tomorrow. I'm off to get a burger like a proper human."

Juan chuckled and shook his head as we watched Sanjay make

a hasty exit. "I'd be offended if I didn't know he's the one who's missing out."

"You've outdone yourself this time." I kissed the head chef's cheek.

"Careful," he said, "or the spice on your lips will burn a hole through my cheek."

"You're the one who made it."

"Yeah, but I can't actually eat it. This batch is just for you. And my grandma. I'm saving some of it to bring her. We'll see which of you is tougher." He grinned before stepping back into the kitchen to help his team clean up. He didn't have to at this stage of his career, but he always pitched in.

The kitchen had closed at nine, and most of the diners cleared out as soon as we finished our set. A few tables remained with people finishing their dinners or enjoying tea or dessert. But nobody was paying any attention to me.

I'd slipped the letter and manuscript pages from Rick Coronado into my messenger bag, and I pulled them out in the empty break room. I looked again at the sketch of a cobra on the first typed page—which I now thought of as a serpent. Was this the Serpent King statue the murdered Luc's mother had hired Gabriela Glass to find?

I did a quick internet search, which yielded unsurprising results. The Serpent King statue was a product of his imagination, as were the Delacroix family and Tristan Rubens. But the Serpent King idea was based on real historical carvings. Serpents, or *naga* in Sanskrit, are revered in India, acting as a protector in many circumstances, including watching over Buddha and being guardians of treasure.

A treasure and a woman in need of help were common themes in the Gabriela Glass novels, but the set-up with Gabriela asked to solve a murder supposedly committed by a ghost was different from his earlier thrillers. This was more like a Gothic ghost story than anything he'd written before. His experience on the secret research trip he'd taken seven years ago was traumatic enough to have caused him to stop writing, so it wasn't surprising it would impact the themes explored in his new book. But a ghost?

Strange facts surrounded Rick Coronado's six-week disappearance. He packed a bag and said he'd be traveling to research his next novel, the subject of which he kept close to his chest. This in itself wasn't unusual. An immersive writer, he was known for his thorough attention to detail.

Seven years ago, he left his oversize mastiff, Clifford, with his business manager brother Vincent, walked down the road with his rucksack—and wasn't seen again for six weeks.

Six weeks and a day later, he was found by two Swiss hikers in a remote region of Thailand, on an obscure trail that hardly any Westerners knew about. A full beard covered his face, and he was fifteen pounds thinner than when he'd left. When the hikers discovered him, he was unconscious and barely breathing. When he woke up in a hospital in Bangkok, he said he couldn't remember anything. Even his doctors questioned this account, but nobody had ever gotten the story out of him.

What had happened during those missing weeks? Did it involve family ghosts, murder, and a thief who stole the Serpent King?

CHAPTER 7

When I woke up the next morning, my eyes popped wide open. I rolled over to check my phone so quickly that I got tangled in the twisted quilt. There were no new messages from Rick Coronado.

Wide awake, I knew what was bothering me most about the two chapters I'd read. The research was too shoddy for Rick Coronado. French colonialists had been in India, but not in Munnar. And *Chaturanga* had already become chess by that time. Rick Coronado wouldn't have gotten those facts wrong. Was this an elaborate hoax by someone who didn't know as much about history as Rick Coronado and me? Or could someone be forcing his hand?

I shivered at the thought—but mostly I was shivering because I was freezing. The roof of my attic apartment was leaking. The rain was helping with the wildfires happening across California, but unfortunately it also meant contractors had more important jobs to take on than a leaking roof over a not-quite-legal apartment. My landlady Nadia's boyfriend Jack had rigged a tarp to cover it, but a recent big storm had done more damage and a draft was still getting in.

I pulled a fuzzy black sweater over my Batman pajamas and headed to my wall of bookshelves. I didn't have enough space for all of my books, so most shelves were two rows deep. I pushed aside a half dozen books on the British East India Company and a dozen more miscellaneous history books (well read) and cookbooks (never opened) before I found what I was after. *Empire of Glass* by Rick Coronado.

I'd read the thriller so many times that the hardcover novel fell flat easily in my hands. I found the Acknowledgments page and scanned the text. There. He thanked his editor, Abby Wu. She'd be able to tell me if it was really Rick. But not if I froze to death first. I'd call her from campus.

Before walking five blocks through frigid wind to my roadster (parking got worse and worse in the city each passing month) I grabbed my favorite sandwich and double espresso with plenty of sugar at Coffee to the People. I finished the peanut butter and egg croissant sandwich before I reached my car and drank the steaming coffee on the drive to campus, finally feeling warmth seep into my fingertips.

From my office, I called Fox & Sons publishing house in New York and asked to speak with Rick Coronado's editor.

"Yes, I understand the editors don't take unscheduled phone calls and I'm not a client," I said. "Yes, but I think she'd want to—if you'd only—my name is Jaya Jones and—oh? She mentioned me? Yes, I'll hold."

She'd mentioned me? I took photos of the pages of the manuscript while waiting on hold. I should have done it the previous night. I didn't have an electronic copy, and I should learn from past mistakes.

As the minutes stretched on, I scowled at the Ganesha statue that filled a quarter of my office and wondered what I was doing. There were less than two weeks left in the semester. I needed to be helping my students and working on my own article. My colleague Naveen Veeran and I had started in tenure-track teaching jobs at the same time, and I'd heard through the grapevine that he was close to submitting his paperwork to apply for tenure. Though our teaching methods were quite different, the two of us taught similar history courses, so we both knew that, funding being what it was, it was likely only one of us would get tenure. Naveen had beaten me to an important first step.

Though my primary job is historian and professor, and I love my students and teaching, recently I'd gotten caught up in a few historical inquiries that took me far from an academic's usual habitat of libraries and archives. As soon as the phrase "treasure hunter" was written about me by the press, my life got out of hand. I wasn't sure if that was a good thing or a bad thing. Because it was both.

For Lane Peters, real name Lancelot Caravaggio Peters, it had turned out far worse. His good deeds with me had cost him his position as a graduate student returning to school in his early thirties after a questionable first career. Not to mention that he'd been found by people in his criminal past and blackmailed into pulling off a heist at the Louvre.

A loud click sounded.

"Jaya? Abby Wu here. Thanks for holding. I'm so glad you called."

"You know what Rick Coronado is up to?"

"One never knows exactly what Rick is up to. But yes, I know he's showing you the draft of his next Gabriela Glass novel before he sends it to me."

"Is this kind of thing normal for an author?"

She laughed. A throaty chuckle, one that I took to be both genuine and well-rehearsed from a lifetime of working in New York publishing. "I've never met a normal author."

"He sent me an overnight package and asked me to call him by midnight last night if I didn't want him to abandon the novel."

"Rick has always been eccentric. I'm not going to feed the stereotype and say the best writers are always like that, but in his case he always got away with it. It's only gotten worse since he stopped writing Gabriela. I think she grounded him. I finally decided to indulge him."

"Have you actually seen him lately? And have you read the pages? I mean..." I bit my lip. "Could it be someone pretending to be him?"

She laughed again. This time it was a bark that convinced me I'd surprised her. "You mean like his plot from *The Glass Deception* coming to life, where the old treasure hunter was killed by the bad guy who's assumed his place, but nobody realizes it until the denouement? No, sadly—or I suppose I should more accurately say *happily*—it's nothing like that. Even though Rick rarely leaves the grounds of his house in upstate New York, he throws dinner parties. He hasn't given up on the world, so he brings the world to him. He had a grand one a few months ago, and there was a look in his eye I hadn't seen for far too long.

"I pressed him, and he confessed he had an announcement he'd make over dessert—did you know he was a great chef? He didn't used to be. But since sequestering himself and feeling unable to write, he said he needed something to do besides read books. God knows he didn't need to spend more time with his brother Vincent. That man is a marketing genius, but a first-class leech—"

"About the announcement?" I prompted.

"Oh yes. I had previously suggested he write nonfiction, since he could do that without writer's block. He did so much research for his fiction that I was sure he'd come across enough juicy tidbits to form a book. But that didn't interest him. At least not before. Over dessert—a soufflé so decadent I hadn't known such a thing could exist—he told us he was writing again. I asked if he was finally trying his hand at nonfiction. He said no, that it was a new Gabriela Glass novel. We all applauded. Until he told us the catch."

"Me."

"Yes, but he didn't mention you right away. He said he couldn't tell us any more just yet. I didn't think much of it, since I know authors can have trouble talking about their work before the story is fully formed. When I contacted him a few weeks later to see how the book was going, he said he had a plan. I thought he meant an outline. But I was wrong. That's when he explained that he had a plan to show the book to you as he wrote it. He said you were the one who'd inspired the story and gotten him out of his funk, so he wanted to share the story with you as he developed it."

"He said he needs me to give him feedback if he's going to write the book."

Abby laughed. "I know. He says there's something missing as

he finds his voice again, and he thinks you can help. If you're worried about him being a stalker or anything like that, don't worry. Watch out for Vincent, but not Rick. When they say Rick is 'eccentric,' they don't mean that as a euphemism for anything else. He's truly inspired by you. He mentioned you to me last year, long before he had the idea to start writing again. He loves that you save real pieces of history, and also that you're a teacher. Listen, I need to jet in a minute, so is there anything else I can tell you?"

"His research is wrong."

"Excuse me?"

"The facts in the book. They're sloppy. Does he write his first drafts like that?"

"He didn't used to, but since he hasn't traveled in the last seven years, he's probably having trouble doing research. That's my bet for why he wants your help." She swore and her voice grew muffled as she spoke to someone else. "Gotta run. An editorial fire to put out—can you believe a typo nearly got through on a book cover? A book cover! Call if you need anything else."

The phone clicked off. I looked at its clock. Two hours before I had a class followed by office hours. I hoped Becca and Wesley would come see me, but I needed to get some work done first. Since my Thanksgiving break trip to Japan had been extended longer than anticipated, I hadn't prepared as well for the remainder of the semester. I didn't want to let my students down.

I scooped up my messenger bag, locked my office, and walked across campus through the whipping wind to a hidden cubby at the library. I needed to go over my lecture notes for the course I was teaching that day. I could have stayed in my office, but even with the door closed and without scheduled office hours, I knew I wouldn't be able to say no to my students if they knocked.

Tamarind knew me well, so she found me in my hidden spot at the library and brought me a smuggled coffee and donut.

"Cop food is good for this time of year," she said, handing me a compostable cup and donut dotted with rainbow sprinkles.

It was cold even inside the library. Tamarind wore pink-and-black-striped fingerless gloves, a faux fur stole, and leopard print tights under a fuchsia skirt. I was in a black turtleneck sweater and had put black tights on underneath my black slacks, but had left my gloves in my office. I accepted the warm coffee with thanks, wrapping my chilled fingers around the paper cup.

I sometimes wondered what would happen to my library privileges if I were to be found eating in the cubicle (in my humble opinion the only thing keeping libraries from achieving their spot as the most perfect places on earth was the rule of no food and drink), but my guess was that Tamarind's presence would smooth things over. She was brilliant at her job (and in life) but she suspected her large stature and misunderstood punk appearance (she used to describe herself as a post-punk post-feminist, but after the year she'd had, she was back to being a self-described feminist punk) served as an asset when she applied for her job at the library. Tamarind was great at dealing with people who caused problems at the library, able to handle tricky situations without calling the police. It wasn't only her appearance. She was good at talking to people who felt like misunderstood outsiders, being one herself.

She grinned at my happiness as I bit into the donut. "Glad you wanted it. I already ate two. It's bribery in case you're slow on the uptake. What else have you heard from Rick? Did he or his captor get back to you?"

"I spoke with his editor this morning. It's really him writing this manuscript, no kidnapping to speak of."

"But?"

I looked again at my phone and swiped aside several messages, none from Rick. "But he's hiding something, even from his editor."

"What?"

"That's the question."

CHAPTER 8

There were two weeks of every semester when students were most engaged: the first week and the last. After an energetic class that ran long with a great discussion, I headed back to my office—with one quick stop on the way. Logically I knew it was too soon to expect another chapter, but I found myself more disappointed than I wanted to admit when there wasn't another package from Rick Coronado waiting for me.

As a historian, I liked the idea of reading it as a serialized novel, like Wilkie Collins's *The Woman in White* or Charles Dickens's *The Pickwick Papers*, with hungry readers eagerly awaiting the new installment each week. But who was I kidding? The suspense was killing me. When would I hear from him again?

I left my office door open so students would know I was available for office hours, and Becca and Wesley arrived right away.

I was again struck by the odd couple appearance of the pair, Wesley in sweat pants and flip flops, Becca with perfectly manicured pink nails and wool coat folded neatly over her arm. But today they seemed more comfortable with each other. Becca especially. She was far more at ease than the evening before.

"It's a good thing I procrastinated on finding an approved topic for my Research Methods final project for Naveen," Wesley said, sinking into one of the two squeaky chairs in front of my desk. "This is the perfect project to show how to research an interesting piece of evidence you find, when you have no idea where it leads and you have to reverse engineer the discovery."

"He didn't approve your first idea?" I asked.

"He said it wasn't historical enough."

"Too recent?"

"Sort of. I wanted to work on a computer code to crack a 5,000-year-old password, to get through that Kerala temple's 'Cobra Lock' password system for the secret inner vault nobody will touch."

Becca pursed her lips. "We shouldn't be wasting Dr. Jones's time."

"I'm not in a rush," I said with only the slightest hesitation. "So a computer code to crack a thousands-of-years-old lock? You think that's possible?"

Wesley shrugged. "I'm not the first person to think of it. But Naveen didn't like the idea as a project."

The temple in India he was referring to had always been shrouded in mystery. Especially recently, when it was discovered the gold-plated temple that legend says was built 5,000 years ago contained billions of dollars of riches. All but one of the known chambers have been searched. Two gigantic cobras are carved into the protective iron door known as Vault B. It's one of the examples I keep handy when students say there's no new historical research left to be done or when I see them getting bored.

"That's the temple the Indian Supreme Court stopped them from opening?" Becca asked.

"Only Vault B," I said. "A *naga bandham*, a snake-binding spell, was supposedly what locked the vault. So a *garuda mantra*, the mantra of the snake's bird nemesis, needs to be recited perfectly to open the doors without causing disaster. If breached by force, all sorts of catastrophes will be unleashed."

Wesley laughed. "Don't tell me you're superstitious."

"Not superstitious. Prudent. If ancient priests wanted to keep people out, don't you think they would have found ways to ensure their warnings were heeded?"

"Like a booby trap?" Becca asked.

"That's the cool thing about trying to get in with a computer program." Wesley became more animated as he spoke, and he kicked his skateboard under my desk without noticing. "If it can find the right order and frequency of sound waves that the Cobra Lock accepts as legitimate, nobody gets hurt, because the priests themselves were supposed to get inside, right?"

"Right," I said. "The theory is that the *naga bandham* is a tonal lock, so the unlocking mantra recited at a certain octave serves as something like a musical key."

As much as I hated to admit it, Naveen was right in this case. It sounded like a fascinating project, but it wouldn't have given Wesley the best application of the traditional research methods Naveen was going for with this assignment. I'm all for creative research, but after you learn the foundations. I was also glad Wesley wouldn't be getting himself embroiled in the on-going political turmoil over that temple.

Becca cleared her throat. "So, our Gold Rush era letter?"

"There's only a week to do research as part of your class projects, but you can do a lot in that time."

"I was thinking I'll use the letter as one of the many forgotten pieces of history that helps tell the story."

"Together," I said, "you two might prove something previously unknown."

"And find our mystery man's treasure." Wesley grinned as his stomach rumbled.

"Not in a week," I said. "Focus on the limited scope of your projects for now. If you find something, you might turn it into a bigger project next semester. Now, how can I help? Do you know your steps for this weekend?"

"We already showed it to the librarian. She said it was real, not a fake," Becca said.

I shook my head. "Tamarind isn't an archivist. And I didn't exactly say it might be 'fake.' Just that we didn't know its age, so it might not be what you think it is. The location is suggestive, but not proof."

"Is that a common thing to do?" Becca asked. "That level of

authentication, I mean. Can't we assume if we find something in a library the librarian says is legitimate, or in an archive, that it's real?"

"What's 'real' though?" I prodded. I was playing devil's advocate, but that was the point of an advanced seminar.

"You mean like we could be in the Matrix?" Wesley stared across the desk at me, his dark brown eyes wide.

Becca rolled her eyes.

"Um, no," I said. "People throughout history have different motives for writing things. That's why different accounts can vary so much—there's another student doing a project about different historical records not matching each other. The fact that you found a letter tucked into a book doesn't necessarily mean what it seems to indicate. It might have been a joke—"

"People back then would have done that?" Wesley stared at me.

"You think people in history had lesser imaginations than now? How do you think people explored the world? The adventurers. Colonizers. Pirates."

"But that was like real life, right? Practical jokes and fiction are different—"

"Storytelling began millennia ago."

"That's different."

"*Beowulf* was written a millennium ago."

Wesley blinked blankly at me.

I sighed. "*Treasure Island* was written in the late 1800s. But it could be something completely different." Which is what I expected, but I didn't want to bias their research. "The letter you found might have been referencing something else entirely and was slipped into the book accidentally, and then forgotten about."

Wesley groaned and Becca laughed. "I do that all the time," she said. "Who knows what a person who checks out my art history library book in the future will say about my *Anthropologie* receipt."

"Exactly," I said, excited she was getting it. "I take it you mean the boutique clothing store, not the academic discipline? But once that store no longer exists, a future historian might think you were using an antiquated local dialect spelling of Anthropology."

Wesley groaned again. "I thought we'd get to go hunting for this underground ship."

"You might," I said. "You just need to put in the work first. It's good to consult experts like archivists. See what you can figure out about the person who wrote the letter. Then back to the library to track down those less obvious sources."

The university library didn't have mysterious hidden staircases or centuries-old thick wooden bookshelves, but it held secrets that by far made up for that. The library had offered up one of its secrets to the students, so I could tell they were eager to go back.

"Do you want me to talk to Professor Veeran about you being able to merge this with your Research Methods project?" I asked.

He shook his head. "It's too late. The deadline was yesterday to get Naveen's feedback before turning in our final paper next week. We were supposed to turn in our proposal last month, and our preliminary research by yesterday at the latest."

"Did you turn anything in?"

Wesley scratched his neck. "Um, nothing. For either. I didn't have any ideas after he didn't like the computer program."

Becca rolled her eyes. When she caught me looking at her, she blushed and tried to pretend she was looking out the window.

"You've got a great project now," I said. "Can you write up a proposal this afternoon?"

He grinned. "Definitely."

"Let me talk to Nav—Professor Veeran—for you."

After talking with four more students, I wrapped up office hours and walked across the hallway to Naveen Veeran's office.

I found him sitting in his desk chair, dressed in his signature three-piece tweed suit and with a pile of papers in front of him and cup of steaming tea at his elbow. His neatly trimmed black hair was prematurely touched with gray at the temples. He did look the part of a professor.

He looked up and beckoned me inside. "How lovely of you to grace us with your presence. I'm surprised you're not jetting off to a glitzy destination and abandoning your students when they need you. Again."

"Thanks for covering my class the other day." Which I'd thanked him for already. Twice. "I'm here about one of your students. Wesley."

"Bright. But no focus. I was hoping he'd get his act together for his final project, but he didn't turn in a proposal for feedback, as I'd strongly recommended to each student. It was due yesterday."

"That's my fault," I said, closing the door and taking a seat. "He found an angle to his project yesterday, and it's related to one of the projects a student is working on in my advanced seminar, so he wanted to consult me—"

"Group work isn't allowed. That wouldn't be fair to the other students."

"Becca and Wesley aren't working together. They're doing completely different projects on an old historical document they found at the library. Something he couldn't have anticipated finding. Wesley is nearly done with his proposal for his new project, so if he gets it to you today, can you give him feedback?"

Naveen blinked at me. "Of course not. That wouldn't be fair to his classmates who followed the rules."

I sighed. Naveen Veeran had no imagination, but I'll grant he was a rigorous scholar. His first book came in at over 500 pages, nearly half of which was made up of its bibliography, and was titled *The Indian Subcontinent from 1937-1947: A Historical Research Methods Case Study.* His assignments for his students mirrored his own work.

He'd also saved my job when I'd been falsely accused of plagiarism. He knew the truth, so he couldn't let it go even if it would have meant his own chances of tenure would be greatly improved without me around.

Naveen rested his elbows on his desk. They were, of course,

protected by suede elbow pads. "Why are you here, Jaya?"

"I just told you."

"May I offer you tea?" He stood before waiting for my reaction.

"Um, sure."

"Students need discipline. Rules." He poured hot water from an electric kettle over chai tea bags in porcelain teacups. "We need to guide them."

"And inspire them, rather than stifle their ideas because they're not perfect." I accepted a cup and breathed in the spicy, sweet scent.

"What better way to inspire than by sharing how much we love our jobs and being here? Which clearly you don't."

"Excuse me?" I hoped I wouldn't accidentally crush the delicate teacup. "My students can clearly see how inspired I am by history. But our jobs? That's not what's important. These are undergrads. They're not training to be professors. We need to show them the value of history first. Get them excited about it. They're several steps away from deciding if they want to become history professors."

Naveen studied my face as he blew on his tea. "I've submitted my application. I wasn't sure if you'd heard. I thought that's why you were really here. You've been so busy that I haven't had a chance to tell you myself. But I wanted you to know."

I knew which application he meant. Tenure.

"Thanks for letting me know. I appreciate it." It was true. Naveen was many things, but he believed in playing fair by the rules as they were established.

I raised the glass to my lips, but couldn't force myself to swallow a sip.

Back in my office, I emailed Wesley with the bad news that Naveen wouldn't be reviewing his proposal. I offered to look at his notes myself if it would be helpful. If this were a real-life project, I'd be able to help more. But based on the structure Naveen had laid out for the students I didn't want to lead Wesley astray.

I was already leading myself astray, and I knew it. By

accepting Rick Coronado's challenge, I was not only risking tenure, but opening myself up to whatever danger had nearly killed Rick seven years ago.

CHAPTER 9

A ghostly fog was descending over the hills as I shifted gears on the winding road.

Why was Rick Coronado writing me a ghost story? I alternated between wondering where Gabriela's story would go and where my own was going. Luckily I was heading to see the man who always helped me see things clearly.

I was meeting Lane at a dinner party in the Berkeley hills. I was disappointed we wouldn't have time on our own until later that night, especially after he hadn't been able to make it to the restaurant the previous night.

Grizzly Peak Boulevard twisted sharply, and I shifted gears again. This was the kind of road my roadster was made for. I'd inherited the classic sports car years ago, and I made good use of it. Driving along the cliff-side road winding through the Berkeley Hills, I had a front row view of the sun descending past the San Francisco Bay. Several cars had pulled onto the side of the road at lookout points, a smart move by the city, because without them drivers would have doubtlessly eased their cars onto unstable edges of the winding road, or accidentally driven right over the edge as their imaginations caught sight of the luminous orange sky and twinkling lights. A city of contrasts, like all cities are. Vast wealth and abject poverty, tourist trails and hole-in-the-wall restaurants only the locals know, skyscrapers stretching toward the sky and the remnants of sunken abandoned ships pressed into the silt of the Bay. My headlights cut through the fog that only partly obscured the view.

Much like part of me wished for my Rick Coronado novel fix all in one sitting, I sometimes wished my real love life could have been as simple as a Gabriela Glass novel. A new man in each novel. No strings attached. Sometimes she got hurt, but she'd bounced back completely by the start of the next book.

I didn't really want that, though. I only wished the baggage of what came before didn't exist with me and Lane. There had always been something both pushing us together and pulling us apart. Since the day we met a year and a half before in his cramped basement office, we'd walked the fine line of wariness and trust, angst and peace, frustration and fire.

But always...always we fit together. I don't mean physically, though that was part of it. I'd resigned myself to my fate of being short, but that's why my head fit perfectly in the crook of his neck. But more important was how we understood each other at an unspoken level. He saw the real me that my brother and my best friend never could, even though I knew they loved me and I loved them dearly. I wasn't nearly as practical or well adjusted as they imagined.

I turned off the main road—using the word "main" loosely, as it was a narrow two-lane street with rare spots for cars to pass each other—and onto a lane barely wide enough for my roadster.

The drive was familiar. Too familiar.

As I rounded a sharp curve, I realized why. This was the same street where I'd looked at a house shortly after I moved to the Bay Area two years before. I'd already moved into my studio apartment, the semi-legal converted attic of my landlady Nadia's Victorian house in the Haight-Ashbury neighborhood of San Francisco. Tamarind had been apartment-hunting, and for fun one weekend we decided to go to all the open houses that looked interesting, even the ones that were ridiculously out of our price range. My favorite house was on this street. Or at the very least, one that looked a lot like this.

The GPS told me I'd reached my destination. Lane had said I'd recognize it because it would be my favorite house on the hill. He was right. This was the house I'd fallen in love with when Tamarind and I had gone pretend house-hunting.

I parked in a section of the street that seemed wide enough to prevent my side mirror being clipped as it had been so many times in San Francisco, and grabbed the bottle of Shiraz I'd brought for my mystery host.

A wooden arch that reminded me of Red Fort in Delhi was the first view of the house a visitor was granted. The rosewood garden arch, carved in an ornate Mughal style, looked like it had sprung to life covered in ivy. Next to it were two small holes, but aside from the gift from the gophers, the landscaping was immaculate. It was even more perfect than when I'd looked at it.

The arch was the entry point to the house, leading the way to a winding stone path flanked by desert plants, rose bushes, and softly glowing electric lights that looked more like fireflies than modern lighting. The house itself was Tudor, with a steeply pitched roof and half-timbered walls. It was neither huge nor small, but perfect.

There was only one car in the driveway, and as I turned on the path, I didn't see many cars parked in the road. How small a dinner party were Lane's friends having? I didn't think I was too early. I walked up the narrow stone path, wondering what I was in for.

The scent of a spicy curry reached my nose before my feet reached the door. Lemongrass and coconut. Lane opened the oversize unpainted wood front door. As usual, he had on the thick horn-rimmed glasses he wore to hide his distinctive cheekbones and distractingly handsome face. He kept his dark blond hair slightly long so it could fall over his eyes to shield half his face when it suited him. He looked as delicious as the food smelled.

A Nina Simone song sounded from a distant speaker, but I didn't hear voices behind him.

"Are people in back watching the sunset?"

"I thought a dinner party for the two of us was called for. We haven't had enough time just for us lately."

I smiled "The offense of not coming to see me at the Tandoori

Palace last night hardly calls for borrowing this perfect house to make a big apology."

"You look gorgeous tonight, Jones." He took the wine and my coat, and closed the door from the chill.

"Now I'm really worried." I was dressed in my standard all-black outfit, from a black cashmere sweater down to black jeans and black three-inch stilettos. And of course my bob of black hair, that in spite of what Tamarind had said, was a couple of inches longer than when I'd met her.

"That look on your face could lure a thousand sailors to their doom. If I didn't know better, I'd say you had a new mystery your mind is working on."

"It's funny you mention sailors, because I've got two new problems I'm mulling over, one of which involves a man who might have been a sailor on a ship that sank at port during the California Gold Rush when all the men were abandoning their ships to go in search of gold. And the other..."

He raised an eyebrow. "The other is clearly one that requires a glass of wine."

I gave him a brief kiss. "In a minute. Right now I'm just taking in this wonderful space. You knew how much I'd love this place, so you borrowed it from a friend who's away..." That's when I noticed the house wasn't furnished. I pushed past Lane. I remembered the grand fireplace and an open floor plan leading to a modern kitchen with an island bigger than my kitchenette.

I thought back to the two holes I'd assumed were from gophers. "This place is sitting empty. Wait, you removed a FOR SALE sign so the neighbors would think someone bought it?" It must have been a house-flipper who bought it when I'd looked at it. But when I saw his face... "You *bought* this house?"

"Guilty."

The man I was hopelessly in love with.

The person I trusted more than anyone else on the planet, and would have even if we hadn't each saved each other's lives countless times.

The former jewel thief.

Had just purchased my dream house.

"You know I've been looking for somewhere more permanent to live," he said. "Tamarind told me you'd fallen in love with this place. It was on the market again, so I went to an open house. As soon as I walked through the entryway arch, I'd fallen in love as well."

He was talking about the house, but looking at me as he said it. We both knew what he was saying.

"You know how competitive the housing market is here," he continued. "I had to move quickly, and they accepted my offer."

My gaze swept across the empty interior. *Mostly* empty interior. A jewelry box rested on the mantle. It was an approximation of the jewelry box I'd once owned before it had been smashed by an intruder. This one was less ornate, but more beautiful. Definitely hand crafted. I walked to the fireplace and ran my fingers over the carved wood.

"I had it made for you," Lane said. "I thought it could be a housewarming present."

"Housewarming?"

"I was hoping you might move in here with me."

CHAPTER 10

"Don't answer yet," Lane said. "Let me give you the rest of the tour." He grabbed my hand and pulled me toward sliding doors that led to the backyard.

The house was the highest one on the street. There was nothing obstructing our view down the steep hillside and outward across the bay toward San Francisco, Marin, and the hazy sunset. Lights from the cities below sparkled, and the distinctive skyline across the water looked like a living painting. The fog cut through the skyscrapers as it tumbled across the bay.

"I haven't signed the final paperwork yet, but this is what I've been busy with. This is why I told you I'd be tied up this week and couldn't make it last night."

"This has been the strangest day."

"Which you're certainly taking your time telling me about."

"You might have noticed someone has been distracting me."

"In more ways than one, I hope." He swept me into his arms and kissed me. "I promise that's the last of my distractions. Now, food, wine, or a tour?"

"All three. Reverse order."

We went back inside, and Lane led me up the hardwood steps to the second floor. With the house sitting empty, I felt like I was creeping up the steps of a mansion in a Gabriela Glass novel.

"You know Rick Coronado?" I asked.

"The author whose books you hide behind the academic ones on your bookshelf?"

"That obvious?"

"Only because the academic books aren't for show, so I've seen what's behind them when you pull them off the shelf. I noticed after I read one of the articles about you where the reporter said they'd seen a beaten-up copy of *Jaipur Glass* in your bag. Or maybe it was *Empire of Glass*."

"Could have been either. I've got both. Rick Coronado read about my being a fan of his. It turns out he's a fan of mine as well. He hasn't written in years, but apparently I've inspired him to write again. He's sending me draft chapters of his latest manuscript, asking for my feedback."

"Do I need to be jealous?" His lips ticked up into a smile that barely held back laughter.

"You're hilarious."

Rick Coronado was a literary heartthrob, so I couldn't deny it was flattering. But I forgot all about the author and his manuscript as we stepped past a bathroom with a claw foot tub and into the master bedroom. Exposed hardwood beams dominated the sloping ceiling of the room, and the view was even more spectacular than the backyard. This alone would have commanded millions of dollars in the Bay Area.

He slipped his fingers into mine. His hand was warm and strong. Standing here, this felt like home.

Lane had an uprooted childhood like my own, which is one of the reasons we understood each other so well. His father cared more about business than his son, and dropped Lane into various international schools wherever he took the family, not caring about the impact on his wife and son. Both were expected to behave perfectly at the many important business parties his father threw, and Lane became good at playing the part. So good that he could drift from one language to another, and without knowing it fooled people into thinking he was a native speaker. As he learned to act the part, he grew more and more angry at his father. His father and colleagues cared more about money than anything else and used ruthless tactics to achieve their wealth.

When I met him the summer before last, Lane was a graduate student getting his PhD in art history. I'd gone to talk with him to get his expert opinion about a piece of Indian jewelry I'd received under mysterious circumstances. Because of complications from helping me, he'd been forced to leave the grad school program. But we'd gone on to rescue several lost treasures together.

I felt so at home here in this house with Lane at my side. Shouldn't that have made me feel comforted? It didn't. The feeling scared me.

"I think I'll take that wine now," I said.

We ran downstairs like kids, and I picked up the jewelry box while Lane set up a picnic basket spread on the floor in front of the fireplace.

As I lifted the wooden box, an object inside rattled. "This isn't empty."

"Of course not. An empty box isn't a very nice housewarming gift, is it? It needs something special inside."

I opened the lid. Inside sat a sparkling ruby bracelet. The dark red gem caught in the light and cast a beautiful reflection onto the side of the box. The box that nearly slipped through my fingers as I forgot I was holding it.

This was one of the Rajasthan Rubies.

I forgot to breathe.

"Jones?"

"You *did* take it," I whispered.

A shy grin spread across Lane's face. "Two of the dozens we found. I saved them for you."

"Two?" I croaked. I turned my attention back to the jewelry box. Opening one of the smaller drawers with shaking fingers, I lifted a solitary raw ruby into the palm of my hand.

I'd always wondered...When we'd found the Indian treasure in the Highlands of Scotland that summer we first met, the ground had already been disturbed.

Five years before that, Lane quit his previous job. As an international jewel thief.

I didn't know the details of the traumatic experience that was the catalyst for his decision, but I knew he'd realized that many of the art and jewels he'd stolen from one wealthy collector had simply ended up in another private collection, away from historians and the public.

"I can't keep these. I mean, *we* can't keep them. They should have been turned in with the rest." But as I spoke the words, I didn't want to let go of the thick gold band with an inset ruby or the ruby as big as my thumbnail. My hands trembled. I closed the jewelry box and set it back on the mantle. I kept the ruby and bracelet in my hand.

"I'm not Robin Hood. I've never lied to you, Jones. I never claimed to be."

"But not *this*."

The flicker of a strong emotion crossed Lane's face. He was good enough at hiding his emotions that I couldn't be sure what it was.

"Where are the rest of the Rajasthan Rubies now?" he asked. His voice was outwardly calm, but now I'd identified the emotion. Not anger. Not indignation. Disappointment.

I stared at Lane, uncomprehending. "What?"

"Where are they?"

"You already know where they are. The British and Indian governments are in negotiations."

"Exactly. Are the Rajasthan Rubies in a museum?"

"No. But that doesn't mean you get to decide what you take for yourself."

"Why not? It would have been lost forever if not for you. You deserve it. So much more than the people who generally end up with riches. I've seen it happen too often. Precious art disappearing because powerful people who want to save face won't bend. They'd rather the art be lost to everyone than for their own ego to be bruised."

"It'll get resolved."

"One day. Maybe. Until then, won't you get joy from this?

Seeing your face—"

"That's not the point. I'd like the Mona Lisa on my wall too."

Lane's lips ticked up into what I'm sure was an involuntary smile. "Would you? God, I always hated that painting. It's like she's mocking us."

"I was making a point with a hypothetical example. But maybe an Ogata Korin painted screen. I'd love that."

"And if you had one you'd loan it to a museum or at the very least have it photographed so people can experience it. I might actually have a contact—"

I choked.

"Legally!" Lane hurriedly continued. "I think I saw that there's one up for auction soon. See—*that* look. That's all I ever wanted. That makes everything worth it. You'd be inspired to rescue more treasures."

"According to you, so they'll end up in a government's labyrinthine secret basement—"

"You can cross that bridge when you come to it."

"Wonderful. My very own Devil's Bridge." I put the bracelet and ruby back in the box, left it on the mantle, and headed for the door.

"Jones, wait."

I didn't.

Lane had tried to end our relationship several times, because he was gallantly trying to protect me, acting like the knight his mother had named him after. He'd been afraid his past would catch up with him. And it had. That past year we'd been blackmailed into working for one of his former associates. We'd come out the other side, and Lane was ready to stay put near me and be together. It all happened so fast that I hadn't been ready to commit. It was my turn to be conflicted. After believing I wanted a more stable life than the one I'd grown up with, I'd found myself unexpectedly drawn to the adventures that had taken me all over the world to save lost pieces of history. I'd always loved the Gabriela Glass novels, but never thought I wanted to be her in real life. Until it turned out I did.

I was so angry I knew I wouldn't sleep that night. I was right, but not for the reason I imagined.

When I reached home, I stormed up the stairs loudly enough that I must have disturbed Nadia. Almost as soon as I slipped out of my shoes and locked the door, she knocked.

"Sorry for the stomping," I said.

Nadia shrugged. "We all have bad nights sometimes. This arrived for you." She handed me a slim package. It was the next chapter from Rick Coronado.

CHAPTER 11

The Glass Thief
Chapter Three
Tristan Ruben's Pigalle apartment, Paris, France

Gabriela was immediately drawn to the handsome, mysterious Tristan, Luc's old university friend who had been present for Luc's strange two deaths.

Of course, nearly everything could be explained and wrapped up quickly if, like Laura, she accepted that Tristan was lying. Nearly everything.

Gabriela wished to hear Tristan's story from his own mouth. And what a mouth it was...

Tristan had agreed to meet her at his apartment, with a view of the Moulin Rouge, on the condition the police weren't involved. Why was that, she wondered? What did he have to hide? If he was guilty, surely he would have disappeared that night, as he easily could have.

Gabriela Glass could sweet-talk men from secret societies across the world into showing her documents in long-forgotten archives; she could learn a local language fluently to pay her respects to tribal elders who would then trust her enough to show her maps no American had ever seen before; and she had braved many a mosquito and snake-filled jungle.

But solve two crimes that had baffled a wealthy family for more than half a century, along with a new murder committed that week? She wished to right a wrong for Laura Delacroix, and she wasn't above admitting that the Serpent King reward intrigued her. This was a challenge like no other.

Tristan Rubens clutched a cigarette as if for dear life, while offering her a glass of port, which he deftly opened and poured with his free hand. She followed his fingertips with her gaze, wondering what those fingers might do to her. Were they the hands of a lover or those of a killer? Perhaps both. Like Gabriela herself.

"I gave my statement to the authorities," Tristan said. They spoke French, Tristan's mother tongue.

"You spoke with them about the death of your friend." Gabriela paused and took a sip as she watched his face for his reaction. Grief. Subtle, yet unmistakable. "I'm sorry for your loss. The authorities don't have much to go on to locate the missing family heirloom. The Serpent King. I was called for that." She didn't mention that she thought he would lead her directly to it.

Tristan laughed without humor. "Keeping up appearances. Any hint of a scandal is worse than the alternative. They cannot say the sculpture was itself stolen, so they cannot give a good description."

Gabriela found her gaze dipping to Tristan's lush lips and sculpted arms, then back to his forlorn gaze. Falling into his arms could be a welcome distraction. And perhaps he would talk in his sleep.

Gabriela had dressed today in knee-high brown hiking boots which she hadn't buffed, well-worn khakis, and a green cloak over a simple white cotton blouse from Nepal. Sweepingly stunning on the outside, and elegantly casual as soon as she stepped inside and removed the cloak. Tristan was a traveler, so she had dressed to put him at ease. Her skills were best used to blend in—well, not exactly blend. She stood out wherever she went. But she stood out as a different person in each location.

"Tell me about that night," she said.

"You know about the family ghost. I expect you also know that Laura Delacroix believes I'm using the legend to cover my own crime. But I swear to you, I'm telling the truth."

"So you believe in the ghost?"

"I didn't used to. But after what I saw—"

"What exactly did you see?"

Tristan told her the same story Laura had.

"Stop," she commanded. "Why are you creating an impossible situation for yourself? Surely you see that if nobody else was found in the house, and the snow was untouched outside when the police and paramedics arrived, that you are the only suspect. Why make up a ridiculous story of a man being murdered two times? Why not simply say it was an accident?"

"Because I'm speaking the truth."

Gabriela pressed her index finger to his chest in frustration. "You're telling me Luc Delacroix was first strangled by invisible hands. Invisible? Surely you mean the man or woman was dressed in black, so you couldn't identify them. And the person must have failed at killing him, which is why he was attacked again."

"No, Mademoiselle Glass. I saw him through the glass doors of the second-floor library. We were only a few feet away from each other. He was alone in that room, and yet he was strangled by an invisible man behind him. I saw the imprint of the fingers gripping his neck. As he struggled, his face became red, then purple."

"Perhaps he was choking. He could have had something stuck in his throat."

"Something that would cause the glass door to slam between us and lock? And for him to fight with his attacker?"

Gabriela thought about the animals of the jungle. Its fiercest predators could be silent until they wanted you to see them. In some ways the predatory animals were smarter than man. But she knew there were ways a man could hide himself. Tristan had surely been too shaken to see the hidden murderer.

"And Luc's second death?"

"I called for an ambulance. There was a slight chance he might have still been alive. I went downstairs to let them in. As they came inside, we all saw Luc being thrown down the stairs by an invisible force. He landed at our feet, his neck broken. For a second time that night."

Gabriela's heart pounded. Surely the words he spoke could not be true. The events he described were impossible.

Tristan continued. "The two men from the service d'aide medical urgante were more frightened than I was, seeing Luc killed by the ghost. Did they think it a joke, or a nightmare from which they could not wake up? One of the men was especially superstitious. He looked around nervously, shouting, 'Where is the ghost!? Where is it!?' When the police arrived, we learned about another strange aspect of the mystery."

"The Serpent King statue was gone," Gabriela said.

"Yes. At first, the police were convinced I had taken it earlier in the day and covered up my crime by murdering my friend. But there were two problems they couldn't ignore, which is why they let me go. First, several people witnessed Luc die as he was flung down the stairs by the ghost."

Tristan paused and looked at Gabriela with naked

fear in his eyes. "Second, there was no opportunity for me to remove the statue. Snow had been falling all day, but it stopped shortly after the Delacroix family left the home for the anniversary night. The snow surrounding the house was pristine. No footsteps approached the house except for mine and Luc's when we entered the house, and those prints were nearly covered by the snow. We never left."

"Laura Delacroix is positive the Serpent King statue was in the house when they departed," Gabriela murmured. She had searched the house herself, thinking that Tristan must have been lying and hidden it. But if there was a secret passageway she'd missed, she didn't live up to her name.

"There's no way for the statue to have left the house," Tristan said, "unless carried out by an entity that can float above the snow."

"A ghost."

Only Gabriela Glass didn't believe in ghosts. She believed in many things in this strange world, but had never encountered a ghost. The secret rested with the Serpent King. The family was hiding its history, as a valuable treasure stolen from India.

To solve the puzzle, Gabriela Glass needed a historian. Not just any historian.

She knew exactly who she would call.

CHAPTER 12

I rubbed my eyes and read the last paragraph again. Like that would make it change. But I'd half expected I'd imagined it. Gabriela Glass was asking for my help.

I read the last lines of the chapter again:

> *Gabriela Glass needed a historian. Not just any historian.*
> *She knew exactly who she would call.*

I have a healthy ego. An overly developed one, if you were to ask my brother Mahilan. But I didn't think I was imagining that Gabriela and Rick meant me.

Rick Coronado had spared no expense getting this new chapter to me quickly, with a same day cross-country delivery leaving New York at seven o'clock in the morning reaching me at five o'clock. What was the urgency? The answer screamed at me from the page. This wasn't fiction. It was real life.

Rick Coronado wasn't asking for my help to write a book—*he was asking for my help to solve a murder and find a lost treasure.*

I reread the pages. He was telling me that Tristan Rubens was guilty of both crimes, but the mystery was solving *how* the murderous thief had accomplished it. The secret lay in the Serpent King statue from Munnar—how had it been removed from the house?

The problem was, I couldn't find any records of a looted

Serpent King statue from Munnar, or anywhere else in India. Not everything could be found on the internet, but surely it was a big deal if Rick was in search of it.

Let's be honest. He was writing the book for me, and quite possibly manipulating me to help him. Damn right I could start thinking of him simply as Rick.

I could also call the man. That didn't mean he had to answer my call, which he didn't. I followed up with a text. *I know you're asking for my help with a real-life puzzle. I need more details if you truly want my help.*

I remembered it was the middle of the night in New York. But if he wanted my help so urgently, wouldn't he have left his phone on? I stared angrily at the unresponsive phone for another minute before turning to more productive tasks.

My immediate impulse was to call Lane. He was the person I could turn to talk through things like this. I was capable of solving problems on my own, but I thought more clearly with him at my side. But if he could keep something so big from me, did I know him as well as I thought I did? I still needed to wrap my head around everything that had happened earlier that night. I couldn't call Lane.

There was no way I was getting to sleep any time soon, so I got down to work.

I knew a lot about Rick already, but it wasn't like I was a superfan. I enjoyed his escapist books. I didn't know much about him personally, but no one living in the United States with a television or internet connection could have missed the coverage of his disappearance seven years ago. Missing for six weeks. Long enough for all sorts of theories to abound, but not too long for the public to forget him.

No passport activity was found (at least none recorded at the time, though the police later found a visa stamp from China in his passport). No credit cards used. No turning up on surveillance cameras. His brother Vincent, who was also his business manager, had been frantic, but commentators had been skeptical that his motives were purely from brotherly love. Vincent lived a lavish lifestyle courtesy of his brother's success.

Born Ricardo Coronado in the Bronx, New York, forty-nine years ago, Rick was a hopeless student as a child. His teachers' notes to his parents indicated he was smart but far too easily distracted. That changed when he was accepted into a high school for the arts. He wrote his first novel at seventeen. This was before the internet. That, he said in many interviews, is what saved him from himself, because he wasn't able to publish it himself. To this day, he hadn't resurrected the self-declared dreck. That "dreck" was rejected by publishers, but was good enough to land him an agent. His first Gabriela Glass novel, *Heart of Glass*, set in New York and Mexico, was published when he was twenty years old.

I looked up from my laptop to the world map that covered the wall above my mini living room. I hadn't realized he was so young when the book had been published. That explained some of Gabriela's more difficult-to-believe backstory, such as infiltrating a drug cartel when she was thirteen to rescue her mother. (Said drug cartel had accidentally discovered Mayan ruins with a hoard of gold, which Gabriela proceeded to rescue for the descendants of the Mayans, after she rescued her mother.)

Over the course of nineteen novels over the next twenty-two years leading up to Rick's disappearance, Gabriela had remained eternally twenty-six years old. Whatever he was working on at the time would have been his twentieth novel.

I'd already looked up the Delacroix family mentioned in the manuscript but found nothing. Rick would have changed the name. I tried searching for a French tea empire. Interesting history abounded, but none of it appeared to be related to a murderous family ghost and a stolen statue. Several prominent families and homes were supposedly haunted, but that didn't get me anywhere. Unless I decided to give up being an academic and move to Paris to become a tour guide. Which I admitted didn't sound completely unappealing.

I was also at a disadvantage because I didn't speak French. I was the antithesis of Gabriela. The only language I spoke fluently was English. Though I'd been born in Goa, India, my parents spoke mostly English with each other and with me and Mahilan, since my dad is American and English gets you far in India. When I was little I used to speak a smattering of local languages well enough to communicate with people (in a country with over seventy formal languages and hundreds more dialects, it wasn't uncommon to have conversations that lapsed into three or more languages), but since we left India when I was eight, I'd forgotten most of them. I spoke enough Hindi to help with my dissertation research, but studying the British East India Company, most of my research was accessible in English.

Research in French wouldn't work—not unless I called my one French friend. But I wasn't going to bother Sébastien Renaud. He was the liveliest ninety-one-year-old I knew, but I still felt guilty that he'd caught pneumonia after we were trapped in frigid waters inside a dungeon of Mont Saint-Michel together, when he was trying to save my life. I had other avenues of research I could pursue. Like Rick's own statements. Rick was handsome and charismatic, and loved to talk about himself. That made him a natural for interviews—at least until he holed up as a recluse nearly seven years ago. I'd seen a few before, and I easily found hundreds more of them online.

My stomach rumbled. I hadn't eaten dinner with Lane as planned. I opened my fridge. I don't know what I was expecting to have magically appeared since I'd last looked. Staring back at me were bottles of mango pickle, ginger chutney, Dijon mustard, harissa sauce, and a package of coffee beans. A takeout container was behind the coffee beans, but the remains of the super-size burrito hadn't survived. Hidden behind it was a foil-wrapped piece of naan from the Tandoori Palace. I tossed it into the toaster oven and hit play on a video that had a lot of viewers. An entertainment television show interview. I didn't care if he liked to eat the same things for breakfast as Gabriela. The toaster oven dinged. The scent of the garlicky bread filled my drafty studio apartment. I slathered chutney over the toasty bread and clicked on another video. Fifteen videos later, I hadn't found anything remotely relevant, but I could tell you all about the stock answers Rick had on standby for generic interview questions. I was falling into the same trap my students did. As I always told them, general internet searches were ranked not for accuracy, but for things like popularity, size of the site, and good keywords a web developer had entered on the back end.

I didn't want pop culture interviews with Rick. I needed details about his research. Though he did in-depth historical research, he wasn't taken seriously by the academic community of historians. I wouldn't find any interviews in academic journals. But what about student projects or amateur historians?

I went back to Rick's website and found an archived list of his past events. On the extensive tour for his last book, only months before his disappearance, he'd done events at several bookstores in college towns.

Bingo.

The sound quality of this college video channel was so bad I nearly gave up on the video—until I heard the next question.

"You're known for doing immersive historical research," she said. The interviewer's voice and expression were serious, but I caught the edges of her lips tick upward as she asked her question. "Have you ever found a treasure yourself?"

They were perched on high stools, two fake plants behind them. A second camera cut to a close-up of Rick's face.

Rick chuckled. Well-rehearsed, yet still charming. "Not yet. But for my next book...Well, I can't spoil it." He gave a shy grin. Was he flirting with her?

"Our audience would love a hint."

He stroked his chin. Another rehearsed move. "I can tell you this much. Sometimes we take the things right in front of us for granted. I really shouldn't say more." He paused. The view was still from the close-up camera. A few strands of gray hair on his temples shone in the harsh artificial light. Fine lines crinkled around his eyes.

I held my breath. He was dying to say more.

"I really shouldn't..." he repeated, looking at the interviewer. All she had to do was prompt him.

A faint clunk sounded before the interviewer spoke again. "Ouch, all right," she whispered, still off camera, before her voice returned to normal volume. "We'd love to hear more."

"I've noticed something," Rick said, "that nobody else has. Not for more than a hundred years. This time, Gabriela Glass will prove herself worthy in the real world."

The interviewer's face betrayed her. She thought he was joking with her. But she was wrong.

I confirmed the number of views for this video with terrible production values. Seventeen. Nobody had put this together with his disappearance, *because they hadn't seen it.*

The treasure. The story. This wasn't fiction. It was what Rick Coronado was after seven years ago when he'd failed. And now, he was asking for my help to find the Serpent King.

CHAPTER 13

I must have fallen asleep at some point, but when sunlight hit my eyes, it felt like I hadn't slept at all. I was hoping a message from Rick would be waiting for me in the morning. There was, but it wasn't what I expected.

Is that your only feedback for now? Do your friends think you're right?

"Do my friends think I'm right?" I shouted at the leaking ceiling. "Why can't you answer a question like a normal person?"

I pulled my fuzzy warm sweater on and called Abby Wu. She didn't answer. Of course. It was Saturday, and I had her work number. I found her email on the publisher's website. My fridge was empty as usual, so I slipped on a hooded jacket to shield me from the rain and went in search of sustenance and warm coffee. By the time I'd returned, Abby had sent a brief reply saying she'd call me shortly.

"Can't you get him to tell us what's going on?" I asked. "Gabriela Glass needs a historian, and I swear it seems like he's asking for my help with a real mystery."

"I see why Rick likes you. You think outside the box. But I think you're reading more into this than is there. He has a quirky sense of humor."

"But the last line of the chapter. It has to be him asking for my help to find this Serpent King statue."

"Wait—what?"

My breath caught. "The Serpent King? You mean it's real?"

"Not that I know of."

"But your voice—"

"I'm annoyed. He's being derivative. Reusing one of his old plots. You remember *Empire of Glass*, set in Cambodia?"

"Of course."

"You know cobras are a recurring motif in his books, that Gabriela is an excellent snake-handler, and the series has a recurring character named Snake. I'm surprised he has that huge dog instead of a snake for a pet. A gold statue called the Snake King is a McGuffin Gabriela wastes her time searching for, not the main treasure, in *Empire of Glass*."

I frowned. "I think I'd remember that." Gabriela had traveled to the real temples of Angkor Wat and Banteay Chhmar, Angkorian era temples with concentric blocks of courtyards with ornate carved structures inside, and Rick had invented a fictional version of the temple of Preah Vihear for Gabriela to discover. A *naga* king was mentioned as part of Cambodia's legendary origin, but there was no snake sculpture.

"Hmm. You might be right. If he listened to my editorial feedback, which he only does half the time, that would have been cut. But it doesn't make sense. He wouldn't reuse an old idea. At least the old Rick wouldn't have done so. I was hoping he was writing something fresh." She sighed.

"This one is set in France, and the Serpent King was stolen from Munnar in India before being stolen from the French family who'd looted it." As I spoke the words out loud, I was again struck by the fact that the location made no sense. The French had colonized parts of India, but not the tea plantations of Munnar. Rick should have known that, just as he should have known the game of strategy he referenced was already obsolete when Algernon Delacroix was in India.

"Could you scan the pages so I can read them?" Abby asked. "I know they're not ready for me yet, and I'll do my best not to take my red pen to them. But I might be able to help figure out what he's doing."

"I've already taken photos of the pages. I'll send them over."

"And on my end I'll see if I can get a better answer from Rick. Hang on a minute."

I nearly choked on my coffee when I heard her gasp.

I held my breath. If this had been one of Rick's thrillers, this would be when the person helping me was conveniently dispatched by the bad guys. But there were no bad guys here...Or were there?

"Abby?" I squeaked. "Are you all right?"

"Damn him," she muttered. Her voice was hollow, as if it was in the distance. "I can't believe he'd—"

"Abby?"

"Sorry, let me get you off speaker phone. Can you hear me better now?"

"Yes. What's going on?"

"Rick got right back to me. Do you know what he said? *That would be giving you a spoiler.* I'm his editor! I'm supposed to get the spoilers! Look, I should call him. He can't do this to us."

"He really hasn't told you anything else about this book?"

"No. And I can't do anything about it because my bosses are thrilled. It doesn't matter to them that he's hit on me so many times over the years, and it doesn't matter to them what he's writing, as long as he's writing. F&S has the right of first refusal for any new Rick Coronado novels—"

"The right of what?"

"Sorry. Industry-speak. If Rick writes another novel, Fox & Sons has the right to make an offer on the book. Rick can't shop it to any other publishers. He's a big enough star at this point that his agent should be asking for a six or seven-figure advance for any new novel. Instead, he's just writing the book before negotiating."

"Do you think he's all right?"

"Do you mean is he mentally stable? He never has been, in my opinion. Not clinically. I'm not worried about him harming himself or anything like that. But he's temperamental like an artist. Look, I should really go call him—"

"If he's set on keeping this to himself, he won't talk."

"Oh, I'll get him to talk to me." Her voice shook. "He and I grew up together, in a sense. I've been his editor for twenty-five years, since I was an Assistant Editor and he was finding his legs with his third Gabriela Glass novel."

"And he never told you what happened for those six weeks when he disappeared?"

She was silent for so long I wondered if she'd hung up on me. But I didn't think so. I waited. It was like when I wanted my students to ask questions but nobody would speak up. You waited them out.

"He never spoke of that missing period of time. Not to any of us." Her voice was different now. As if she was questioning what she thought she knew about this man she thought she knew well. I knew the feeling.

"What about a girlfriend he might have confided in?"

"There was a new one every few months. They threw themselves at him, but none of them lasted. He always said he was waiting for his true love. And obviously he wouldn't have confided in Vincent."

"He doesn't trust his brother?"

"Vincent would have tried to convince him to televise his exploits for a reality TV show. That man tries to monetize everything. So no, there was nobody he'd confide in."

"I read that some of his doctors weren't convinced he had amnesia."

"Be careful about believing everything you read. One doctor doubted it, and he spoke to the press. I believed Rick. And since we'd grown up in this business together and all...We told each other things we didn't tell other people."

"What kind of things?"

"I'm the one who kept him from killing off Gabriela more than once—he said he wanted to write a series with a male hero, a more realistic character than Gabriela. Sure, she can speak two dozen languages, survive without her own food and water for weeks in the jungle, and kill a cobra with her bare hands. But that's what readers *want.* At least that's what they expect from a Rick Coronado novel. He wasn't writing *War and Peace.*"

"But the missing six weeks? Abby?"

"The bastard," she muttered. "I sat with him in the hospital and he swore to me he couldn't remember. *But what if he did?*"

"And he wants my help to do what he couldn't."

"Be careful, dear. He's a master at his craft. With Rick, nothing is what it seems."

CHAPTER 14

I turned up the volume on my headphones and ran through the rain listening to bhangra beats. I did a five-mile loop through Golden Gate Park.

Sanjay jokes that I'm a terrible Indian, and I can't say he's wrong. I can't explain what Ayurveda is except to say I know my eating habits would horrify a practitioner, I don't know how to wear a sari, and I've never made it through an entire yoga class (and no, I don't wish to discuss the circumstances under which I was kicked out for disturbing the tranquility). But playing the tabla and going running are the two activities where I achieve close to a meditative state. As I was on mile four on the home stretch of the winding path, I knew what I had to do.

At the edge of the park, on the cusp between the protected greenery and the concrete consumerism of Haight Street, I paused to stretch and let my breath return to normal. I lifted my face to the sky to let the cool rain wash over me, receiving more than one judgmental glance from pedestrians carrying large umbrellas.

I brushed wet hair from my eyes and made a phone call.

"I'm out," I said, then hung up after I'd spoken those two words into Rick's voicemail.

I knew it was the right thing to do, but I wished I hadn't been put in the position that made it necessary. Now I knew it was better not to get to know your heroes personally. It was a good thing Egyptologist Amelia Peabody had lived a century before me, so I could imagine she was as incredible and brilliant as she was in her memoirs and the biographies written about her.

My phone rang as I trudged up the outer stairs leading to my apartment. I didn't know the number, but it was a New York City area code.

"Jaya."

I knew that voice. Deep and charming, even with a single world.

"Rick?"

"We need to talk."

"Too late." I wished Tamarind had been there to witness it.

"There's more going on here than you realize."

I almost laughed. The words sounded like something Gabriela would say. But something in the worried tone of his voice told me he wasn't joking.

"I understand that the Serpent King is real." I unlocked my door and kicked it shut behind me. "If you want to salvage any chance of getting my help—"

"I'm coming to San Francisco."

"Stop right there. I'm not waiting for you to come to San Francisco." I'm fairly certain I was shouting now. "You need to tell me *now*. We can video chat if talking by phone isn't enough."

"That's not why." There was a break in his words and a muffled sound. "I'll be there soon. In the meantime, don't do anything else."

"But—"

"Tomorrow—no, Sunday is too soon. First I need to...Make it Monday. Monday at dawn. Under the clocktower at the Ferry Building. I'll call if anything changes."

The line went dead.

Monday at dawn? Under the clocktower? Rick had been reading too many of his own novels.

In the meantime, *don't do anything else?* Not likely.

Tamarind was working that day, so once I arrived on campus she took a break to join me in the secret courtyard. The spot wasn't technically a secret, but you had to walk through a back hallway to get there, and it was mainly used by the library's staff on their breaks. A picnic table and benches were bolted into place on the square concrete tiles, and my favorite part was that it was encased by plants in oversize rectangular planter boxes with a mural of San Francisco painted along the outward-facing surface.

I groaned when I saw her hair.

"You don't like it?" Her short hair was now emerald green. "It's in honor of Gabriela."

"That's why I groaned." I told her about my revelation that the manuscript was fact rather than fiction, Rick's cryptic text asking what my friends thought of my theory, my conversation with the reclusive author, and how he wanted to meet at dawn under the Ferry Building clocktower.

"Shut. Up. Rick Coronado has truly lost it and thinks he's in one of his books?"

"I believe him."

"And you've lost your mind too?"

"Help me think through the research to see where to go next. If we come up with nothing, I'll happily go back to my office and prepare for the last week of the semester."

"Well, at least I'm honored that you came to me instead of staying in bed all day with Lane on this gorgeous Saturday. No...You two had a fight?"

"How is it possible my face is that obvious?"

"Oh, fine. I was going to drag out the gag, but that's cruel. Your face doesn't betray you. He did. He came around the library as soon as it opened, hoping to catch you. He thought we might have gotten coffee together before my shift. So why *didn't* you seek my advice this morning?"

"I've been busy. I was up half the night—"

"Rebound already? I did *not* expect that from you, Jaya Jones."

I glared at her. "I was doing research into Rick Coronado.

Which is what convinced me he's onto something real."

"Okay. I'll help. But what gives with Lane?"

"We're not talking about my love life while there's a ticking clock."

She whipped her head around and shifted into a guarded stance. The soles of her purple combat boots had done some damage in their heyday. "Is there? A ticking clock, I mean."

"I have no idea. But I plan to find out. What with Rick's secret messages..."

"OMG you just did that thing with your face, like you figured it out!"

I reached into my messenger bag and pulled out the handwritten letter with the snake he'd sketched.

"This snake," I murmured. "It's a cobra. A serpent."

"Tomato, to-mah-toe."

This was a pretty simple drawing, but its hooded head was clearly meant to be a cobra, so I'd taken it to be a doodle related to Gabriela. Could there be more to the sketch than was visible to the naked eye? I grabbed my phone and texted Sanjay.

"Well done," Tamarind said. "Half a day for a rebound ain't bad."

My glare deepened into a scowl. "We need his help."

"We do? Because we're helpless women?" She crossed her arms and returned my scowl.

"We need Sanjay because we're not magicians."

"Touché."

While I waited for Sanjay to be free after a rehearsal, I got to work at the library. I was on my own, as Tamarind got pulled into doing her job. Fair enough.

"Why do students only realize they need a librarian's help when it's the last week of the semester? I'll come find you when I'm done pointing the next generation in the right direction. So it'll be a while."

Historical research has been made easier in recent years through the digitizing of archives and newspapers. It's a development that allows people who otherwise wouldn't have the means or access to discover history, but it also comes with pitfalls. The old dearth of information has given way to a flood of data. Finding the relevant pieces in the glut of noise can be a challenge. I didn't have a name. I didn't know which facts Rick had changed, so I began where Rick began the story. With the first ghostly death. I pulled up newspaper archives from Paris in 1950.

An hour later I had nothing to show for my efforts except for feeling ravenous. Tamarind was helping four anthropology students, so I slipped out of the library for a cappuccino and croissant at the student-run coffee shop. I'd eaten half the croissant before I realized I'd copied Gabriela Glass's usual order.

Before I could dig into the second half of the croissant, the pastry disappeared before my eyes.

"You spotted me heading here from the library?" I said to the person I knew was behind me.

"This was a more fun way to say hello." Sanjay popped the last of my croissant into his mouth and sat down next to me.

For a brief window of my life I'd wondered if Sanjay and I would become more than friends, but now the universe had realigned. Sanjay was my closest friend, so much like a brother to me that he often felt like more of a brother than my real one. Because with Sanjay, I had all of the comfort of knowing he'd fly around the world for me (and he had) but none of the baggage of stupid childhood fights. Though apparently I still had to wrangle over food. As long as it wasn't spicy.

"I'm still hungry," I said. "Are you going to buy me another one? And how are you not at all wet when it's pouring rain outside?"

"All I get for bringing you my invisible ink kit is half a croissant?"

"I should have gone to the kid's section of a magic shop instead of waiting for you."

Sanjay clutched his hands to his heart. "You wound me. This is a *high-end* kid's invisible ink kit. What have you got?"

Though he was acting like his usual self, his dark eyes revealed how tired he was. He'd had bad luck with assistants recently, and the Napa Valley theater where he used to perform two sold-out seasons a year had burned in recent fires that devastated the region, so he was trying to figure out his next steps. He'd been rehearsing a new act, inspired by his trip to Japan, that he hoped would be a big success. I'd helped him with a couple of his shows in a pinch, so I knew how much practice it required to be a successful magician. Sanjay had mastered the mix of rigorous sleight of hand, physiological manipulation, and showmanship.

I showed him the cobra sketch Rick had presumably drawn. "I think there might be six or eight more snake heads around this central cobra head."

"Like a *naga*?"

"Exactly a *naga*. And maybe more clues."

"Clues? Okay, Velma. I'll see what I can do."

I already knew Rick had changed fact into fiction with the names of the family and missing treasure. What other details had he hidden? If Rick was searching for an Indian treasure he called the Serpent King, could there be more clues in the drawing I'd dismissed?

Seven- or nine-headed *naga* statues were found across India. The *naga* could be worshiped on its own, but was more widespread as a protector—either watching over the Buddha, as it was depicted in bronze and sandstone sculptures, or guarding treasure, as in the Kerala temple with a cobra lock that nobody had yet breached, the lock that had intrigued my student Wesley.

I got us each another pastry while Sanjay got to work. When I handed him the puff pastry, he shook his head. "All I've got so far is the visible sketch. And an amateur one at that."

"He's a writer. Not an artist."

Sanjay steepled his hands together. "He's a dude who's manipulating you." With a flourish, he produced a hardback copy of

Mayan Glass. "Look at his photo on the back cover. Is it humanly possible to look more pretentious?"

"Because he isn't smiling?"

"Of course not. I don't smile in my professional photographs. Men don't smile. It's his jacket. Patches for all the places in the world he's visited? Really?"

I tried to snatch the book away, but it disappeared.

"What's the deal with this sketch?" Sanjay asked.

"It's a long story, but it looks like there's a real treasure he wants my help finding. And since he's an eccentric author, he won't tell me exactly what's going on. He's asking for my help through his fiction."

"That's actually pretty cool. I wonder if I could do something similar in one of my acts. Hmmm..." His eyes wide, he turned back to the paper, but shook his head a moment later. "Nope. There's nothing more here."

"Nothing?"

"This is just what it looks like: a pencil sketch of a cobra."

I was back to where I started. No clues in the real world. No hidden drawings. Whatever Rick was trying to tell me was hidden in his text.

"Why don't you ask him?" Sanjay said. "He said he wanted feedback, right? Your feedback is his artwork sucks and you don't appreciate being jerked around."

"Right. Because that's the way to win someone over when you meet them."

Sanjay blinked at me. "Meet them? You're going to New York for this—"

"He's coming here."

"This is getting weird, Jaya."

"I know."

CHAPTER 15

I spent Sunday answering student emails and preparing for the last week of the semester, and barely slept Sunday night, in anticipation of my meeting with Rick Coronado.

Tamarind insisted on going with me to the Ferry Building at dawn for, in her words, my "clandestine meeting with the delusional author."

"I'm your BFF number two," she'd said, holding up her arm to pre-empt any objections. "Don't try to object. I know Sanjay is BFF number one. But he's a creature of the night. No way he's in top form before sunrise. Librarians get the job done."

Tamarind kept a lookout from behind a manga comic at the coffee house with glass walls, while I paced through the central corridor of the Ferry Building. We kept in touch by chatting with each other through our phones hidden in our jacket pockets. The sun was beginning to rise over the bay from the east, but Rick was coming from another time zone. What counted as sunrise?

"Have you thought about a strategy to get him to talk?" she asked. "You could seduce him—"

"I'm *not* seducing him." I turned and gave her a sharp look.

"Don't look my way! That's the whole point of me being over here and us talking on these walkie talkies."

"They're phones."

"In walkie-talkie mode. Over and out."

"He *wants* to talk to me. I don't need a strategy."

An hour later, I wasn't so sure. Rick Coronado hadn't arrived and I'd called him three times.

"I need to get to work," Tamarind said from my side, having given up on our walkie-talkie phone plan. "Sucks that he blew you off. It's definitely after sunrise."

"I have to get to class too."

"Doesn't look like you're moving."

"I'll stay a few more minutes."

A few more minutes turned into an hour. Because I couldn't believe he'd ditched me and wouldn't answer his phone. He was the one who'd asked for my help in the first place!

Damn, it was the height of rush hour. I'd never make it to campus before my class started. I hated to ask for a favor, but...

"Naveen Veeran," he answered on the second ring.

"I'm not in your phone contacts?"

His sigh was audible. "It's the polite way to answer the phone."

"Are you on campus already?"

"Of course. It's a busy week."

"Listen, I might be a few minutes late to my History of the British Empire class because of traffic. Could you check on my students, and cover for just a few—"

"I have my own work to do. You should be more prudent with your time."

"Could you walk over and—" The phone clicked off. "Leave a note on the door," I finished, speaking to nobody.

I wished I'd been on a landline phone so I could have slammed it into the receiver.

I sent a quick email to the class list saying I might be a few minutes late, hoping at least a few of them would see it in time to tell the rest to wait, then drove as fast as my roadster would go.

I arrived on campus twenty minutes after the class was scheduled to begin. The classroom doors were both closed, which was a good sign. I skidded to a halt, my heels wet from the misty rain outside, and eased open the door at the back of the classroom. Naveen was standing at the front of my class answering questions.

"Here she is," he said, then lowered his voice as I reached him. "I did it for them."

"Thank you. I'd be happy to return the favor."

The look of indignation on his face shouldn't have surprised me. Of course the punctual Naveen Veeran had never needed anyone to cover for him in his life.

"You didn't cover research methodologies?" he whispered, packing up the papers on the lectern.

"This is an intro class."

He left, shaking his head.

I put all thoughts of Naveen out of my mind as I taught. I stayed for half an hour after class ended to answer more questions, then closed the door to my office and enjoyed the first silence of the day.

"Why couldn't he simply have a phone conversation like a normal person?" I said out loud. Yes, I was completely aware I was the only person in my office. Except for Ganesha. Who I wasn't in the habit of speaking to.

Rick still hadn't gotten in touch to explain why he stood me up.

I would have lost my mind if it hadn't been the busiest week of the semester. In my twenty-student advanced historical research seminar that afternoon, the projects ranged from a comparison of the vastly different ways historians described a single event, with the student tracking down original sources to try and determine which historical account was closest to the truth; to a student interviewing professors of different disciplines that involved historical research, including archaeology, anthropology, and sociology, to see how each area approached history.

And then there was Becca's project showing each stage of lesser-known facts about San Francisco's sunken ship landfill. Given how much time she wanted to spend asking me questions, I was betting the project would be the most comprehensive paper. I didn't think it was likely she and Wesley would find their missing sunken ship, but I was hardly disappointed about that.

After class I went straight to office hours.

Before I could drop my bag into my desk drawer, Becca stepped into my office with a look of concern on her face.

"Are you all right, Dr. Jones?"

I hadn't thought my distraction over wondering what had happened to Rick showed on my face.

"Is it a guy?" she asked, then immediately reddened. "Sorry! I don't know why I said that."

I laughed. "It is, but not in the way that you think. Tell me what's going on with your letter about the sunken ship. How can I help?"

I was surprised to see a flash of annoyance cross her face.

"I've actually got one more thing I want to look up first," she said. "You've got a long line of people waiting to see you, so I'll come to your next office hours."

Ah. That explained the annoyance. She was frustrated at herself for not being further along in the project.

The following student asked if the due date was firm for properly formatted footnotes as well (it was), and the next asked if I could help her untangle her thesis statement that had gotten muddled (I did). Wesley Oh was the fourth student to arrive. His orange skateboard was poking out of the top of his backpack as usual.

Wesley gave me an embarrassed smile as he tugged at his uncouth hair. "I know I'm not one of your students and there's a line out here…"

I returned the smile. "There's time. Come in."

Since Naveen hadn't budged on helping Wesley with his research methods class proposal because it was one day late, I gave him some ideas for various ways to track down the origins of an unknown letter from clues about the writer to authentication.

When the last student left at the end of an especially busy afternoon, I stood to see him out, and found one last person waiting for me in the hallway. One who wasn't a student.

They say people can smile without the sentiment reaching their eyes, but in Lane's case, his eyes were so expressive I could see their hopeful smile, even though the expression didn't reach his lips.

"Jones."

"I'm sorry," I said. "But I can't do this right now. I'm not—"

"I know." Lane didn't step into the office, but as he leaned forward and handed me an envelope, I breathed in the faint scent of sandalwood that brought a tidal wave of memories. "A peace offering."

"This isn't the bracelet," I whispered, accepting the thin envelope. "Or the ruby."

"No. And it's not to open now, but when you're ready."

"Ready for what?"

"To know something about me I should have told you a long time ago." He smiled, but now his lips were turned up into a forced smile while his eyes held a sadness I didn't understand. I already knew the worst about him. What else could he possibly have to tell me?

I wish I'd been ready to ask him more then. I didn't realize how precious this time together could have been.

Because the following day, Rick Coronado's body was discovered in the San Francisco Bay.

CHAPTER 16

The body hadn't been identified yet, but I knew it was Rick. It was his unique bomber jacket with patches from places he'd visited. It was the one from his author photo. Nobody else in the world owned the same jacket.

I saw the story on the news when I stopped by the student coffee house, which was nearly deserted now that many of them had already cleared out for winter break. The sound was too low to hear, so I asked the barista if she could turn it up.

I felt like the air from my lungs was being squeezed out of me. My whole body felt heavy. Rick Coronado was dead. He'd been coming to San Francisco to see me. I alternated between feeling a numb sense of shock—surely there was some mistake—and grief for the great writer. And also, anger at Rick's choices. What hadn't he been willing to tell me? What had he gotten me involved in?

I didn't think I was actually hyperventilating, but I was close. I wished I'd paid more attention in those yoga classes I'd gotten kicked out of when I was younger. I never gave any credence to how one's breathing matters. But as I became light-headed and felt my palms begin to sweat, I would have traded my skepticism for a full gulp of oxygen.

It took me several seconds to realize the ringing I heard wasn't buzzing in my ears but the sound of my phone.

"Jaya," Miles said. "Thank God you answered. We need to

talk."

"You saw the news too?"

"Your threatening letter made the news? How did they—"

"Threatening letter?" I felt woozy again. "I'm talking about Rick being dead."

"Rick is *dead*?"

"Where are you?" I asked.

"You mean dead like you're not going to help him 'cause he's a jerk so he's dead to you?" Miles's voice shook. "Ha ha? Right? Please tell me you're joking."

"Dead like murdered. Where are you?"

"Outside your office. I was going to organize your last batch of mail when I found it."

"Stay there."

"Hell no. Didn't you hear me? A whack job left you a threatening note. And now I know he's a murderous whack job. I'm coming to you."

"Fine. I'm at the student café."

"Where's the note?" I asked when Miles found me five minutes later.

"It's evidence. I didn't touch it."

I groaned and stood up as Miles sat down.

"We're calling the police," I said. "Will you go back inside my office with protection?"

"I trust Tamarind to protect us more than the police."

"You can call her too."

I called to report the break-in and threatening note. Only when I said it was related to the murder of Rick Coronado did that get their attention. They agreed to send someone immediately.

Tamarind, Miles, and I waited in the hallway outside my office for the detective to arrive. It turned out to be two of them.

"You knew Coronado?" the younger one asked after getting our names.

"Not well, but I recognized his jacket when I saw it on the news, and they said he hadn't been identified—"

"We're waiting to get in contact with the family before releasing the details," the older one said. "The press only got a hold of it because the people on the beach who found the body posted about it on social media. None of that, all right?"

"You knew who he was already?" Tamarind asked.

"You said your break-in was related to this matter?"

"I'll get the door." I got out my key.

"Don't touch the handle," he said. "We might be able to lift prints." He took the key from me and eased open the door.

"Where's this threat?" his partner asked.

"Right on the center of the—" Miles broke off and swore. "It was right there! On the top of her desk. I swear—"

"Uh huh." The older detective looked almost bored.

"Hey," Tamarind said, "if Miles said there was a threatening note, there was a threatening note." She turned and whispered to Miles, "Didn't you take a photo of it?"

"Why would I think to take a photo? Like I'm going to stick around a room where someone wishing us bodily harm left a threat? I'm a pacifist."

The detective ignored them, but I'm fairly certain I saw him roll his eyes.

"You didn't see this note?" he asked me.

I shook my head.

"Your door wasn't forced."

"It wasn't?" I followed his gaze to Miles.

Miles scratched his neck nervously. "I didn't say the door was broken down. I said there was a note—"

"Miss Jones," the detective said, "is anything amiss?"

"Not that I can tell." I scanned the office. It wasn't the first time someone had gotten into my office. Perhaps it was time I considered installing a video camera hidden in Ganesha's broken tusk. Before I could decide how to explain the complicated situation with the manuscript chapters, the older detective spoke again.

"Thank you for doing your civic duty to make sure we knew the identity of the man in the Bay. I'm sorry for your loss. Good people are investigating. Now if you'll let us get back to it."

We stared after them.

"Our tax dollars at work," Tamarind muttered.

"Rick was famous," I said. "They assume Miles was making it up for attention. I'm sure they're getting tons of crank calls."

"Fair. But they didn't have to be such jerks to Miles."

"I swear a note was right here, Jaya," Miles said. "A handwritten note, written with black marker in creepy serial killer all-caps style, was in the center of the desk. It said *FORGET ABOUT THE RICK CORONADO NOVEL.*"

"Shut. Up." Tamarind said.

"We should go after them," I said. "The Gabriela Glass chapters—"

"They're not going to believe anything you say now."

I closed my eyes. "Even if they did, we don't even know how they're related. The chapters don't tell us who killed Rick."

"Them," Miles corrected. "Not us. The chapters don't tell the police who killed him."

"No," I agreed. But if we could figure out what the chapters were hiding, it might tell us what the killer was after.

Tamarind had to get back to work, and after I promised I'd have dinner with the two of them that night, they left hand in hand. I was left with my own thoughts to sort out what had just happened. I sat down at my desk, and that's when I noticed it.

The desk drawer was ajar. A drawer I never left open.

It was probably Miles who'd opened it before he saw the phantom letter. I pulled it open. My hand flew to my mouth and I pushed backward, sending the chair tumbling. A dead snake was curled inside the drawer.

My survival instincts kicked into high gear. I flung open the single door to the office and peered into the hallway. Life carried on as usual. The dean of students was chatting with the department secretary at her desk at the end of the hallway and two graduate students were walking together.

My heart raced as I tried to make sense of what had happened. If the person who'd left the note had second thoughts, why not take their snake as well? *Unless they'd been interrupted.* Tamarind's voice always carried down the whole hallway, so the intruder would have had ample warning to get out of the office before we returned. I leaned against the door and closed my eyes. Miles hadn't been making up the threatening note. Not that I'd thought he was, but now I could stop doubting myself.

I had no idea what to do with a dead snake, but at least it wasn't alive. I wasn't Gabriela Glass so I'd have had zero chance of killing a snake with my bare hands. With my jiu-jitsu, I could hold my own against a human adversary, but I doubted flipping a snake onto its back would do me much good.

I forced myself to get a better look at the poor dead creature. Only...This wasn't a dead snake. It was a *fake* snake.

My fear turned to indignation. Did they really think they could scare me off like this? The culprit who'd left the threats clearly understood nothing about psychology. No, they did. They realized they'd acted rashly and tried to take it back. Or could it be two people working together? Is that why the first one thought a note would be a good idea, and the second thought better of it?

I groaned. I needed to face the fact that I had no idea who—or what—I was up against. I locked my door and headed to the library.

"Miles wouldn't lie to you," Tamarind said when I appeared at her desk.

"I know. I believe him about the note. That's why I'm here. We need to find the Serpent King."

CHAPTER 17

Tamarind steered me to the secret courtyard. "I don't want to frighten the students with talk about dead authors. They're stressed out enough with only a few days left in the semester."

Rain was no longer falling, but the stones and benches were slick with rainwater.

"To find out what happened to Rick," I said, "we have to follow the clues he laid out for me. I think we know more than we think we do. If we start with the Serpent King—"

"Um, Jaya. It's time for me to stage an intervention."

"You have somewhere else you need to go?"

Her nostrils flared. "Rick Coronado is dead, Jaya. Someone killed him and tried to scare you off. The police are looking into Rick's murder. The intervention is for *you*."

"He's dead because of me." I looked away. I couldn't face her. "He was coming to see me. I hadn't figured out enough—"

"He was manipulating you." She grabbed my shoulders and spun me around. "Go home. Get some rest before I make a big plate of enchiladas for dinner. Everything will seem better with good food and great friends. Do you want to invite Lane too?"

"Definitely not. I'm too emotional. That's been the problem with our relationship from the start. I've been making decisions when there's some crisis throwing us together."

"Which doesn't make for the best decisions. I get it. But there are only two days left in the semester. You told me you're totally behind. Rick isn't your concern. Not anymore. You need to be more concerned about Naveen Veeran. You know he wants to steal tenure out from under you."

"I can handle Naveen."

"Maybe. But just because a handsome celebrity had a wild theory he convinced someone was worth killing over—"

"It's not just a theory."

"Seriously, Jaya. Go home and get some rest. You're totally messing with my image of myself if I need to be the responsible one in our friendship."

"I can't go home."

Tamarind gasped. "You think they've gotten to your house?"

"What? No. It's freezing at my place—" I broke off and we both started laughing hysterically.

"I'm glad you didn't start bawling," Tamarind said in between hiccups of laughter. "I was primed for any emotional outburst."

"You're right. I'll go home. I didn't find anything in the archives before anyway."

"You got through the newspaper archives already? You weren't here for that long before."

"The digitized archives make it fast to look things up."

Tamarind frowned. "Our digital archives are behind the times and don't have images linked yet. But you miss the photos if you don't look at the microfiche scans. Dammit. Your eyes just lit up. Why did I say that?"

"Because your librarian genes make it impossible for you not to."

"Stay where I can see you," she called after me as I ran back inside the library.

Two hours later I was still looking through images of old newspapers. Text searches of old materials that had been digitized made a lot of research easier, but it couldn't tell you everything. When Tamarind came to remind me the library was closing soon, I was staring at the photograph. I couldn't quite believe what I'd found.

I'd already searched for snakes, *naga*, cobra, and the Serpent King. Those key words weren't in the text of any of the articles, but something was in the photos from the time when Beauregard Delacroix was pushed down the stairs. The mansion. The one with the serpentine art nouveau designs on the facade.

"The mansion," I whispered. "The mansion is real."

Rick had altered the names and the story to hide the real history, but he'd described the house exactly as he'd seen it.

"Shut. Up." She looked over my shoulder. "That's the house Gabriela Glass described. The Durants. He didn't change the name *that* much. The Durant family, who suffered tragedies across generations."

"Beaumont Durant, who broke his neck when he fell down the stairs in the mansion his grandfather Aristide built, shortly before Christmas in 1950. His wife Daphne, a celebrated artist who slipped in the same spot a year later. Their grandson Marc, traumatized by the family curse so he got drunk on the fateful anniversary and fell down the same stairs."

"Huh," Tamarind said. "No mention of the woo-woo ghost story or of Marc being raised from the dead after being strangled. He was just a lush who slipped on the stairs. Closest we get to the ghost is this quote from a cop who showed up and was scared of being at a haunted house."

"Look at the timing of the most recent death," I said. "It's not a new crime like in a Gabriela Glass story. It was seven years ago. *Seven years ago*, Tamarind."

"You don't think—"

"I do. Marc Durant was killed shortly before Rick Coronado disappeared for six weeks. Marc died in a supposed accident at his ancestral home in Paris. Rick Coronado thought it was murder."

Tamarind swore. "This is big."

I scanned the rest of the article and searched for others now that I had a name. There was speculation that depression ran in the family and that these were all suicides, because no evidence of murder came up in any of the cases. No reputable news sources mentioned a ghost.

"Don't you think they would have realized those were some dangerous stairs and built new ones?" Tamarind mused. "Though I suppose if we believe Rick Coronado's manuscript, they did take precautions."

"By leaving the house on the fateful anniversary when they expected the ghost to strike, you mean?"

"Yeah, since they believed that was the only day of the year the ghost was a danger to them." Tamarind frowned. "It's so sad. All of this took place right before Christmas."

"There's nothing mentioned about them leaving the house two nights before Christmas each year, but they wouldn't have broadcast to the press, 'Oh, by the way, we're freaked out by our family ghost so we're leaving our home full of riches on the same night each year.' So we don't know if the real life Delacroix's—the Durants—weren't as superstitious as their fictional counterparts."

The lights overhead flickered. I stared at Tamarind.

"The alert that the library is closing in ten minutes," she said. "Though pretty good timing, right?"

"We need to hurry."

"As in hurry our little butts to the police station, right? Okay, fine. You're right. I know you're the only one with a little butt." She rested her hands on her ample hips.

"We can't tell anyone what we've discovered."

"Why not?"

"Rick wasn't just killed because he was going after a real-life treasure," I said, feeling a tremor emerge from my voice as I spoke. "He knew that someone had murdered Marc Durant in Paris. Someone smart enough to have covered their tracks got away with a murder seven years ago. If that person finds out we know what Rick's been trying to tell us—"

"I don't want to go into Witness Protection. Does that even work anymore with facial recognition technology?" Tamarind's chest heaved with distressed breaths. "OMG will I have to disguise myself with boring hair and no piercings? I'll be honest. I don't know if I can handle that."

"Nobody is going into Witness Protection."

"Really?" Tamarind's breathing calmed slightly. "Why not?"

"Because we're not going to wait for multi-jurisdictional police forces to be convinced our story is true and catch whoever killed Marc and Rick. Rick said the Serpent King statue was the key to solving Marc's murder. It's the key to solving Rick's murder too. That's one thing Gabriela Glass and I have in common that we do better than the police—we can find missing pieces of history."

The library plunged into darkness.

CHAPTER 18

An eerie glow from the screen gave enough light to see each other as silhouettes.

"Don't worry," Tamarind said. "That's just to convince the students to take us seriously that we're closing. The lights will come on again in a few seconds. Um. I think."

"Do we really need to leave?" I asked.

"I'm supposed to be doing a sweep for lingering patrons right now, so we've got five minutes at most."

"I only need two. I need to finish reading this one article about the Durants. I saw something in there."

The lights came on.

"Here it is," I said. "The Durants made their fortunes when France was a protectorate of Cambodia, not in India. Rick's shoddy research—" I broke off and gasped so dramatically it would have done justice to Gabriela Glass. "That's what was wrong with Rick's research for the book! *He was talking about Cambodia the whole time*, not India."

"Wait," Tamarind said. "I read the pages. He clearly said India."

"I expect it was to get me interested because he wanted my help. And if he planned on publishing the book, he wouldn't want to get sued by the Durants. India and Cambodia have so much of a connection that his misdirection worked. And the Serpent King statue—I should have seen it. *Naga* are much more prominent in

Cambodia than India. Where Rick set *Empire of Glass*."

I examined the few grainy photos of the art the family had collected. Two other statues from Asia. Numerous paintings by artists I didn't recognize. A small collection of ostentatious antique jewelry the family claimed was from a noble French family in the Middle Ages from whom they were descended. Nothing was officially catalogued, and there was no mention of the Serpent King by name, which is why I hadn't found it in my initial search, but the family had proudly displayed their art collection in the fortress-like library.

The sandstone Naga King sculpture was larger than I'd imagined from Rick's novel. More than a foot high, carved as a slab with bas-relief snake heads that looked as if they were crawling out of the stone. The central cobra figure—presumably the king—was larger and fiercer than the rest. It spoke to the skill of the artist that Rick hadn't taken dramatic license when he said there was a regal quality to the king. The poise of the serpentine head and the baring of its sharp fangs conveyed strength, not malice.

There was something else about the small image of the seven-headed *naga*. The shape was odd. Had a portion of the stone been chipped off toward the bottom? No, I didn't think that was it. I zoomed in.

"Tamarind!"

"I'm right here. And now I'm deaf."

"The *naga* is a guardian, either watching over Buddha or guarding a treasure. And look at this." I pointed at the flat lower portion of the sculpture. "This is similar to what Gabriela Glass described, but not quite. Gabriela wondered if the sculpture was incomplete because of a flat portion on the bottom. But look, the base of the stone juts out several inches and has been smoothed."

Tamarind leaned over my shoulder. "Like a pedestal to set something else?"

"Exactly. The *naga* is a guardian of treasure. The treasure our *naga* king was guarding isn't here."

"Shut. Up." Tamarind whispered.

"The Serpent King statue itself is a treasure, but it also points to something more important. Something it was guarding. Seven years ago, Rick Coronado realized the significance of the stolen statue. He knew Cambodia intimately from his research for his most ambitious novel. This all started with *Empire of Glass.*"

"Wasn't he found in Thailand at the end of his missing six weeks?" Tamarind asked. "Not Cambodia."

"The countries share a border. A disputed border. And there are undeveloped areas with thick jungle canopies."

Lost for six weeks. Found in Thailand, a country that not only bordered Cambodia, but controlled access to one of Cambodia's temples because of land routes. Fifteen pounds thinner, as if he'd been in the jungle searching for the treasure the Serpent King was meant to guard.

"His amnesia was a sham," Tamarind said.

I nodded. "That explains the reason he publicly feigned amnesia. He knew someone had killed Marc Durant and stolen the Serpent King—a family heirloom looted from Cambodia that was meant to be guarding another treasure that was still out there, waiting to be found. Rick's editor told me how he was unfulfilled by success and wanted to kill off Gabriela to be something more."

"A real-life treasure hunter. A hero. But look where it got him—"

"Excuse me," a voice said. "The library is now closed. Tamarind? Are you still helping a student? Do I need to remind you of the library policies?"

"Sorry, Betsy," Tamarind said in a saccharine sweet voice. "We're leaving." She clicked off my screen and hoisted me up by the elbow.

We stayed arm in arm as she led me to the locked front doors. "God, I hate that woman," she hissed. "My apartment. Two hours. Promise me you won't do anything stupid in the meantime."

"I promise."

*   *   *

I really had meant the words at the time.

But when I returned to my apartment, Nadia was sitting on the porch swing with a martini in her hand.

"Shall I make you one?" she asked, raising her glass. Her Russian accent was stronger than usual, so I suspected she'd had a couple already. "You look as if you have aged five years in the three days since I have seen you."

"Bad week. Sorry I didn't make it to your weekly brunch on Sunday."

"Ah, that explains the untouched food. You did not see my note on the table to help yourself to food in the fridge. Jack and I took a last-minute trip to Guerneville. That reminds me."

She eased herself out of the porch swing more elegantly than I would have thought possible in the awkward swing and slipped into the house. She returned a minute later not with a martini for me, but a stack of mail.

"Your mail since Saturday."

Poking out from the bottom was a rush delivery from Rick Coronado.

CHAPTER 19

The Glass Thief
Chapter Four

"The Serpent King was damaged when it was brought to France?" Gabriela asked.

She sat at the mansion's fifteen-foot dining table in the uninviting room that was brightened only by a narrow stained-glass design at the top of each window. She sipped a glass of sherry and studied the few black-and-white photographs that existed of Algernon Delacroix's prize. The base of the sculpture bore not the signature of the stone carver, but a series of deep, overlapping scratches.

"If you believe your reward won't be valuable enough," said Laura Delacroix, "I have additional funds to pay you."

"You misunderstand me. I don't think this is damage. This isn't how sandstone breaks down. Someone intentionally made these markings." Gabriela pointed at the intersecting lines in the photograph. They looked almost like a partial grid, except the lines were squiggly. A map?

"But why?"

"I was hoping you knew the answer."

Laura clutched her pearls and stood at one of the

cold windows. "I know only what I told you, that my husband told me his grandfather won it in a foolish game in Munnar, but I believe he looted it from there."

"Now it's you who are lying."

Laura gasped. "How dare you—"

"Ship manifest records show Algernon Delacroix returning not from India, but Cambodia."

"That can't be."

"If you wish me to help prove the thief Tristan Rubens murdered your son, you need to tell me the truth. What else are you hiding from me, Madame Delacroix?"

Laura Delacroix proceeded to swoon. Gabriela couldn't be sure it was a fake reaction, but the woman conveniently slumped into her chair rather than crashing into the table.

Laura had lied to her. Or had Luc's mother been deceived as well? The family had not wished their ancestor's looting to be discovered, so they lied about the history of the grand sculpture they proudly displayed with their other treasures.

The Serpent King sculpture was Cambodian.

Gabriela had slapped her forehead and cursed her stupidity when she found the records the previous day. How could she have been so blind? She had simply accepted what she had been told by her client, which was never wise. A naga didn't necessarily mean it was Indian. Nobody else had seen the truth because the two styles of iconography were so similar.

Indian culture and religions had spread throughout South and Southeast Asia, and the folklore of the Kingdom of Cambodia's origin was intertwined with India. Gabriela remembered the story because it involved a nagini princess and naga king—the rulers of the cobras. And Gabriela had always been fascinated by the majestic snakes.

As the legend went, a Brahmin prince from India had been an adventurer, much like herself. He'd braved the unchartered waters and found himself in a strange land where rice sprang from lakes. Along a tributary river's edge he saw the most beautiful woman he'd ever seen. A princess. Her father was the king of the land. A naga king. The prince proved his bravery, and the naga king blessed the union of his daughter and the valiant and handsome foreign prince. The king drank up the waters so his daughter and her husband would have a new land of their own. He named it Kambuja.

The naga king's underground watery kingdom was filled with precious gems. Gabriela closed her emerald-colored eyes and thought back on the hundreds of precious stones she'd rescued for women in need, always saving one for herself.

She opened her eyes and took a sip of the dry sherry Laura had insisted on serving. The Serpent King was the naga king of this legend. The snake was guarding his kingdom. The sculpture wasn't incomplete as she had originally thought. The smoothed-out base wasn't a blank canvas that hadn't yet been carved. It was meant to hold and protect something else. What could be more precious than his beloved daughter and her prince?

Gabriela hadn't yet solved the murder and theft that had taken place in the Paris mansion. She understood violent murder, but this trickery that had killed Luc Delacroix was something new to her. As Luc's mother had suggested, the best way for Gabriela to solve the murder would be to find the missing treasure. Only Gabriela now suspected there were two treasures: the Serpent King and the princess and prince that he guarded.

The king had been spirited from the mansion. Had he gone in search of his beloved daughter and her *prince?*

Gabriela's work in France was nearly done. Then she would visit the sacred temples of Cambodia's Angkorian Empire to find the prize the Serpent King was protecting.

She knew she might not find the treasure the Naga King was guarding on her own, but no matter. The historian would be meeting her in Siem Reap one week from today.

CHAPTER 20

Rick Coronado had discovered what the Serpent King was guarding. The Brahmin prince and *nagini* princess from Cambodia's mythical origin story.

I stared at the chapter until my eyes could no longer focus. Rick had made the same deduction I had: the sculpture was Cambodian and only one piece of a larger treasure. If I could take Gabriela Glass's latest revelation seriously, Rick had gotten one step further and discovered what that treasure was.

And if Rick meant for me to believe Gabriela, he was serious about something else too. The last line. *The historian would be meeting her in Siem Reap one week from today.*

Siem Reap. The modern city near Angkor was the jumping off point to reach the famous temples of Cambodia. Had Rick figured out the *location* of the second half of the treasure?

Rick had mailed me this chapter as a rush delivery on Saturday before he'd traveled to San Francisco. The day he referenced would be the first official day of the university's winter break, when Rick knew I would be done with my teaching responsibilities. Was he really egotistical enough to think I'd drop everything and fly to Cambodia to help him find the Serpent King and his missing daughter and her prince?

I hated that he was probably right.

The note accompanying the chapter read, *I look forward to hearing what you and those closest to you think of this chapter.* I should have thought more about the brief message, but the last words Rick conveyed to me before he died were at the forefront of my mind. *The historian would be meeting her in Siem Reap one week from today.*

The information from Rick was the start of a quest, but there wasn't enough information to complete it. I couldn't ask Rick about the next phase of the journey beyond Siem Reap. But there was no way I could ignore it. Not now.

"Couldn't you have given me a name of the treasure, Rick?" I whispered to my water-stained ceiling. "Or anything more to go on? Why the games?"

Rick had been manipulating me. Reeling me in by allowing Gabriela to be drawn into Cambodian history in the same way I'd originally been drawn to it. The women who'd done so much for their country had been erased from written history, but their stories were still alive through stone carvings and local oral histories. What else had been lost to history through war, genocide, and looting? What had become of the princess and prince, if they truly existed?

I closed my eyes and tried not to let guilt wash over me. I was supposed to receive the latest Gabriela Glass chapter before he was killed, but because of my not-quite-legal living arrangements, I never received my mail when Nadia was out. Would I have done anything differently if I'd received the chapter on time? Could I have saved him?

I couldn't help feeling like I could have helped him avoid whatever had caught up with him. If only Rick had asked for my help in a more straightforward way, I would have known if there was more I could do. It was true that I turned down hundreds of requests from amateur treasure hunters. Did he think I would have refused to hear him out?

I sent a message to Tamarind that Nadia needed me that night, but that I promised to make it up to her with dinner at my place soon. Nadia was dramatic enough that it was a believable lie. I hated lying to Tamarind, but she wanted to convince me not to act, when I knew I had to.

I sat in my drafty apartment feeling sorry for myself. There wasn't anyone left I could turn to. I tapped my finger on Lane's name on my phone. In addition to the brief visit to my office, he'd texted and called, but only once in each medium, but hadn't pressed further. Damn him, why couldn't he make it easier to hate him?

The photo attached to Lane's name on my phone was one where I'd captured one of his rare unguarded smiles. A moment before he'd been deep in concentration, cooking a Scandinavian dessert he'd learned to bake from a childhood nanny. When he'd noticed me watching him he grinned like he was the same seven-year-old boy who'd gotten away with creeping downstairs to steal a slice of her cake.

I slammed down my phone. Cake wasn't the only thing he'd been stealing for decades.

I wasn't ready to deal with my complicated feelings about Lane's past. An understandable yet problematic history that I believed he'd left behind not only for me, but for himself.

What would Gabriela do? Not sit around indecisively. I've never been good at sitting around doing nothing and feeling sorry for myself, so I got back to work. Whatever Rick had stumbled onto, it had gotten him killed. And now they were after me. I wasn't going to stick around and wait for the next attack.

In spite of Rick's deception, I already knew a lot.

The first four chapters of the Gabriela Glass novel I'd seen mirrored true crimes, both murders and a theft. Someone wanted to make it look like a family ghost had killed two people three quarters of a century apart on a deadly anniversary in the ancestral Parisian mansion.

Two Frenchmen who were old college friends decided to steal family heirlooms. One of them ended up dead, the other swearing it was a ghost who killed him—twice. And the sculpture that had been in the family for generations disappeared. This took place seven years ago, around the time Rick Coronado disappeared for six weeks. The murderers were never caught, and the theft went unreported because the sculpture was obtained illegally.

I had only one more day of the semester with classes to teach. Rick Coronado had asked for my help. Maybe I could have turned him down then. But not now. To finish what he'd started, I needed to follow Gabriela's footsteps. I booked a flight to Paris for the following night.

CHAPTER 21

I landed at the Charles de Gaulle airport in Paris as the sun was setting. A light snow was falling on the tarmac as the plane approached the gate.

I turned on my phone and it lit up like a Christmas tree. When I was boarding the flight, I'd texted both Tamarind and my brother where I was going and where I'd be staying. I was impulsive, but not too stupid to live.

As the plane taxied to the gate, I read their messages of concern and also checked the university portal where students submitted their final papers, which were due today. I'd been disappointed that Becca hadn't been in class the previous day. It was an optional class for students who needed help finishing their research projects, rather than a formal lecture, but I'd been hoping for an update on the sunken ship project.

Darkness had fallen completely by the time I took a taxi to the tiny apartment I'd rented online. As I stepped out of the cab, I could see my breath in front of me, and light snowflakes dusted my cheeks. I breathed in the cold air. Paris smelled like cigarettes and sweet cream. In my black clothes and three-inch heels, I fit right in. Except for my red messenger bag, which couldn't be considered a classy handbag.

Though I'd traveled extensively in Asia and lived in London, until the last couple of years I hadn't seen much of continental Europe. My last memory of Paris was being coerced into stealing a hidden item at the Louvre. Lane and I had pulled it off together.

And I'd loved the thrill of it more than I'd admitted to anyone, even him.

My apartment was in the 7th Arrondissement, home to the Eiffel Tower. I quickly discovered how it had been possible to find the rental so close to Christmas time. It was a fifth-floor walk-up with no elevator, and the apartment itself was roughly the same size as the bathroom of the luxury hotel in Paris where I'd stayed the last time I'd been here. At the time, I'd been essentially kidnapped (though my captor insisted it was friendly coercion), so I much preferred this cramped abode.

I leaned my head out one of the two narrow windows, affording me a view of half of the Eiffel tower, which was easy to spot as its golden lights sparkled in the dark night sky. The mansion wasn't too far. Had Rick Coronado had a similar view when he was here seven years before? He'd never set a Gabriela Glass novel in Paris before *The Glass Thief*, so I didn't have much of a sense of how he and Gabriela thought of the city. In spite of owning a New York City penthouse, Gabriela was more at home in the wild corners of the world than metropolitan habitats. A flurry of snowflakes blew into my face, bringing me back to reality. I closed the window.

The apartment was charming in an impersonal way. Vintage black and white photos of Paris were framed in faux-aged wood, pillows crocheted with fleur-de-lis symbols had been tossed on the narrow couch that converted into a bed (more to say "you're in Paris" than to indicate the nobility the symbol had once signified), and most of the countertop space in the minuscule kitchenette had been taken up by a welcome basket. Champagne with two glass flutes tied with a red bow, a box of Godiva chocolates, shelf-stable fancy cheeses. I'd planned on dropping off my bag and finding the mansion, but as I got settled in the warm, cramped apartment, the snow began to fall harder.

I opened the champagne and poured myself a glass. "Here's to Gabriela living on forever," I said as I raised the glass. "I'm sorry I couldn't help you, Rick."

I took a sip, then left the glass on the counter.

I'd slept for most of the ten-hour flight, so I wasn't tired. I'm one of the only people I know who can sleep so well on flights. I'm only five feet tall in socks, which helps. I'd dreamt, unsurprisingly, of noble serpents swimming through winding waterways, and the legend of the Indian prince and *nagini* princess who married and formed Cambodia. I'd always been annoyed by that story, because in the version I'd learned, the prince had shot an arrow into the princess's boat to frighten her into marrying him. Not the greatest start to a marriage.

Gabriela's version of the story was different. She mentioned the prince proving his bravery, not asserting his might. In each version, the legend was slightly different, which wasn't surprising. In one version I'd read, the *naga* king's daughter was named Soma, meaning the moon, and the prince Kaundinya represented the sun. Soma was also a historical queen with a husband of that name. In a Chinese version, Kaundinya was given sailing directions in a dream, and enchanted winds guided his ship. Yes, historical research has its challenges.

I knew what I wanted to do, but it felt terribly selfish. There was one person in France I could turn to. Sébastien Renaud, the retired French stage magician who'd been devoted to me since we'd saved each other's lives.

No, that statement wasn't quite true on two counts. First, he'd sacrificed more to save me than I had him, so I didn't deserve the devotion. Second, though he'd retired from the stage, he refused to retire from magic. He was a magic builder, one of those behind-the-scenes geniuses who think up the mechanisms for an illusion and who build the props to bring an act to life. He was brilliant at building mechanical automata for the *Machines de L'île* in Nantes and at coming up with ingenious additions to classic magic acts.

Sébastien's home in Nantes, including its adjacent mechanical workshop converted from an old barn, was one of my favorite places on earth. To gain admittance to the house, you had to appreciate the unconventional doorbell, two mechanical birds routed along the gutter of the roof to follow and serenade visitors. Once their song was over, a mechanized claw would spring from the door and hand you instructions.

His home was almost as much of an amusement park as the *Machines de L'île*, where machine-powered animals from giant flying herons powered by hydraulic lifts to sea creatures spinning on carousels entertained children and those young at heart, and a giant mechanical elephant roamed the grounds.

"As much as I love hearing your voice," Sébastien said, "you call me once a month and it hasn't been nearly that long. I take it this isn't merely a social call?"

"I'm in Paris."

"Another vacation already?"

"Not exactly on vacation."

"Why doesn't that surprise me?"

"Because I never go anywhere these days without some breaking and entering." I told him about the family mansion I was interested in.

"Ha. I'd leave now, but my eyes, they're not what they used to be. I'll leave at first light."

Nantes was a four-hour drive from Paris, so I had a few hours on my own after I woke up. I got an espresso and a croissant across the street at an impossibly cute café. I would have thought of it as romantic with the cozy seats if the purpose of my visit had been different. While waiting for Sébastien, I tried to do research by looking up French library archives, but, not surprisingly, everything was in French.

The snow had stopped falling, and the sun shone brightly on the horizon. I donned my running shoes and jogged the mile to the mansion. I remembered the exact address, as I'd looked it up to give it to Sébastien the night before. But I didn't need it. I knew I'd found the right place as soon as I rounded the corner on the block.

I stopped running in front of the house and pretended to

stretch. Technically, I really was stretching. I simply didn't need to at this point in a run.

The house had been radically modern when it was built over a hundred years ago, and it retained that same radical feel. Rick's description had captured the spirit of the serpents that slithered up the iron balustrade. Neither his words nor the old photographs could do justice to the fierce faces carved intricately into the design. But Rick had come close.

Dammit, why had he felt the need to see me in person? Why couldn't he have stayed safely at home? Wasn't he supposed to be a recluse?

I reached out and touched the cold head of the wrought-iron snake. A light covering of snow had fallen across the railings leading up the house. I flinched. I could have sworn I heard a hiss. I knew it was my imagination, but it felt real.

A moment later, I saw why. My stealthy accomplice had arrived. Sébastien stood leaning against his Porsche Panamera. His wild white hair stuck out from under a black beret; he pulled off the look as if he'd invented it.

He gave me a hearty hug, and I was happy at the strength of his arms. He'd lost too much weight after catching pneumonia.

"I had foresight," he said. "I brought my four-seater, so whatever is in store for us we can take my car. Where's Lane? Oh dear..."

"He tried to get to me through you too?" Now that was getting to be too much.

"No. I haven't spoken to Lane. Your face. Don't forget Christo and I had a mentalism act. Your poker face is half decent, but you show your emotions when it comes to love."

"Speaking of which, I believe I see some of that on your face as well. You're seeing someone." I put my right hand to my temple. "A younger man."

"Ha! All men are younger than me."

"Fitz is... seventy-nine?" I lifted my left hand to my other temple, trying to look as if I was deep in concentration reading his mind. "He was bored in retirement, so he began doing some work at the *Machines de L'île*." I laughed at the look of horror on Sébastien's face. "Don't worry. I haven't debunked your magician brethren's life's work. Sanjay told me."

"I take back what I said about your poker face. You're frighteningly good. Now, are you going to tell me why you're in Paris on your own, standing in the snow in front of an old mansion that looks as if it would be perfect for one of my magic acts?"

CHAPTER 22

I hefted a birdcage covered with a silky black cloth up the steps to the apartment. "New pets you couldn't leave alone?"

"All will become apparent," he said enigmatically.

Sébastien had brought a small overnight bag of worn leather that looked simultaneously in pristine condition and hundreds of years old, and two oddly shaped containers he said he'd explain later.

"Did you bring Démon so he could bite holes in another pair of my shoes?" I asked.

"I'm sure he misses you too."

Démon was Sébastien's demonic bunny. A real rabbit, not an automata like Sébastien's butler Jeeves. Also unlike Jeeves, who didn't do much beyond fetching tea, I swear that creature was at least as smart as a dog. And he loved chomping on my shoes.

"Démon?" I said hesitantly to the bird cage. The sound of cooing was my answer. Bunnies didn't coo.

"You hinted you'd need to get inside that mansion you just showed me," Sébastien said. "I didn't think you'd have a key, so I brought some options."

Options. Right.

I told Sébastien about the strange tale from Rick Coronado and his death on his way to see me. I ended with the reason why I'd come to the mansion: the impossible double murder (of the same man) and the disappearance of a valuable sculpture even though the snow outside the mansion hadn't been touched. I assumed those elements would appeal to his curiosity, but it was something unexpected he latched onto.

"A death threat?" he repeated. "You received a death threat and decided to step into the lion's den?"

"It wasn't a *death* threat. Just a threat to forget about whatever Rick was trying to tell me. And the dead snake wasn't even real. It was plastic."

"But the person who wrote the note has killed a man, Jaya. Possibly two, if the author was killed by the same person who killed Marc. Therefore it's a death threat."

"It's a good thing I have you to look after me then." I kissed his cheek and took his mug to refresh it with more tea.

"And it's a good thing I'm an agreeable old man. I know there's no stopping you, so I might as well help."

"Back to our plans for getting inside the house."

"To reenact what happened?" Sébastien asked. "How very Belgian of you."

"English, if you want to get pedantic," I said. "It was Agatha Christie who invented Poirot."

"If you're going to ignore my fatherly advice and refuse to go home, at least let's stop discussing fictional detectives and get back to what we know."

"I don't think we can exactly reenact the crime, since we don't have enough facts. I want to see what's real and what's fiction. Enough of it is real to have gotten people killed. What's really in that house?"

"You're frightened."

I glared at Sébastien. "I'm not scared. I'm frustrated. None of this speculation matters if we can't find a way into the house."

"That?" Sébastien's eyes twinkled. "That I've already figured out."

"You just got here!"

"It took me all of five minutes to work out the details," Sébastien said. "Why do you think I wished to see the house first?"

"I know we have to wait a couple more days until the

anniversary when the household is out—"

"Do we?" Sébastien sighed. "For a brilliant historian, you can overlook the most obvious facts."

"What am I missing?"

He chuckled, then a sadness swept over his face. "Do you really think that parents who had their son die in their home would choose to remain there? Especially if they had the means to go anywhere they wished?"

I should have thought of it.

"*Alors*," Sébastien said, "while you were fixing tea, it was an easy search to find that the parents of Marc Durant moved to their country chateau in the year following the death of their son. He was already divorced from his wife Gail, and she didn't take the house. The Paris mansion hasn't changed hands, so I expect it has been sitting empty since then."

"The curtains were drawn," I said, thinking back on what we'd seen from the outside, "but the house and garden had been kept up."

"Again, money buys many things. Including the security system that I'm certain is in place to prevent burglars or squatters."

He showed me the mechanical birds in the trunk I'd lugged up the steps. They were similar to the ones at his house in Nantes that he used as his doorbell, but something about their construction was different.

"These little fellows will do the work, and my living friends will be the misdirection."

Sébastien explained his plan. It didn't matter what type of security system it was, only that the "birds" needed to set it off and peck through the wires so that the security company would investigate and determine it wasn't worth fixing in the dead of night. If there were security cameras, they would see the mechanical birds, which looked quite realistic from afar. And the living birds would be present when the disturbance was investigated. Neither people nor valuables were in the house, so one night of having no electricity would be the logical result. We hoped.

"Why do we need to wait until nighttime, then?" I asked. "It might be marginally easier to hide outside, but wouldn't it look more natural/less suspicious if someone spotted us during the day?"

"Hiding in plain sight, you mean? Yes, that can help in some contexts, but here we need human nature."

It clicked. "The employees of the security company," I said. "When it's freezing and late at night..."

"*Exactement.* They will not wish to stay outside and fix the system for an empty house with no people making them do so."

"Won't they realize birds wouldn't be there that late at night?"

"Only if there's an ornithologist who's called out. Otherwise it's not the first thing you'd think of when you think you are seeing real birds. That's a risk I'm willing to take. Especially when it helps mitigate another risk we haven't spoken of."

"The fact that someone killed Rick Coronado and tried to scare me off. We need to be on guard for that person. I wish..."

"You wish he was here with you."

"I hate how you read minds, you know."

He laughed. "A curse and a gift." When he continued, his voice was softer. "You love him, Jaya. Why are you fighting it?"

"You know how the two of us met?"

"In the Highlands of Scotland. If I wasn't a Frenchman down to my bones, I'd concede that was a romantic place to meet."

"I didn't meet him there, but that's where I got to know him."

"When you were searching for the Rajasthan Rubies."

"Which we found, but..." Sébastien knew the partial story of Lane's past. Not everything, but enough to know there were very good reasons Lane didn't wish to catch the attention of the police. In multiple countries. "What I'm going to tell you, you can't tell anyone, even Sanjay."

"I'm a magician. I know how to keep secrets."

"He kept two of the ruby artifacts."

Sébastien waited. "Is that all?"

"Is that all? He wants me to have them, but those pieces of jewelry and gemstones belong in a museum."

"And are they? I mean the rest of the hoard."

"It's still tied up in court, as Scotland and India argue over it. And I know, I know, the people who technically own things aren't necessarily the people who deserve it. But that's not the point. Do I deserve it either? That's ridiculous."

"Is that what this is about?"

"What?"

"Whether you deserve the ruby?"

"I don't need to be psychoanalyzed, Freud."

"Ha. He was still alive when I was born, you know. That was a long time ago. Living a long life gives one perspective. And a more nuanced position on right and wrong. As it applies to the law. My very nature was once illegal. And still is in some countries. Laws themselves can be immoral. Practical in most cases, but far from morals to live by."

"It's not that I think it's wrong that he broke the law when he stole the rubies for me."

"It isn't?"

I buried my face in my hands. "Not exactly." It wasn't a single instance of breaking the law—it wasn't any of them. Lane's foray into crime began when he went to college in England. There he met a man who showed him how easy it could be for someone with Lane's talents to take advantage of corrupt wealthy people. So Lane had become a thief. He followed his morals, meaning he never stole from anyone who he believed didn't deserve it and couldn't afford the loss, and he never used a weapon. Lane had never hurt anyone.

But the case of the rubies was different. In this case, he'd taken something *for me*. A choice had been made for me.

"Why can't there be a simple answer?" I whispered.

"Life, my dear, is rarely simple. That's who he is, Jaya. You knew that going in." He paused and waited for me to look up. "Let me tell you a story about Christo. We were together for nearly fifty years before he died. Do you know how we first met?"

"Because you were both stage magicians."

"He wasn't when we met. He was an actor. He loved the spotlight. I didn't. I wanted to perform magic, and I loved seeing the audience react in the moment, but I hated the fame he thrived on. We were a grand success once we started working together. Too much so. He knew I hated it. I never asked him to change his true nature for me, and when he saw I was trying to change mine for him, he put a stop to it. He saw what I needed and we found our balance. I became a magic builder, creating new magic tricks and acts, and I mentored young magicians. He went back to the stage. He didn't need magic; he needed the venue of the theater. I didn't want him to change his true nature." He clasped his hands together. "Enough sentimentality! How did your Rick Coronado get involved?"

"Because of the vanishing statue."

"Then let's get to work making it reappear."

CHAPTER 23

"Your role," I said to Sébastien, "will be getting us into the mansion later tonight."

He wriggled his white eyebrows. "And looking for trickery inside. I assume a killer will have taken whatever contraption was used, but there is always evidence left behind."

"We've got time before it'll be late enough to break into the house, so we can look into the vanishing statue itself."

"The vanishing statue." Sébastien mulled over the words. "I take it the name in the Coronado manuscript, the Serpent King, isn't real?"

"Not that I can find, but I could use your help with the French."

"I hate to disappoint you, but the French word for serpent is—"

"Serpent. I know. That's not what I meant. I need help with the Durant family history that's publicly available. They were a prominent family in France, and the mysterious deaths were reported in English-language papers, but nothing else. I want to know more about the man who looted the treasure in the first place. Aristide Durant."

We had a full day before we could break into the Durant mansion, and we made good use of it.

I was hoping to visit the Labrouste Reading Room of the Bibliothèque Nationale, the National Library of France, after seeing photos of the inspiring room with ornate domes stretching high above massive pillars. It reminded me of the British Library's reading rooms in London, where I'd spent countless hours researching original historical documents. But like the British Library's reading rooms, you needed to arrange for a Reader Pass. Sébastien had a better, albeit less atmospheric, idea.

"We're in the modern age," he said. "Now that we know what we're looking for, we can find much of the history of the Durant Tea Company online."

"In French."

Sébastien grinned. "That's what I'm here for. Though it's a shame you won't get to see Labrouste's creation today. He was a magician, you know."

"The librarian the reading room was named after?"

"Henri Labrouste was the architect. Decades before anyone else put pneumatic tubes into practice, he built a complex system of air-pressured tubes to deliver research materials to library researchers. Along with Jean Eugene Robert-Houdin, the French clockmaker turned magician, Labrouste's creations were part of the inspiration for my mechanical doorbell in Nantes."

"You're not doing a good job convincing me we shouldn't go to the library."

"Ha. Once you've solved this mystery, I'll help you apply for a Reader Pass."

I didn't get to spend the day in a historical building with dramatic vaulted ceilings, but Sébastien knew me well. After two errands to prepare for the evening, he insisted we do our research not in the apartment but at a café overlooking the Seine River. "Better for the mind not to be in a cramped space," said the man whose magic studio was a sprawling barn at least ten times as large as my apartment.

We sat at a small table on the sidewalk, a heat lamp above us and cappuccinos to warm our hands, as Sébastien translated the French sources. The art nouveau mansion was only a small indication of their lavish lifestyle. While in Cambodia, Aristide

Durant had built a grand house and filled it with furniture made by French artisans who were bringing French culture to the country. He even employed a French cook. Which seemed to me would defeat the purpose of traveling across the world, especially under the conditions a nineteenth-century traveler would endure.

"Aristide lived in Cambodia for longer than he intended," Sébastien said. "When he fell ill, he tried to return to France, but there was a problem with his ship. He was forced to remain in Cambodia, where he died."

"Wait," I interrupted. "That can't be right. He died in Cambodia? Then how did his sculpture get to France?"

"His possessions were returned to his family." Sébastien paused to read more. "Some of them, at least."

"You're suggesting Cambodian officials simply let him take the valuable sculpture he'd looted?"

"It was easier for Europeans to take works of art out of poorer countries in the past than it is now. You're the historian, Jaya. You know this."

"I know it still took effort. Bribery, at the least. Which would be much more difficult if Aristide was dead."

Sébastien stroked the white stubble on his chin. "Perhaps a fellow explorer who saw to it his wishes were honored. Many of my countrymen went to Cambodia. I presume they stuck together and looked out for each other—"

I gasped. "Or not. Someone could have taken the prince and princess."

Sébastien shook his head. "Why not take the whole thing? I'm inclined to think Aristide made multiple trips. Records from the time are sure to be incomplete."

"Maybe," I murmured. But something wasn't fitting together. "This is all speculation. We don't have enough information yet. There are too many unanswered questions to know how he got his treasure out of Cambodia."

Sébastien nodded and looked out over the water, and for a few minutes, he was oblivious to my presence. A wave of emotions overtook his face. Memories, good and bad, must have filled his mind. How much must this scene have changed over his long lifetime? I knew only snippets of his life, and didn't even know how much time he'd spent in Paris. What memories had I dredged up by inviting him here?

"This family has certainly suffered more than most," he said, breaking the silence.

"After the men in the family did their part colonizing and looting Cambodia, ignored their children, and abused their factory workers."

Sébastien grinned and it was clear he was firmly back in the present. "I never said they didn't deserve it. At least some of them. I do feel sorry for Marc. Remember even before he died, his wife had left him. Not only that, but she went to America with their only child. It was no wonder he became a drunken fool who thought it amusing to tempt fate."

A frigid wind blew my hair into my face.

"We'll be tempting fate if we stay in the cold sitting still," I said. "Let's get back to the apartment."

"Life is too short to sit in a tiny apartment. We're in Paris. With several hours before we can put our plan into action. There's something else we can do. No, there's something else we *must* do."

"More research?" We'd already made a brief stop at the Musée Guimet, the Asian Art museum in Paris, as one of our errands before settling into the scenic café, where we saw many *nagas* but none related to the Durant family.

"Not exactly. If we're about to be arrested, at least we can enjoy Christmas in Paris. We're going to a Christmas market."

"I love you, Sébastien."

"Of course. What's not to love?"

My brother Mahilan was spending Christmas with his fiancé and her son in Switzerland. My father was in Goa with old friends he'd been close with before my mother died. Lane hadn't seen his parents in a long time, so he'd decided that in spite of his fraught relationship with his father, he wanted to see his mom. Tamarind was flying to Mexico City to spend Christmas with extended family, bringing Miles to meet them. Therefore I'd resigned myself to not doing much for Christmas this year. Nadia had invited me to Christmas Eve dinner with her and Jack. Even though we considered each other friends as well as tenant and landlord, it still felt rather depressing.

As we approached from across the Seine, a towering Christmas tree adorned with bright blue lights came into view in front of the Cathedral of Notre Dame de Paris.

"The Marché de Noël à Notre Dame market is across from Notre Dame." Sébastien pointed. "You can see the lighted cathedral in the background. Nothing can keep down the spirit of the French, not even a tragic fire."

I squeezed his hand and we walked into the festivities. A band was playing amongst the matching booths with their white steeple-topped coverings that protected against the light snow that began to fall.

We agreed to skip the mulled wine, but I ate my fill of gingerbread.

"This couldn't be more magical," I whispered.

"It couldn't?" Sébastien produced a three-inch wooden Christmas tree out of thin air. I smiled and was about to lift it from his gloved hand, when I saw this was no simple tree. The branches folded inward before opening again. As they opened, green pine needles sprouted from the branches.

A little girl next to us squealed with delight. She asked him a question in French, and Sébastien knelt on the ground and spoke a few words to her. She nodded and grinned, and he handed her the tree. She ran toward her parents and brother, showing them her prize.

"I can make another one for you," Sébastien said as he stood back up. "But since you're not a budding young engineer, I thought the tree belonged with her."

"Agreed. I'll be happy with a hot chocolate before we head back."

"If this is my last evening of freedom," Sébastien said, "I couldn't have picked a better way to spend it."

CHAPTER 24

At 10:30 p.m., we put our plan into action. Late enough that the streets were no longer crowded, but early enough for us to reenact the tragedies exactly as they'd happened.

At 10:31, CCTV cameras picked up the image of a drunken man walking home on the street of the mansion, singing an opera aria at the top of his lungs and feeding a string of birds with breadcrumbs. As he passed the Durant mansion, he tossed the remainder of the baguette next to where we'd identified a key component of the house's security. Of course, the drunken man was really Sébastien in disguise.

He continued down the block in disguise, and five minutes later walked back down the street as himself. He let himself into the apartment across the street.

Our other errand that morning was to find a vacation rental across the street from the mansion that had a perfect vantage point. Since it was so close to Christmas, it was of course occupied. If we'd been working with Henry North, the man who'd coerced me into robbing the Louvre, he would have had half a dozen ways to sweet-talk the family out of the rental. Sébastien was more pragmatic. He saw that the rental went through a large agency, so the renters wouldn't know everyone. He'd then found a way to get water through the door to make it look like a leak, arrived to say it was a burst pipe, and upgraded the family to an apartment twice the size and far more luxurious, free of charge, and no paperwork needed.

This place was now Sébastien's apartment for the duration of his stay, so we didn't have to share the shoe-box-size one I'd rented. He was thinking of inviting Felix to join him, but thought better of it when I pointed out we were about to commit larceny.

"Bluebird and Celine are ready to get to work," Sébastien said, sitting next to me in the window across the street from the mansion.

I gaped at the two mechanical birds in Sébastien's hands.

"These," he said, "are drones."

On the outside, the two birds looked like the old-fashioned brilliantly constructed mechanical pieces Sébastien loved to create, made of both intricately jointed wood and feathers, but these creatures had computers in their bellies.

"Courtesy of Felix. My almost-octogenarian beau is bringing me into the twenty-first century. My classic design built around this computerized contraption. What would someone your age call them? Automata 2.0?"

"5.0 at this stage, I'd say." I took one of the birds in my hand. If I'd been even a few feet away from it, I would have sworn it was real. As it was, there was something unsettling about how lifelike it felt. My hand jerked as it cooed.

"Careful," Sébastien murmured, petting the jarringly realistic bird and lifting it from my hand back into his. A chill swept into the room as he cracked the window. He set the birds on the sill, then lifted a black device from his pocket.

The two mechanical birds took flight. The birds first went for the breadcrumbs, then flew up to the security system on the front of the house.

They pecked through important wires as Sébastien made it look like they were going for the bread, the curated scene we wanted the security cameras to pick up.

The larger bird pecked away at the wire until a glaring alarm began to sound.

"Celine is stuck," I said.

"That's Bluebird. And this gizmo is supposed to fix her." He banged his head against the controller in his hand.

"I don't think it responds well to force."

"*Merde*. This would have been easier with my old methods."

"Sébastien, we don't have much time. I'm serious. We—"

"Got it!"

I let out a sigh of relief. I would have been terribly embarrassed if I was the one hospitalized for a heart attack.

With Celine and Bluebird back, we next released two of Sébastien's trained pigeons.

By the time the alarm company arrived, the real pigeons were in place. We waited inside the flat with a view, able to hear the conversation through the microphone we'd planted.

The two men from the security company left quickly when they noticed the pigeons, thinking the alarm had been triggered by birds.

Sébastien laughed and backed away from the window, further into the darkness.

"*Ça m'est égal*," he repeated. "They don't really care if they solve the issue tonight. They're leaving the system off."

"That was the idea."

"Yes. But I wasn't sure it would work. Remind me never to hire this security company."

"I didn't know you used a security company," I said.

"I don't. My traps for burglars are much more fun."

CHAPTER 25

With the power cut off, it was easy to get into the house. Staying undetected was the bigger challenge. Without power, we had to use flashlights, which could be easily spotted from the street. The drapes had been drawn so onlookers couldn't tell the house had been closed up, so it wasn't as bad as it could have been, but we used the low settings even though it made it more difficult to see.

Sébastien locked the back door we'd come through. Though we were inside, when I breathed out I saw my breath in front of me. I closed my eyes. It was perfectly natural that the house felt so cold. It was the dead of winter and there was no heat to warm the sprawling mansion. The concrete floors didn't help, though at least my shoes didn't squeak underneath me.

White sheets had been draped over the furniture, covering everything from low sofas and tables to higher shelves that towered over us like abominable snowmen. I alternated between feeling like I was trapped in a Scooby-Doo cartoon and like I was in a house of horrors. I was on high alert, half-expecting one of the sheets to come alive, until I realized the reason they were hanging at odd angles was because there were items on top of the furniture.

I sneezed as I eased a sheet off a small mahogany desk. A glass blown paperweight and a wooden model of a clipper ship remained on the desk. The Durant family hadn't taken their furniture with them when they'd moved to a chateau in the countryside. That somehow made me even more on edge. It was as if the house had been abandoned in a heartbeat. This was nearly a time capsule of what had taken place the night Marc Durant died.

Sébastien removed the cloth draped over the grandfather clock and let out a sigh. "Several minutes after twelve. I don't know if I'm relieved or disappointed that it didn't stop at midnight on the dot."

"You're relieved," I said, eyeing the creepy, oversize clock. "Definitely relieved."

It was an eerie sight as our flashlight beams cut through dust motes and shone over the uneven heaps of white as we made our way to the central part of the house. The only sound was our breathing and the light pat of our footfalls.

We stepped further into the house, and as we came around a curve of the back hallway, we reached the grand entryway with the infamous staircase and library above.

A chill began in my ankles and made its way up my body. I couldn't tell what I was reacting to. Not consciously. I'd already adjusted to the white puffs of air left by my breath.

"Oh my God," I whispered. "The scent." I'd learned in Scotland one of the signs a ghost was present was that you could smell a scent strongly associated with his last moments in life.

"What are you—?" Sébastien began. "Ah, the scent of pine. A Christmas tree? But how could there be a Christmas tree? Unless..."

He didn't have to finish the sentence. I knew what he meant. Unless the ghost was making us smell the Christmas tree that had been there when the previous deaths had occurred.

"There was a tree here seven years ago," Sébastien said.

I rushed forward and came to a stop in the sprawling foyer, with the grand staircase in the center. This was where three people had fallen to their deaths. In the story, Beauregard Delacroix. His wife Delphine. Their grandson Luc. Rick hadn't disguised their names much at all. Beaumont Durant. His wife Daphne. Their grandson Marc.

Here in the foyer, we were bathed in dim light. I half expected to see a pool of blood at the foot of the stairs. No, it couldn't be...The cast of light wasn't white—it was red.

"The moon," Sébastien said as he reached me. "It's the moon

casting that ethereal light through the stained-glass window above."
Above us light from the moonlit night sky was coming through
a crimson stained-glass skylight. I thought of Soma, the Cambodian
princess who represented the moon.

"The scent of pine is stronger here," I said. "But there's no
tree." I clicked off my flashlight. Between the moonlight and my
eyes adjusting, it was easier to see without the harsh glare of white
light and darkness. And, to be honest, less creepy. I would always
think of the china cabinet covered in a sheet in the hallway as an
abominable snowman with stubby arms raised above his head.

Sébastien whisked a sheet away from a low table next to the
base of the staircase. As he did so, a smattering of dried pine
needles scattered across the floor.

"They packed up hastily," he said. His gaze moved from the
dry remnants of the Christmas tree up the staircase.

Dark wood furniture filled the room, looking out of place with
the walls barren of their previous art. All except for one painting
that had been left behind. A portrait of a solitary, unsmiling man.
The ghostly portrait from Rick Coronado's novel.

The sweeping staircase was also just as Rick had described it.
Wide at the bottom, with wrought-iron railings cast into Art
Nouveau style twirls that followed the narrowing stairs upward to
the landing. It must have once been an enticing welcome as visitors
stepped through the front door.

"To the library?" Sébastien asked.

"To the library."

One glass door leading into the room was still broken, so we
stepped carefully through the double doors. Sébastien lifted the
sheet from one of the bookshelves in the library. Most of the art
that had once hung on the walls had been removed, but the books
remained on the bookshelves. The sheets had protected them from
most of the dust they would have accumulated, but it wasn't
necessary. Sébastien shook his head, and I knew why. These books
hadn't been read. They were fancy hardbacks I expected had been
purchased for show. I pulled one off a shelf and sneezed.

"This gives me ideas for a new act..." Sébastien murmured.

"Didn't you stop performing fifty years ago?" I whispered.

"For some lucky young magician. Perhaps Sanjay would appreciate it."

We searched methodically, going from room to room. I looked for the types of hiding places that existed in historical buildings, like priest holes. Sébastien looked at the sizes of the rooms themselves, in case they were smaller than they should have been and hiding secret rooms. We even checked inside the large pieces of furniture, in case they included false panels. We found no evidence of mechanical devices that could have convinced people there was a ghost in the house, but those could have been removed in the intervening years. But neither did we find any secret passageways where a murderer could have escaped with the statue. They would have been more difficult to conceal. And none of the walls or furniture held any false panels—Sébastien's long experience as a skilled magician would have seen through any such deceptions.

"It's a tragedy," he said. "A house like this should not be built without at least one secret passageway."

I picked up a framed photograph of a younger Marc Durant and a blonde woman holding a toddler. A toddler with vaguely familiar features. This was Marc's family that had left him and gone to America. Their clothes were out of style, but not too much. Taken a decade or so ago. Marc's family...the age of his daughter...Three names were engraved on the frame: *Marc, Gail & Rebecca.*

Rebecca. The name of someone I knew. Only I knew her by her nickname. Becca.

Everything about Rick's strange manuscript now made sense. As much as I didn't want to believe it, her actions now made perfect sense.

"Oh no," I said. "I know who's behind this. Marc's daughter. She's my student, Becca Courtland."

CHAPTER 26

Becca. The young woman who'd transferred to the university at the start of this year and had tried to get close to me from the start. What if it wasn't academic curiosity, but something else? So many of her reactions had struck me as odd, as she'd tried to get close to me but then being frustrated by innocuous things I said. And the timing. She'd come to the restaurant the same night Miles brought me Rick Coronado's rush delivery. *She was watching for my reaction to the pages.*

As I told Sébastien about Becca, everything clicked into place. My head spun as my eyes darted around the haunted mansion. Shadows looked more jagged and threatening than they had minutes before.

"The timing can't be a coincidence," I said. "Rick Coronado's story is the same as her family's, so they have to be connected." I shone my flashlight around the room, so well described by Rick. "He's been in this house. Why did they lead me here? Why me?"

"The treasure is why Becca thought you could help. You receive so many inquiries, no? But she knew you couldn't say no to your idol."

"That article telling the world I'm a fan of Rick Coronado and that he was a fan of mine brought me nothing but grief. But that information is public. There's no reason for either of them to pretend they didn't know. Why didn't Becca simply tell me she wanted my help solving these unsolved crimes? Why go to all the effort of convincing Rick Coronado to tell me the story as a novel?

Why manipulate me?"

"You've pointed out the answer many times," Sébastien said.

I groaned. "The statue was looted."

"Do you suppose your author was looking for a looted treasure when he disappeared?"

"His disappearance in Southeast Asia." I thought again of that missing chunk of time when Rick claimed he had amnesia. He'd done so much research for *Empire of Glass*. When Marc was killed seven years ago and only incomplete details were reported, Rick could have realized more about the sculpture than the family. The theft details hadn't been reported, but the timing was too much of a coincidence. He was already interested in this crime. Had Becca met him then, when she was still only a kid? Becca was smart. I didn't yet know how, but she'd put it all together.

Sébastien shone his light onto the photograph. "They've had no answers. Only mysterious deaths, fear of a ghost, and the seemingly impossible theft of a valuable antiquity—"

"Which their ancestors stole."

"You see! Exactly why they didn't come to you directly. Becca is an impressionable young college student who's had no closure after losing her father, so she deserves some sympathy. But it stops there. I'll feel no additional sympathy for someone who's doing this to you. She's using her mother's surname?"

"I presume so. She's not using Durant. I would have put it together if it was."

"What else do you know about her?"

"Well, she tried to scare me off after asking for my help—" I gasped. "No."

"What are you thinking?"

"That she could have killed her accomplice."

Sébastien blinked at me. "You believe she killed Rick Coronado?"

As he repeated my idea back at me, I heard how thin it sounded. I didn't quite believe it myself. "I don't know what to think. But Rick told me something more was going on than I realized when he was on his way to San Francisco. Becca was in San Francisco."

"Along with millions of other people."

I scowled at him.

"*Merde.*" Sébastien looked at his watch. "More time has passed than I thought. We shouldn't risk staying too much longer. I'll put the sheets back where we found them. Starting with the other rooms. As soon as I'm done, we should leave this house."

Ten minutes later, we were safely back across the street.

"What's your next move?" Sébastien asked.

"We confront Becca."

CHAPTER 27

It was after two a.m. when I called Becca. Five p.m. in California.

It took her four rings to answer. "Dr. Jones?" A yawn. "Um, I'm on Christmas break."

Not only had she yawned, but her voice was groggy. I was right.

"I know. And you're in France."

She had no reply to that.

After Sébastien and I had slipped out of the house and made sure we'd left nothing behind at the apartment across the street, we'd returned to our original apartment where I looked up more of Becca's online presence. Unlike most people her age, she didn't have much of a digital footprint. At least not a public one. One social media account was private, and she didn't use any others I could find. Which made sense, because she'd been planning this for a long time. She could have deleted her accounts.

"I know you're in France, Becca," I said. "Visiting the French side of your family. I know it was you. It was you who set up Rick Coronado."

"How did you—? No, it doesn't matter. We knew you'd put it all together eventually."

My mouth went dry. I was right. It wasn't a coincidence. I hadn't thought it was, but to hear her say the words. "Is that why you killed him?"

"What?" The tiredness was gone from her voice. "Rick is dead?"

"Don't pretend you don't know."

"He was fine when he came to see me a few days ago in San Francisco!"

I stared at my phone. It was resting on the table so we could both listen. "Rick came to see you in San Francisco?"

I scrunched my eyes shut, disgusted with my egotistical stupidity. When Rick said he was coming to San Francisco, I'd assumed it was all about me. But I was far from his first priority. He'd gone there to see his partner—Becca. I thought he was coming in response to my ultimatum phone call, but he'd said more was going on than I realized.

Becca didn't answer right away. But she hadn't hung up. She was flustered. She hadn't planned on this. "You're manipulating me." Her voice shook. "To get back at me."

Sébastien scribbled a note and handed it to me. *She didn't kill him. She's never going to believe you. She needs external validation.*

I nodded and spoke again to Becca. "Look at the news on the man pulled out of the Bay."

More silence on the other end of the line, but again the connection hadn't dropped. I hoped she was looking it up.

"No, no, no!" The words came a minute later, and not directly into the receiver. She must have been looking it up on her phone. "This can't be happening. You did this!"

"He didn't show up when he was supposed to meet me," I said. "He was already dead."

"He'd changed his mind about seeing you. I convinced him—" She stopped short.

"What did you convince him?"

"It doesn't matter."

"It matters. A man has been murdered. We need to meet."

"Not likely. It's not a crime to talk to an author about my family's tragedy."

"Would you like me to tell the police you were the last person to see Rick Coronado alive?"

"Is he there with you? Telling you what to say?"

Sébastien and I exchanged a glance. "Um, didn't you look up and see that he's dead?"

She gasped. "He's dead too? What the—"

"Aren't we talking about Rick Coronado? Who are you talking about?"

Silence.

"Becca?" My heart raced. *Who was she talking about?*

"You really don't know, do you?" She laughed bitterly.

"Don't know what?"

"I'll meet you. But somewhere public."

"Fine." I'd planned on suggesting a public meeting spot, and I'd already thought of the spot that would give me strength for whatever followed. I swallowed hard. Who did she think was here with me? "Tomorrow at noon. Meet me at the glass pyramid in front of the Louvre."

I barely slept at all that night. At a few minutes before noon the next day, I stood in front of the towering glass pyramid that served as the entrance to the Louvre Museum. A light snow dusted the ground and the hundreds of glass panels that formed the pyramid.

Becca Courtland appeared in a baby blue coat, matching hat, and fluffy cream-colored gloves and scarf. It was probably my imagination that the crowd parted for her as she approached.

A crowd of tourists might not matter to a murderer, but it couldn't hurt. I stood by myself, but my phone was on in my coat pocket, both recording and on the line with Sébastien, who was several yards away in the courtyard that was crowded even in the cold, taking photos and generally acting like a tourist.

As Becca reached me, my initial impression of her perfectly put together appearance didn't hold up. Her eyes were bloodshot, and concealer hadn't disguised the dark circles. She looked around nervously.

"I didn't call the police," I assured her. I was so far from having pieced together what was going on, I wouldn't have known what to tell them.

"Funny." She rubbed her gloved hands together and pulled her coat more tightly around her. "Of course you wouldn't dare call the police. Where is he hiding?"

"You think I faked that news that Rick Coronado is dead?"

"If you still want to play this game, fine." Her eyes darted around the courtyard. Had she spotted Sébastien casually watching us? "What do you think you know?"

"No. That's not how this is going to work. You've already shown how manipulative you can be. I'm not giving you more ammunition."

"I *want* this all to come out. That's the whole point! Just because I'm agreeing to tell you what I've done, this doesn't mean you've won."

"Fine. I'm listening." My toes were just about frozen, but I wasn't going anywhere.

"Courtland is my mother's maiden name. She's American. My dad is French—*was* French. It's not fair I have to talk about him in the past tense. My father was Marc Durant. And he shouldn't be dead."

"I'm sorry." I really was sorry. I knew what it was like to lose a parent.

She narrowed her eyes. "Spare me your sympathy. We're both here because we want answers. I'll tell you what I know, and then you'll do the same. The truth."

"The truth."

Becca looked at the pyramid. "Did you know that Rick wanted to call one of his novels *The Pyramid Thief*? It's a great title, isn't it? But Fox & Sons wouldn't go along with it, since it didn't have *Glass* in the title."

I shook my head. "I didn't know that."

Becca looked back at me, almost as if she'd forgotten I was there. "When I read about you and Rick being fans of each other, that's when I had the idea. The press never paid any attention to my family's story. There was no demand for justice for Marc Durant. Everyone forgot about him. But if a famous author were to take up the cause, and to tell the true story through fiction, revealing a killer that even the police had overlooked? That's something else altogether. Something people wouldn't be able to ignore.

"I was able to convince Rick to write my family's story as a manuscript because it would be a win-win situation. He was interested in the lost *naga* statue that had been stolen from my family when my father was killed, and I wanted justice for my father's murder.

"Rick had declared his writer's block and fear of travel, so his career was effectively over. But I had a story I knew he'd be interested in, because he'd been interested in it seven years before. I had details known only to my family, so I could give him the whole story for a Gabriela Glass thriller."

"You had the plot," I said, "and he could write it."

"He was hooked before I told him what I wanted to do."

"You found out about his time in Cambodia when he went missing. His searching for the treasure that goes with the *naga* statue. The one you've taken up the search for."

"Treasure? You think I care about that? I want justice for my father. Rick is the one who wanted the treasure."

"But the treasure is real."

"A family 'treasure' was stolen," Becca said. "A stupid old statue of a creepy snake. But to Rick, a small theft like that wasn't enough for Gabriela Glass. He needed to make up more to the treasure, so he took family gossip someone made up about one of our ancestors and a jewel-encrusted prince and princess, and made it into a big deal in the book. He said even though I couldn't find it online that didn't mean it wasn't real. Whatever. I didn't care, as long as the story would still solve the crime of proving who killed my father."

"A jewel-encrusted prince and princess?" I repeated.

"Aren't you listening? It wasn't real. Don't you think they would have displayed it with their other treasures if it was?"

"Rick thought it was still in Cambodia. I think that's where he went when he disappeared—"

"Forget about the treasure," Becca said. "I should have realized he'd kill again if provoked." A tear rolled down her pale cheek. "I was naive, I admit."

"You know who killed Rick Coronado?"

"I'm not surprised he didn't tell you he killed Rick. But I was sure he'd have to tell you about his earlier crime when you showed him the manuscript pages. Maybe not the murder itself, but the theft. I believed you were smart enough to put two and two together."

My mind reeled. "Rick's notes. His insistence that I show the pages to those in my inner circle. He didn't want feedback. He wanted me to show it to someone so I'd see their reaction."

"Ding ding ding. Give Dr. Jones a prize."

"Tamarind and Miles read the pages, but Tamarind is a *she* so that's not who you're talking about. And there's no way Miles had anything to do with a murder."

"Not those two," Becca growled.

"None of my inner circle had anything to do with France—" I gasped. Did she think *Sanjay* was involved? Sanjay, who'd introduced me to Sébastien. I couldn't speak. She *couldn't* mean Sanjay.

The impossible crime element of the earlier theft had the trappings of stage magic. Sanjay was a busy guy and didn't read much fiction, so I hadn't shown him the manuscript. God, had he gotten himself into something bad when Sébastien was mentoring him?

"Your boyfriend Lane Peters," Becca said. "He's the man who killed my father."

CHAPTER 28

Lane Peters. *My* Lane Peters?

I focused on the details of Becca's face as I took in her accusation, from the firm set of her jaw, visible above the scarf that had fallen, up to the anger in her eyes.

She was dead serious. As I watched her breath turn to mist in the frigid air, I knew she was telling the truth. *Her* truth. I didn't believe for a single moment that Lane was a murderer, but that the manuscript was meant to tell his story, as Becca understood it.

I understood something too. *It was the story Lane had hinted at since I'd known him.* The reason he quit his old life.

Like an ostrich sticking its head into the sand, I had assumed the tragedy that made Lane quit his old life was something like nearly getting caught and a friend of his winding up in jail. But being involved in a murder? I hadn't pressed for details when he told me about it two summers ago when we first met. The memory had still seemed too raw.

I groaned. "The name. Tristan Rubens. The name of a Knight of the Round Table and a Baroque painter. Just like Lane's given name, Lancelot Caravaggio."

"Rick was giving you a big hint."

And I'd missed it. I'd let my ego take over, wanting to believe Rick was enlisting my help as a historian who'd found other lost treasures.

There was no question. Becca wasn't lying about that. Tristan was meant to be Lane.

"There's no way Lane Peters is a killer," I said. "That's more ridiculous than a ghost killing anyone."

"I was so sure he'd confess everything to you after he saw the writing on the wall that exposed what he'd done. I guess he's not sticking around after all. No matter. The actions of a thief might not merit an international man-hunt, but a murderer? His time is coming." She smiled maliciously.

"Lane has told me all about his past," I said as carefully as I could. Now that I knew this was all a trap, I was aware she might be recording the conversation.

"But not what happened to my father. You must have shown him the pages! I was so angry he stood you up that night at the restaurant. I'd planned the timing so carefully! Rick's demand for an answer that night, and making sure the package wouldn't arrive until the end of the day, so you'd be sure to talk it over with your boyfriend. You showed him the pages. That's why he killed Rick—"

"He didn't kill Rick. He didn't kill *anyone*. Lane never saw the chapters from *The Glass Thief*."

"You're lying," she said through gritted teeth "I waited for as long as I could for Lane to show up at the restaurant that night. I'd so wanted to see his reaction when he realized he was about to be discovered. It was a risk, of course, that he'd disappear and the authorities wouldn't catch him. But I didn't think he would. Because of you. Either way, I'd get to see him destroy himself. Give up his freedom, or give up the love of his life. Probably both, since the novel was going to be a sensation. True crime novels are all the rage. Rick's book was going to be huge. Everyone was going to learn about Lancelot Caravaggio Peters, the murderer who ruined my life. And I'd get to watch his downfall from the start. But because of stupid Wesley..." she trailed off.

"What does Wesley have to do with this?"

She glared at me. "He's more polite than I thought. He didn't want to take credit for finding the letter in my book that afternoon, and didn't want us to linger any longer at the table that night. He said we'd be rude, since so many people were waiting for a table."

"The letter?" I repeated. No...

More pieces clicked into place. The timing was even more specific than I thought. Becca and Wesley "found" the letter the same day Rick Coronado's first manuscript pages arrived. That was the plausible reason for Becca to be at the restaurant when she thought Lane and I would both see the opening of Rick's novel. Becca had orchestrated the whole set-up perfectly. But perfectly on paper doesn't translate to real life. She could fake a historical letter and have a friend "accidentally" find it that afternoon where she'd left it in plain sight, but she couldn't control the people around her as much as she'd anticipated when she dreamed up her revenge. Wesley had taken the bait of the letter, but he was a decent guy who acted respectfully at the Tandoori Palace. And Lane was supposed to meet me at the restaurant that night, but had canceled because, as I later learned, he was busy filling out paperwork to buy the house.

It was my own biases that had fooled me. In a highly publicized case, I'd discovered a treasure my great grand uncle Anand had saved here in San Francisco, shortly after the Great Earthquake of 1906. The discovery involved the sunken ships underneath San Francisco. I was primed to respond to a similar discovery. A discovery that Becca and Wesley brought me, leading me to spend more time with them.

Becca had been unable to get close enough to me at a large university, so she faked and planted a historical document in the book Wesley found. She was smart and knew finding it herself would have been too obvious. She didn't want to show her hand. She needed a fellow student to find it. Her family had money, so she could have easily created a document that looked superficially aged. I should have seen it myself, only she knew exactly how to play on my weaknesses.

"You can't expect to control people like this," I said, hoping my voice wasn't shaking.

Becca shook her head sadly. She'd experienced far more than

she should have for a twenty-year-old. "Both of us are victims. I see that now. I'm sorry now that I had to bring you into this, but it was the only way."

"How did you find Lane?" I asked. I could have feigned ignorance, but I wanted answers. I knew in my heart that Lane was Tristan Rubens. I didn't believe the fictional facts, but I knew there were many grains of truth in this story. I needed answers.

"The most horrible thing about it is why I recognized him." Becca laughed and a tear escaped and rolled down her pale cheek. "The man I thought was my father's old friend from university. The man who was really Lancelot Caravaggio Peters. I should have known he was younger than my father, but when I was thirteen, adults simply seemed like adults. When I saw them talking, I didn't know what they were planning, but I thought he was the most handsome man I'd ever seen. I had the biggest crush on him. That's why I knew every aspect of his face. That's why I was able to recognize him when his photo was posted by the press the summer before last, even though he'd done something different to himself— or rather, I now know that he was in disguise back when I first saw him. He's hot, so there was a meme about him for a heartbeat. Everyone else forgot about him a couple of days later when a football player proposed to his girlfriend on live television. Except me."

"He *didn't* kill your father, Becca."

"He might be a changed man since you've known him. But that doesn't forgive what he did. He took my father away from me. He ruined my life."

The look of rage and indignation on my own face must have been apparent even from yards away, because Sébastien, who'd been keeping his distance, walked directly toward us. When he was a few feet away, his shoe hit a slippery piece of ice. He faltered and stumbled.

"Seb—"

"*Mesdemoiselles!*" He caught our arms and righted himself. "*Je suis desolé.*"

"Are you all right?" I asked in English.

He gave me a sharp look before turning a kindly one toward Becca. "*Je ne comprends pas.*"

Becca answered in French. I didn't catch most of what they said, since I spoke probably twenty words of French at most, but it was obvious she was concerned for the frail elderly man who'd stumbled. What was he up to?

Becca's face turned cold when she glanced my way. She switched to English. "This gentleman needs assistance getting back to the metro safely. Since you and I are done, and the remaining members of my family need me, I'm going to escort him. Don't worry. I won't ever take another of your classes. Don't you dare give me a failing grade as retaliation for telling the truth, though."

"Your faked historical document will do that all on your own."

She gave me a saccharine smile. "An irrelevant old letter that didn't make it into my final paper, which you'd know if you were doing your job and grading papers instead of traipsing around the world. I'm sorry my new friend here doesn't speak any English to witness your defeat. Even though Rick won't be here to see his manuscript published, I'll make sure a ghostwriter finishes it. I'll have to wait a little longer to see justice, but I've already waited for seven years."

"Wait," I said. "Who else did you tell? And why did you try to scare me off?" She had to have been involved with the threatening note or its disappearance.

She linked her arm through the crook of Sébastien's elbow. "Goodbye, Dr. Jones. I'll be seeing you again across a courtroom. If you decide to stick with him, that is. I won't blame you if you don't."

Sébastien shook my hand as he murmured his thanks in French. More importantly, as he did so he used sleight-of-hand to slip a note into my gloved hand.

CHAPTER 29

I was stress-eating bonbons in my apartment rental when Sébastien arrived.

"She didn't kill the author," he said.

"Judas."

"You don't believe it either."

I pushed aside the half-empty box. "No. She might have left the threatening letter but then thought better of it. But I don't think Becca killed Rick. From the facts I know, it doesn't add up."

"Yes. And she was far too caring. My stumble was inconvenient timing for her, yet she reacted compassionately. And yes, let me stop you before you interrupt. I know anyone is capable of murder under the right circumstances, so I can't rule it out 100 percent, but she's intelligent. It doesn't strike me she was boxed in enough that she'd react by killing someone. She wants justice for her father above all else."

"Which she planned so meticulously that the plan fell apart when the smallest thing went wrong. She's a mastermind who's been planning her perfect revenge for years."

Sébastien eyed the number of bonbons I'd eaten by myself. "There's no need for that. I don't believe Lane is a killer either."

"Obviously. But the meticulous research Rick always does…"

"You believe Lane is the Tristan character."

"There are things you don't know about Lane, even though you're one of the few people who know some of his past life."

"I know the important things. That he's a good man. That he loves you more than anything. That he's been trying to atone for his past sins for a long time."

"Two summers ago when I met him, he told me about his past. He told me there was a job that went very wrong five years before—making it seven years ago now—which is why he got out of his old life. He never told me the details."

"Perhaps it's time you asked him."

I told Sébastien I needed space to call Lane and speak in private, so he left for his apartment rental. I hated lying to Sébastien, but I had too many feelings to work through. I knew it would be worse to talk to Lane before I was ready.

The sun was low in the sky. I bought myself a bottle of wine at the market below the apartment. A delicious Bordeaux that I planned to finish on my own, along with the box of bonbons, and then I'd be ready to call Lane.

Lane. There was zero chance he was a murderer. But why hadn't he told me about this mess that had made him decide to turn his life around? He *had* told me it was so disturbing he upended his entire life because of it. And even if only half of what Rick had written based on Becca's facts was true, Lane didn't come off in the most flattering light.

I understood the impulse to hide from our embarrassing oversights. I was no better myself. I clenched the stem of the wine glass. Becca had faked the San Francisco gold rush letter so she would have an excuse to spend more time with me. She'd set up the timing perfectly, orchestrating Wesley's forced "discovery" for the same afternoon as the first Rick Coronado chapters that arrived with his demand for an immediate answer that night—and late enough in the day that she'd be able to innocently show up at the Tandoori Palace the night Lane was supposed to meet me there.

I was still mad at Lane, but at the same time, I loved him and trusted him more than anyone I'd ever known. I looked at myself in the small mirror with fleur-de-lis flowers on the edges. The independence in my eyes gave me away to myself. I was reacting more to my fear of losing that independence than to the ruby bracelet and gemstone.

The only men I had ever lived with were my father and brother. Neither relationship had gone especially well. My dad brought my older brother Mahilan and me to California after our mom died in Goa, where my parents had met when my American dad went to India as a young man to find himself. After arriving in Berkeley when I was eight and Mahilan was ten, we weren't given the most stable of childhoods. Our dad self-medicated his grief with relatively harmless drugs and vastly mediocre music. Our house smelled like pot and was filled with the discordant notes of the music students my dad took in to pay the bills. He taught sitar, an incredibly difficult instrument to learn.

Our doors were always open to neighbors in need, but those in need were often ourselves. We didn't have much money, so our frequent "potluck" dinners meant that friends would bring food and my dad would play music. We were evicted several times before a small inheritance helped my dad buy a tiny house. We always stayed close to Berkeley because of the strong social network there. My dad's long line of female friends babysat me, and my wardrobe was made up mostly of thrift store selections of my dad and his friends, which meant I wore a lot of tie-dye. Even though the sixties had ended decades before. Was it any wonder my brother went to law school and I got my PhD?

I left home after finishing high school. I traveled around the United States making a living as a waitress for several years before starting college. I needed to understand more of the real world. Waitressing is the hardest job I'd ever had, far more difficult than being a professor. Academia was challenging for sure, but in a different way. And academia was what I thought I'd always wanted. I certainly paid my dues. I lived with Mahilan, sleeping on his couch, while I was finishing my dissertation.

I'd always wanted the life of a mild-mannered academic. Yet

here I was in a hastily-rented apartment in Paris. I'd been manipulated by one of my college students and one of my favorite authors. The college student wanted revenge against the former thief I loved, the author wanted to get his hands on a treasure from Cambodia that had probably been stolen by French colonialists. And that treasure potentially led to a larger treasure, which somebody had killed for—more than once.

I looked back in the little fleur-de-lis mirror and tossed back the last of the wine. When I caught another glimpse of myself, I could have sworn it was Gabriela Glass looking at me from behind the glass.

Clearly I was far too drunk to call Lane. The alcohol and chocolate left me with a strange combination of nervous energy and lethargic bloat. I donned my running shoes.

I wasn't reckless. I took my passport and a few essentials in my messenger bag, keeping it light and tightening the strap across my chest. I left my headphones in the bag rather than on my ears, skipping bhangra beats in favor of listening to the world around me. I had enough sense to know I needed to stay alert. I didn't think the killer was interested in me at the moment, but I was in an unfamiliar city and the alcohol was far from wearing off.

I ran along the edges of the serpentine Seine River, thinking that even though I wasn't following a recommended guidebook loop, if I followed the river, how lost could I possibly get?

Paris at Christmas time was like stepping into a romantic movie. Or it would have been if I hadn't been tipsy, alone, and ridiculously confused about Lancelot Caravaggio Peters. Christmas trees filled public squares and could be glimpsed through lighted windows of apartments. Trees that had lost their leaves for winter were brought to life with glowing, festive lights strung through their branches. The scents of cozy, wood-burning fires and chocolate filled the air.

I was exhausted, half-drunk, and freezing cold from sweating on a cold night when I got back to the apartment. As I started up the narrow stairs, a pounding headache began to take hold.

I was in bad enough shape that I didn't fully register something was wrong as I rounded the winding steps to the fifth floor of the apartment building. But part of my brain knew. As I looked at the door of the apartment, pulled almost, but not completely shut, I knew the door had been forced.

And that someone was behind me.

Before I could reach out and touch the doorknob, hands wrapped around my arms and pulled me backward.

CHAPTER 30

I spun around and faced my attacker, who wasn't my attacker at all. Just the way Gabriela had been so wrong in a scene of *Empire of Glass*.

"My savior," I said, then burst out laughing.

Lane sniffed my breath. "You're drunk."

I held up my index finger and thumb with a small space between them. "Just a little."

"That," Lane Peters said, "was one of the stupidest things I've ever known you to do." He pulled me back, away from the door that had been forced. "At least you have your purse with you. Stay here while I check inside."

"It's not a purse," I mumbled to the empty hallway. "It's a messenger bag."

He was back minutes later, shaking his head. "Whoever was here is gone." He crouched down and examined the door more closely. "Sloppy break-in. Not professional."

"Should I be relieved?"

"Not yet. Do you know who's been following you?"

"Besides you?"

That almost got a smile. "Yes, besides me."

"Gabriela Glass?" I pushed past Lane and stepped into the tiny apartment. "She wanted to meet me."

He raised an eyebrow. "I have no idea how to—"

"You're Tristan!" My head was spinning, and only partly from alcohol and adrenaline. "And you're here. In Paris."

"I thought both of those points were rather obvious by now. Tamarind was worried about you. She told me what was going on and where you'd gone. Let's get you some coffee and figure this out. It's not safe to stay here. Come on. We're going to—"

I stopped his words with my lips. I didn't care what he was doing there. I just needed to feel his touch. His arms wrapped around me and his hands caressed the small of my back before abruptly pulling away.

He held me at arm's length. "There's no time for that."

"You said whoever was here is gone."

"And you're drunk. I'll gladly accept the turn of events if you're no longer upset with me. But first, we need to sober you up and figure out what's going on."

"On no," I said, stumbling backwards and falling into the fleur-de-lis pillows on the couch. "You're here where it happened—"

He misinterpreted my reaction. "I saw the door had been forced. That's why I grabbed you, to stop you from going in. Jones, you can't think I'd—"

"I'm not afraid *of* you, I'm afraid *for* you." I grasped the starchy edges of the couch cushions, willing the sinking feeling to stop. "You're being framed."

Becca...Rick...Gabriela...Tristan...the haunted mansion...the ghost covering up the murder of Luc—no, his real name was Marc...the vanishing sculpture...My mind wouldn't focus.

Lane pulled me up from the couch and wrapped his arms around me. I listened to his heartbeat with my head resting on his chest. His heart was beating too quickly. He wasn't as calm as he was pretending to be.

"I'll figure it out," he murmured into my hair. "This isn't your mess. You shouldn't feel—"

"Stop being stupid." I held onto him more tightly. "Whatever is going on, you're not on your own."

I had to save Lane. I wouldn't let a killer get away with letting Lane take the fall. Did he really think I'd let someone I loved—

"Sébastien!" I cried, pushing Lane away and scrambling for my phone. If I'd put my dear friend in danger yet again, I'd never forgive myself.

Lane swore. "You've involved Sébastien?"

"You didn't know?" I stared at Lane while the phone rang. "Come on," I whispered to myself. "Pick up."

"Jaya?" The sound of Sébastien's voice. "What's happened?"

I was so relieved I didn't care that Lane was glaring at me. Sébastien assured me he was safe, having met up for dinner with old friends after he'd left me. I was thankful he was better at answering his cell phone than I was.

"We're going to my place," Lane said. "Now."

Lane's "place" was a safe house I'd visited after our Louvre escapade. Two separate keys unlocked a narrow door that led to a studio apartment smaller than 200 square feet, which was a generous estimate. The largest piece of furniture was a couch that doubled as a bed, followed by a wooden table with two small chairs. I hadn't remembered how small it was because the thing that had always struck me about it was how he'd filled the space. There used to be times when he'd need to hide out there laying low for more than a few days, so nearly every inch of wall space was put to use: a combination of bookshelves crammed with well-loved books on philosophy, art history, and fiction, and reproductions of artwork from around the world. And inside a pewter frame, a photograph of me.

Lane steered me toward the bathroom. "A cold shower will do you a world of good. You'll thank me later."

I didn't thank him. But at least freshly brewed coffee was waiting for me when I stepped out of the bathroom wearing one of Lane's dress shirts, which nearly reached my knees.

"The intruder didn't bug your luggage," he said, tossing my bag of clothes to me. "You can have your clothes back."

"In a minute." I dropped the bag at my bare feet and accepted the coffee. "My head is clearer now. Which for some reason is making things make *less* sense than they did before. You followed me to Paris—"

"Which I had to learn about from Tamarind." Color rose in his cheeks, and he couldn't keep the anger out of his voice as he continued. "She told me about Rick Coronado's murder, the letter in your office, and she showed me the chapters. You should have—"

"You should have told me some things too."

"I know. Those chapters...I need to tell you about them—"

"They're your story. I know. And Tamarind doesn't know everything." I rummaged through my bag until I found the papers I was after. "There's one more chapter."

Lane read the pages in silence, spinning a pencil between his fingers, while I finished a second cup of strong coffee with plenty of sugar.

"This complicates things," he said, throwing the pages onto the small wooden table so forcefully that they slid into my mug.

"How much do you know?"

"Apparently not nearly enough."

I told him what I'd learned from Becca. How she'd convinced Rick Coronado to write her family's story, knowing he was interested in the stolen statue, and then used him to avenge her father's unsolved murder, before transferring to my university and getting close to me so she could watch Lane's downfall.

"She used me to get to you," I said.

It was my fault. They'd found Lane through me. Lane had tried to stay out of the media coverage that had followed our discoveries, leaving me to take full credit without him. But dammit, why had he taken two of the rubies? Why couldn't he leave well enough alone?

I had to focus. I could go back to being mad at him later.

Lane wanted to stay hidden, so no one would look into his past. But his photograph had appeared a few times, leading to people in his past to find him.

"I see the gears in your head spinning, Jones," Lane said softly. "You're wondering how she knew it was me."

"That part, I know."

"You do?"

"She saw you with her father seven years ago. She was thirteen and had a crush on you."

"But when I was in Paris with Marc for that job, I was dressed as his old college friend—the one he thought I resembled already. There's nothing that should connect me to this. Yet she knew."

"You're not just paranoid that you have a distinctive face. If someone has feelings for you and they're looking closely, they'll see through your disguises. At least the subtle ones."

"I'm sorry. For all of this."

"Don't be. It's mostly my fault. I'm the one who let my ego get in the way, allowing her to fool me. She's trying to prove you killed her father. Becca is the one behind everything that's happening now, but she's not the one who killed her father—she's seeking revenge, but against the wrong person."

Ending up in the spotlight was the worst part of saving lost treasures. I hadn't asked for any of it. I blinked back tears.

"I'm sorry," I whispered before turning away. But I didn't get far. He pulled me into his arms. I rested my head on his chest. But only for a moment. I pulled away and looked up at him.

"We need to figure out who actually *did* kill Marc Durant and Rick Coronado," I said. "Because otherwise, you..." I couldn't finish the rest of the sentence. I couldn't lose Lane.

"I couldn't solve it seven years ago."

"That's before you met me." I looked into his hazel eyes. Flecks of emerald green shone in the light. "I refuse to lose you. I'm going to solve this. I need you to start at the real beginning of this story."

CHAPTER 31

"Marc Durant was the man who got me involved," Lane said. "You've heard all about him."

"The man you watched die seven years ago," I said.

"Twice."

"Wait, that *really happened*?"

"Almost exactly as it was told in the pages by Rick Coronado."

I sat with my feet in front of the radiator, warming my cold toes. I'd gotten dressed in my own clothes but had kept Lane's fuzzy wool socks. "The impossible murder in the Rick Coronado manuscript was real?"

"The key facts, but not the details. I wasn't really an old university friend of Marc's—Luc in the story. I wasn't really much of a friend of his at all. Not at first. But I came to think of him as one in the short period of time we spent together. Stupid, on my part, though I don't know that feeling otherwise would have changed anything."

"You were so sure you wouldn't be recognized not only because you looked different back then, but because they thought you were someone else. Someone French."

Lane nodded. "Marc knew that one of his friends from university was away from his apartment traveling abroad, and it was a man who looked similar enough that I could disguise myself as him. It was a precaution only. Nobody was supposed to see me. Nothing was supposed to happen that night."

"You're skipping ahead."

"Right." Lane adjusted his glasses. "I'll start with the beginning. Marc Durant. The heir to the Durant Tea Company fortunes. He was in his early thirties, and his father was about to retire as the head of the company.

"I'd met Marc more than a decade before, when I was a teenager forced to attend one of my father's parties. Marc was in the same position, though a few years older than me. I was paraded around to speak with business associates in their native language, since my father knew how to take advantage of a manipulative ploy when he saw one. Marc's father was much the same, already grooming him in the cutthroat business practices he and his father before him had used to grow their tea empire. When he hated business school, his father insisted Marc at least become a doctor, so he tried medical school and hated that even more. He couldn't win.

"Marc and I slipped away with a bottle of Calvados and a pack of Gauloises cigarettes. He told me how he lived in a miserable old mansion with the ghost of his grandfather. I thought he was making up an entertaining story, fueled by alcohol and boredom. But the story is the same one in Rick Coronado's manuscript, and the same one Marc told me again when we met up years later. How his grandfather was a brutal man, feared by his factory workers and family alike. When someone pushed him down the stairs of that mansion in 1950, everyone who was there that night claimed to have neither seen nor heard anything. Because his murder was unsolved, his spirit decided to stick around for vengeance. The painting that had once resembled the dead man's own grandfather, who'd built the mansion before the wars, now morphed into looking like him. I laughed at the time, as we finished the bottle of *Calvados* and the last two cigarettes, and told Marc he should become a writer.

"He insisted it was all true, and that his family story had a tragic ending. His grandfather's ghost killed his own wife on the anniversary of his death. Pushed down the stairs by an unseen hand.

"That creepy story ended our evening together. Marc and I didn't keep in touch, but we met again at an auction here in Paris, more than seven years ago. His family was selling one of their pieces of art, one of Marc's favorites, and he was there to say goodbye to it. I was there for other reasons, which aren't relevant to this story. But what is relevant is that I wasn't *myself* at the time. I was in disguise, as it were. A down-on-his-luck Frenchman from a noble family."

"What exactly does that look like?" I asked, wriggling my toes for warmth.

"You're cold." Lane pulled a tartan blanket from a shelf under the bed.

"And you're ignoring the question."

"*Moi?*" He lifted his glasses onto his head and shrugged. The mannerism was small, yet that of a completely different person. A downtrodden wariness had replaced the confidence present a moment before.

"You scare me sometimes."

He tilted his head and his glasses fell back into place. "I stayed away from Marc as much as I could, because no matter how good a disguise is, it's never wise to put yourself in close contact with people you know. We were near each other only once during the evening, and there was indeed a flicker of confused familiarity, which I didn't return, so we each went our separate ways. But watching Marc from afar, I saw that he was miserable, so after my business was done, I became myself again and bumped into him. We went out for a drink.

"He told me how his awful father was about to retire and hand him the business, which was struggling and needed an even more ruthless hand at the helm to save it. He'd told his father he wanted to sell the business and maybe even the house—why did the family need to pay upkeep on the drafty old haunted mansion? They had a museum's worth of artwork in the house that could easily pay for his own daughter's future several times over. But when Marc proposed this to his father, his father decided to sell only one piece of art—the one piece he knew Marc loved more than anything, but wasn't worth much money. That's what had been on auction that night. There was an ancient statue his great grandfather had brought back from India that was worth a fortune—"

"Wait," I interrupted. "Cambodia. The statue is from Cambodia."

Lane raised an eyebrow. "I read Rick's manuscript. The Serpent King...Damn. A *naga*. I hadn't studied as much Asian art then, but yes, it could have been Cambodian."

"It is. But we'll get to that later. Go on with your story."

"There was a condition in the family trust that prevented the family from selling the statue. Marc didn't know what he was going to do. He was a writer like his mother and a painter like his grandmother. Not a businessman. Especially not one like our fathers.

"Marc was living with his family in a tiny apartment in Paris, refusing his mother's offer to live in the mansion with them, even though there was plenty of room. He didn't want his father's malice to infect his family. Or their superstition. His wife had left him and taken his beloved daughter. He wanted them back."

"His daughter Rebecca."

"Ever since the death of his grandmother on the anniversary of her husband's unsolved murder, nobody had slept in the mansion on that December anniversary. They always cleared out and left for a hotel, so the ghost couldn't kill anyone.

"You know the story of how I chose my initial profession. To get back at my father and his corrupt associates. Never stealing from anyone who couldn't afford it. Especially fond of jobs where I could make someone like that suffer. It was *my idea* to steal the sculpture for Marc. I proposed it subtly at first, just mentioning how it was a ridiculous way to live, and couldn't someone simply walk out of the house with the statue? He said there was an impenetrable lock. I joked that such things could be overcome.

"After I said that, I saw the flicker of recognition reignite in Marc's eyes. 'I knew I recognized you earlier tonight,' he said, 'but I didn't know it was *you*. I only knew it was someone from my past. You looked very much like an old university classmate of mine. I suspect there's more to you than you've told me.'

"I didn't say anything more then. But we exchanged contact information, and I looked into him. His story was exactly what he told me. I trusted him because of our similar fathers, and because we trust people we knew when we were young. He felt the same way. When he invited me to coffee, he made the next subtle move, letting me know his father was so miserly that he refused to put video surveillance security in the house.

"We understood each other then and dropped the pretense. I told him I knew exactly what needed to be done. It was a month before the anniversary of the earlier murders that had never been solved. The day that everyone cleared out of the house. That would be the night to steal the statue and several other valuable items kept in the library. As one of our several safety back-ups, I would disguise myself as his old friend from university—the one he'd mistaken me for at the auction. The man now lived only half the year in France, and we learned through social media that he'd be in a much warmer part of the world through winter. If Marc and I were caught, we could say we were old college friends who got drunk while reminiscing, decided to spend the night in a haunted house, and surprised an opportunistic burglar. It was a perfect plan. Until midnight..."

I blinked at him. "You aren't telling me the ghost story is true, are you? A ghost who floats above the snow and can bring people back to life to kill them again?"

"I know what I saw, Jones. I watched as a ghost killed Marc Durant through a locked glass door, only to see him die again on the staircase that had claimed his ancestors before him."

CHAPTER 32

Lane leapt up from the table. He paced the apartment, spinning a pencil (which I knew he wished was a cigarette) between his fingers. "God, I went over this so many times in my mind the year after it happened. But since I quit that life and began my art history PhD, I've forced it from my mind. It began to feel like a nightmare—horrifying, but a dream I'd long-since woken up from."

"I'm sorry you have to relive it," I said. "You can take a break," I added, even though I didn't mean it.

Lane smiled for the first time since he'd begun his story. "You don't mean that. But thank you for saying it. It's all right. I'll tell you what I saw." He paused and took a deep breath. "We'd entered the house though the back to avoid street cameras. The outer doors to the house had good security, but Marc had a key and knew the code into the house. It was the inner doors to the library he couldn't breach himself. Military-grade glass with a lock like that of a safe. Through the library's wide glass double-doors, the room's treasures were on display for everyone to see as they ascended the grand staircase. His father was the only one who knew how to unlock the door, but he wanted everyone to see his riches inside the room."

"Sounds like a charming fellow," I murmured.

"You see why I empathized with Marc's situation."

"But don't tell me you're an expert safe cracker now. If I've stepped even further inside a Rick Coronado novel, I'm going to scream."

Lane laughed. "No. A lock, yes. A safe, not a chance. But I'm a creative thinker."

"The glass."

"Exactly. Glass that's meant to be unbreachable serves its purpose in the moment, but it's no match for time. And we had time that night. The plan was to set off the alarm and force the door on our way *out*, so it wouldn't look like an inside job. But we never got that far.

"After half an hour of work, I broke through the glass and got us into the library. The room was on the second floor, directly off the landing at the top of the grand staircase, with hallways to the left and right leading to bedrooms.

"I was supposed to follow him inside after making sure the house was indeed empty. But when I reached the outside of the room, the glass door flung itself shut. I could see Marc's horrified face from inside the room. His hands flew to this throat. I ran to the door, but it was locked. As I shook the door handle, I watched as Marc's face turned red. His hands remained on his throat. It looked like he was fighting with an invisible assailant. It yanked him upward, and his feet left the ground. But still, I couldn't see who was strangling him."

"The ghost," I whispered.

"I didn't know what to think at the time. Or rather, I didn't have *time* to think at the time. I was watching my friend die before my eyes, and I was trapped on the other side. I grasped the door handle, but it didn't give. I reached through the circular opening in the glass I'd cut to unlock the latch, but it was jammed. I knelt at the door and tried to force it open any way possible, but it didn't give. Through the glass, my eyes locked on Marc's. His hands were still on his throat, but now blood was pouring from his lips."

I gasped and covered my mouth.

"He—" Lane's voice broke. "He fell to the ground, and his hands fell limp at his side. His eyes stared at the ceiling, unblinking. I knew it was too late. He was already dead."

Lane got himself a glass of water before continuing.

"As one of our precautions, I didn't have my cell phone with me. Easier to pretend to be someone else when you don't have your own phone or a suspicious burner phone. I ran downstairs to use the landline. I called for an ambulance but didn't stay on the line with them. I ran through the house, looking for open windows or doors. There had to be someone else inside the house with us. Someone who'd killed him. I thought it might have been a rope around his neck, which I'd been too distracted to see, so as soon as I got off the phone I ran to the attic above the library. That was the only thing that made sense—someone pulling a rope from above. But the attic was empty. It showed no signs of a hole where someone could lower a rope, and it was *dusty*. Nobody had been there. But while I was in the dusty attic, I heard the scream. It was his voice, Jones. I rushed back down and found the glass doors open—and Marc's body was gone.

"I knew I'd seen him be strangled by an invisible force. But now he was gone. Banging at the front door startled me and drew my gaze to the stairs. That's when I saw where Marc's body had reappeared. He'd been flung down the stairs. His twisted body lay at the bottom of the staircase. For the second time that night, there was no question Marc Durant was dead."

"You didn't see him alive in between then?"

He shook his head. "I didn't see him, but I swear I heard him. The detail Rick Coronado added in his manuscript about the medical crew seeing him thrown down the stairs was fiction."

Hadn't I read something about witnesses in the initial reports seeing a ghost? I couldn't place the recollection, though.

"I let the paramedics into the house," Lane continued. "The police and a second ambulance arrived shortly afterward. They took me to the hospital for a gash I'd gotten on my arm when I tried to break through the glass to help Marc, and said they'd follow up with more questions after I received treatment. That was a conversation I knew couldn't happen. So I called someone I knew could help.

"It was a strictly mercenary transaction. In exchange for a substantial amount of money, he asked no questions and provided me extra bandages for my arm, dropped me at a neutral location I requested, and left without looking back. I got back to my apartment without being seen.

"I had no idea what to do. My friend was dead. I was about to turn thirty. I'd had a good run getting back at unethical people like my father. But I was an adult. One who'd screwed up far beyond what I would have thought possible. Even though I had followed my self-imposed rules—no weapons and only stealing from people with questionable ethics who could afford it—someone was dead. It was time for me to take a good look at what I was doing with my life. So I called John."

"Seriously?" The man who'd introduced him to his old life of crime.

"When one is in dire straights, calling one's mentor is a perfectly natural reaction."

"That only applies when your mentor isn't an international jewel thief. In your case this sounds more like jumping out of the frying pan and into the fire."

"John got out of the game before I did."

"For a similar reason?"

"No. A far better one. A woman. His wife, Vicky."

"She's not in the same business, is she?"

"No. She's an art historian at a museum. She terrifies me. Because she can see through anyone." He smiled. "You two are a lot alike."

"Did John help you figure things out?"

"Vicky did. She wrote me a letter of recommendation that got me into my graduate school program." Lane blinked at me. "Hang on. I've been so absorbed in what happened seven years ago, I haven't thought about this week. It's still fall semester. It's not just the police you're fleeing. Finals—"

"Ended at the end of last week. I have a ton of grading to do by a little under two weeks from now, which I can do. And you're supposed to be visiting your mother for Christmas."

"My mother is the least of our problems. I'll make it up to her."

"So what happened after you disappeared? Did the police try to find you or the man you'd impersonated?"

"The police were mostly convinced at the time it was death by misadventure, with two drunk friends acting stupidly. They hadn't yet discovered the other missing piece of the mystery, because the family never asked them to look into it. The missing piece I hadn't fully comprehended at the time because I'd been so focused on Marc. *The sculpture was gone.* The one we'd set out to steal. Marc certainly hadn't taken it, and I hadn't either.

"But it was impossible for it to have gotten out of the house. The snow had stopped earlier that night. The only footprints before emergency services arrived to help Marc were my own and Marc's, walking up to the house. Nobody else had entered the house after us, or left before us. I searched the house. There were no secret passageways."

"I know."

"You know?"

"Sébastien and I have been busy."

"You've—?" He swallowed hard.

"Don't get off track yet. Finish the story. I wasn't far enough into Rick's manuscript to know how the seemingly impossible murder got resolved. What was the answer? How did it happen?"

"I'm afraid that's the end of the story." Lane went back to twirling the pencil between his fingers. "Gabriela Glass's interview with Tristen Rubens never happened, and the university friend was never involved." Lane snapped the pencil in half. "To this day, I still don't know the answer."

I stared at him. Gabriela Glass believed the thief was lying. That was how she explained the impossible crime. I had no such luxury. I knew Lane wasn't lying. That meant what he'd witnessed was truly impossible.

CHAPTER 33

In the morning, we regrouped with Sébastien at the apartment across from the mansion. We took two metro lines and two cabs to get there, just in case whoever had broken into my apartment attempted to follow us.

I wondered at the futility of the exercise, since we were across the street from the lion's den. Then again, I knew we weren't yet done with that haunted house.

We discussed what we'd each been up to. Sébastien said he'd been thinking about Becca's story and saw some major gaps. "We don't know how much the charming girl hounded him," Sébastien said, "but..."

"I know," I agreed. "It was certainly convenient for her to convince Rick of her plan. It was too easy."

"The lure of the treasure he'd been after for seven years," Lane said.

"That's it," I said. "I don't mean you're right. I mean that's the problem. If we're all so convinced that's what he was after when he disappeared for six weeks, how did he know about the Durant family treasure in the first place? Didn't the family cover up the theft of their statue, which according to Rick's novel was a bigger deal than the family expected?"

"I can't help," Lane said. "At that point I was running from my old life. I'm not sure how things were handled then."

"The theft wasn't reported in the press," I said. "Tamarind and I looked. It was only the suspicious death in the news, and gossip about the wealthy family in other media."

Thinking of Tamarind made me think about my students.

"I need to check on something," I said. "You two keep talking. I'll be in the kitchen."

I felt guilty that I'd been ignoring my job. Wesley needed to know the letter was fake. And I'd tell Naveen it was my fault if his project for Research Methods had shoddy research. I logged in and checked the electronic submissions of my student's papers. Becca had told me the truth: she'd left the fake letter out of her paper. I doubted she'd had the courtesy to tell Wesley not to use it in his own research.

I emailed Wesley to tell him the letter was a fake and that I'd put in a word with Naveen. It was eight a.m. in Paris, so eleven p.m. in San Francisco. I didn't know if I should get my hopes up that he'd reply right away.

My email inbox was overflowing, so I skimmed it for important messages. Probably best not to ignore a message from the dean of faculty. Especially when he'd emailed me twice. One was an alert that I'd missed a voicemail message from him at my university extension, the other was a "per my message" email.

I winced. I hadn't thought to check my university number since I'd left. One of the simultaneous up- and downsides of being an academic is that it's far from nine-to-five hours. I called in and listened to my messages. Two students asking for extensions, and the dean's voicemail message, with an unexpected question.

In our process of, er, what I meant to say is that an accusation has been made against Naveen Veeran. We are investigating, but as it overlaps with your area of expertise, I thought you might be able to shed light on this without our having to make a broader, more embarrassing enquiry. A graduate student who works with a different advisor recently published a paper, and a chapter of Naveen's newest in-progress book is quite similar. I'll email you the details.

Tenure applications were generally confidential. I expected that was why he'd stumbled over his initial words, not knowing

Naveen had told me he'd applied for tenure. It was that same moral code that made me skeptical of the accusation. But if the student had published his paper first...

I opened the aforementioned email and found the student paper and the book chapter. I knew immediately what I was looking at. When Naveen and I had started at the university at the same time, in the glow of securing such great first jobs out of graduate school, we'd been more collegial than we were now. We'd critiqued each other's work. And I recognized the content of the chapter. It was Naveen's work from more than two years ago, long before the student's paper was published.

This was the kind of thing that could sink Naveen's application. He'd eventually be able to prove he hadn't plagiarized the student's work, but without quick validation, the seed would be planted in people's minds that maybe he couldn't be trusted. And tenure was voted on by a committee of humans with the same biases as the rest of us.

I closed my eyes. There was no question that I had to speak up on Naveen's behalf.

By the time I'd replied to the dean to assure him I'd seen Naveen's draft work two years before, and it was the student who'd gotten hold of the work to pass it off as his own, Wesley had emailed me back.

Jaya, thanks for the warning, but I already authenticated the letter. It's real, dated to more than 100 years ago, and the paper is French!

—W

Wait...what? He'd even attached the authentication. From a reputable person I knew. That wasn't possible. A second email popped up while I was still processing the first.

Thanks for thinking of me, though. Your

encouragement is why I didn't drop out last year. I was in your Intro to History class, and your lectures rocked. And now you're helping me with a project for another prof's class. I didn't know teachers could be so cool.

I didn't know how to react to either email.

This kind of authentication was expensive. Wesley was a charming kid who must have learned how to be resourceful to survive without money.

But that meant I'd jumped to the conclusion that if Becca planted the letter that the letter itself was a fake. But if it was a *real* historical letter, simply put somewhere it didn't belong, that meant the *information* in the letter was real as well.

I looked up the photo of the letter I'd taken on my phone. It was in French, so I entered the words into a translator as we'd done before.

Son,

> *My ship sank at port. Most of my possessions are buried at sea with the ship. But your inheritance is hidden safely. As for the fragile pieces, I will need to go back for them. I hope to return home soon.*

No name had been signed. But if facts were telling me what I thought they did, that the letter was real, written in French over 100 years ago on French paper, and it was something Becca had obtained from her own family's archives.

Becca was smart enough to know I'd spot an obvious fake. But if she used a *real one* that was simply unrelated, she could get the attention she wanted at the time she wanted it.

My heart thudded. The letter in Becca's possession was referencing not a San Francisco treasure, but *this one*. It was telling us the *naga* statue was indeed only one piece of a treasure. "Fragile pieces." This was our link to the prince and princess.

Everything else had been at least partly manipulation, impossible to tell fact from fiction. Lane filled in the blanks about what he'd seen seven years ago, but he knew nothing about the statue and where it might lead. He hadn't even known it was Cambodian. But this letter filled in one of the key missing pieces.

"You guys," I called from the kitchen. "You guys!"

They were at my side in seconds.

I showed them the image of the letter that Becca had put in a San Francisco Gold Rush era book for Wesley to find. "This letter is what Becca used to get me to pay attention to her. She lied about what it really was, so I thought it was completely faked, but my student Wesley had it authenticated."

Lane took my phone and read the words in French. My stomach gave a little lurch, and I wasn't sure if it was more from the realization that we had confirmation of our theory, or the sound of Lane's voice.

"If I'm right," I said, "this shows that Becca's ancestor knew of something bigger in Cambodia. *The treasure that the naga statue was guarding.* Rick had learned from Becca about a jewel-encrusted prince and princess. It's real."

"Let me see that," Sébastien said, squinting at the phone. He made his own translation, but the words were very similar to the translation we'd gotten from the Internet on my phone. Close enough that the meaning was the same.

"*Your inheritance is hidden safely. As for the fragile pieces, I will need to go back for them,*" I read aloud.

I closed my eyes and thought back to *The Glass Thief.*

"What are you thinking, Jones?" Lane asked.

"Gabriela mentioned markings on the base of the Serpent King statue. I didn't think it was relevant since we've already discovered where it was pointing us. But Rick drew attention to the fact that the markings weren't damage, but purposeful markings."

"Gabriela was right," Lane said. "That's not how sandstone breaks down. If there are really markings on the base of the *naga* statue, they could be a map. A perfect place for it, since stone markings have conveyed information for thousands of years. The author of the letter says he had to go back for the most valuable pieces."

"If we believe this to be a real map on a real sculpture," Sébastien said, "we need that map."

"And we need to find it tonight," I said.

"Tonight?" Lane repeated.

"Gabriela Glass was scheduled to meet a historian in Cambodia this weekend."

Sébastien laughed. "Surely you can't think..." His expression turned serious. "You really think someone will be waiting in Cambodia for you?"

"With Rick dead?" I shook my head. "I don't know. But someone knew that Rick Coronado had put the pieces together. They killed Rick and broke into my office to scare me off. They're following in Gabriela's footsteps too."

Sébastien frowned. "This should make you *less* interested in traveling to Cambodia. Not more."

I took Lane's hand in mine. "I'm not risking your freedom. I don't care about a looted treasure." I paused as I felt their skeptical gazes boring into me. "All right. I care. But not a fraction of the amount that I care about making sure Lane's life isn't ruined because of what happened in that mansion seven years ago. The killer is after the treasure, so we follow the killer to catch them. I'm not going to sit around and wait for them to follow through on whatever their plan is. We can't ignore anything."

Lane squeezed my hand. Before he could do anything else, Sébastien cleared his throat.

"Back to this map, then," Sébastien said.

Lane let go of my hand. "There aren't generally photographs of the base and back of sculptures. And the family wasn't forthcoming with details about it. All we have are regular photos of the expensive artwork in the library. I don't think we'll find a photo of the base of the sculpture."

I thought back to the haunted mansion across the street, with its scent of pine needles from a long-ago tragic Christmas. "We need to figure out what happened to that sculpture after it disappeared."

"Well then," Sébastien said. "Let's find that sculpture. The secret to where it went is in that mansion. Lane, are you up for setting foot inside that house again?"

CHAPTER 34

Sébastien wanted to play the part of a frail old man to check if the house security was still off by knocking on the front door and pretending to have the wrong address if his forced attempt inside tripped an alarm.

"Too risky," Lane said. "A good Samaritan might try to help the confused old man. That won't get us inside unobserved."

"And your karma of crying wolf is going to catch up with you one of these days," I said. "How am I supposed to know if you really need help?"

Sébastien took my hands in his. "Your concern is touching, but unnecessary. I have outlived Christo and far too many of my friends. No, no. I know you will say I have a new beau, you two, Sanjay, many friends, and my menagerie of illusions that is still growing. But I do not fear death. When it's my time, it's my time. Until then, I plan to enjoy this world and its mysteries. Including this one. It must be a magic trick of some kind, as nothing truly impossible happened. There was no ghost. Of this I am certain."

"You have a better plan to get us inside?" I asked Lane. I couldn't let myself get sentimental

"The simplest plans are usually the best. You already went to the effort of disabling the alarm. All we need to do is test it without drawing attention to ourselves. Sébastien's plan was almost right. He should go to the back door as if he belongs. If no alarm is triggered and nobody shows up within fifteen minutes, Jaya and I follow in construction worker attire."

"He's good," Sébastien said.

An hour later, we were all inside. As we entered the grand foyer with the staircase, Lane stumbled backward and crashed into a covered side hutch. The remaining contents rattled. It was daytime and a bit warmer than when Sébastien and I had visited, so it wasn't ghostly breath that had startled him.

He was looking up at the one thing that dominated this space more than the central staircase: the painting of Aristide Durant, who had built this mansion a hundred years before. Or, if the legend was to be believed, that now held the visage—and spirit—of the first man who'd been pushed to his death here. Aristide's grandson Beaumont.

Lane was eyeing the painting as if he'd seen a ghost. I agreed that the portrait of an angry man looming over us was dispiriting, but Lane didn't usually overreact.

The oversize painting that hung high on the wall overlooking the stairs hadn't been removed with most of the other paintings, nor had it been covered with a sheet. Above us, the chandelier near the stained-glass skylight hadn't been covered either. Both were high enough that it wouldn't have been easy to reach them. It was another indication the occupants had departed quickly and not overseen the house being closed up.

Lane inched up the first few steps, getting a closer look at the eerie portrait. The man had sunken eyes and pallid skin and was seated in a stiff position. The orientation of the artist wasn't head-on, but captured from the viewpoint of someone in a lower, subservient position. A background of dark gray conveyed power but not warmth. Even as the sunlight shifted and the daytime sun cast red and blue light onto the wall next to the portrait, the mood of the room didn't improve.

Lane stopped and shook his head.

"What's the matter?" I asked.

"The portrait...It changed again. That's not one of Marc's ancestors. The man in the portrait is now Marc himself."

"It can't be," Sébastien said. "Surely you're mistaken. Family members resemble each other."

"You're sure that's your friend?" I asked.

"Positive." He'd recovered from the shock and was now halfway up the stairs, where he could get a closer look at the painting. The stairs weren't bound by any walls, but floated in the center of the foyer leading to the second floor gallery, like an atrium. The painting was on one of the walls that stretched the full height of the mansion.

Frustrated that he couldn't get a closer look, Lane came back down the stairs. When we looked around, Sébastien was gone.

Lane swore. "We never should have involved him."

"Really, what would you two do without me?" Sébastien came into the room carrying a ladder. "Though at my age, ladders are heavier than they used to be."

Lane took the ladder. Sébastien and I held it while Lane climbed the rungs to get a closer look at the painting. He tugged at the frame. "It's bolted to the wall. We're not getting it down. But that's okay. I can tell what we need to see from here. Someone painted over the face."

"Obviously," Sébastien said. "The question is *who*."

"And when," I added.

Lane sniffed the canvas. "Not recently."

"Who was it meant to frighten?" I asked, but I thought I knew the answer. "You don't suppose it was to get Marc's parents to move out of the house?"

"This paint job is sloppy," Lane said. "It looks far more like Marc than his grandfather, but the painting I remember from seven years ago was good."

"The painting of the supposed ghost?" I asked. "Which was already painted over in 1950."

He nodded. "It's only the face that's been painted over, which is why the overall appearance is so jarring. A different man's face in the same old-fashioned clothes and setting."

"It's so high," I said half to myself as I craned my neck. "And it's got to be ridiculously heavy. It had to have been a conspiracy. Multiple people working together."

"Or one very daring one," Lane said.

"Come down," Sébastien said. "You're making me nervous perched up there on this old ladder."

"Whoever this man is," I said as Lane climbed down, "he's not someone I would have wanted to be friends with."

"I knew men like this in my youth," Sébastien said. "It's one reason I was glad to retire to the countryside." He pulled the ladder away from the painting.

I put my hand on his arm. "Hold on."

"The painting has been faked," Sébastien said. "There's nothing more we can learn from it."

"There's one more thing. This painting is designed to frighten. To keep people away from it." I climbed the ladder and stood eye to eye with the creepy portrait. "What's the one place we didn't search for the missing *naga* statue, which we know couldn't have left the house? Lane, do you have a knife?"

"Please don't tell me you're going to do what I think."

"What choice do we have? Seven years ago, someone killed Marc, framed you, and stole the missing *naga* statue which they think leads to a bigger treasure. Now that same person has resurfaced and killed Rick, and they're going after us and the treasure."

He tossed me his Swiss Army knife.

The portrait was bolted to the wall. *But what was behind it?*

I opened the knife and ran the blade between the canvas and the frame. It took less than a minute.

No, this couldn't be right. Behind the canvas was a mildew-spotted portion of the stone wall. There was no secret passageway or hiding spot.

I banged my fist on the wall. I pretended it was because I wanted to see if the wall was solid, but honestly, it was in frustration.

"It was a good idea anyway," Sébastien said.

"But it couldn't have left the house," I murmured. "Should we search again?"

Had Rick visited this house? Did he tell the family he wanted to write a book about their family history? Considering how they tried to keep things out of the papers, they surely would have refused. What did they do to him that traumatized him so much he disappeared for six weeks and hadn't written a word in seven years?

I snapped out of my reverie as Lane and Sébastien crept up the stairs.

I held my breath as I stepped over the landing where three people had died, and ascended the stairs leading to the library where Lane had witnessed a ghost killing his friend.

CHAPTER 35

We examined the scene of the crime in the library. The plan was both to stir memories and to see if there was any evidence remaining.

"This is where the first murder happened," Lane said, standing in the center of the room.

"Since we're recreating the scene," I said, "I'll go outside the room to the landing."

"With Sébastien," he said firmly, looking at the older man.

"No," I insisted. "Not before we test the lock with all three of us on the outside. You said yourself the lock was jammed so you couldn't get in to help Marc."

Lane nodded and we tested the door. The lock was still broken, but instead of jamming to keep the door shut, now the creaking hinges refused to allow the door to close completely. I nodded my assent.

Sébastien and I left the library and closed the glass doors as much as possible.

As I looked through the heavy glass, Lane put his hands to his throat. I knew he was only reenacting what he'd seen seven years before, but my own throat felt as if it were constricting.

"Breathe," Sébastien whispered in my ear as he squeezed my hand. I grasped his thin fingers and he squeezed back. We were keeping each other from rushing into that room.

"Where could it be hiding?" Sébastien asked softly, looking away from Lane to the corners of the room.

I took my eyes off Lane for a second to gape at Sébastien. "You don't think—"

"Not a ghost. No. But something else that wasn't a person."

"You think it was a mechanism?"

"It's a possibility."

Oh no. And we'd left Lane inside with it.

"Then what are we doing out here?" I reached for the door handle, but Sébastien held me back.

"It was only activated once," Sébastien said calmly. "Dozens of people, if not more, have been through the library countless times since then."

But as Lane clutched his throat in agony and fell to the floor in a limp heap, I couldn't stay put and watch from beyond the glass doors. I rushed inside so quickly that I tripped over the pile of sheets and went flying. I landed hard—on top of Lane's prone body.

He grunted and cursed. The noise of a very annoyed man. But one who was very much alive.

Sébastien was already inspecting the crevices of the walls. He looked up at the ceiling. "You're certain that's exactly where Marc was standing?"

Lane cursed once more as I extricated myself from his limbs and helped him up. "Positive. And Jones, I appreciate the sentiment, but maybe you could put a moratorium on searching haunted houses in high heels."

"Pity it wasn't two meters to the left," Sébastien murmured. "Then it would have been easy to get a rope through the light fixture. But here?" He shook his head.

"I thought of the same thing at the time." Lane rubbed his shin. "The way the invisible assailant yanked him upward, it had to have come from above."

"We could check the attic to be certain," Sébastien said. "We should also have Lane show us what happened with the second death of Marc Durant on the stairs. Jaya, are you listening? Your face..."

"There's no need to check the attic again," I said. "Or to reenact the fall down the stairs. I know who killed Marc Durant. And how."

CHAPTER 36

"Think about what we witnessed at the mansion," I said to Sébastien once we were back at the apartment. "Not what we think is logical, but what we really saw when we watched Lane through the glass doors of the library, reenacting what he believed he saw seven years ago."

Sébastien threw his hands into the air. "We were standing together. We saw Lane pretend to be strangled by an invisible rope or invisible hands. We both saw this. Ah! Unless you mean since I'm a foot taller—"

"Nope, not that type of misdirection." The more I thought about it, the more certain I was that I was right.

"There were no mirrors."

"And I know what I saw seven years ago." Lane, who'd been looking out the tiny obscured window, turned to face us. "I know it was a long time ago, but I'll never forget it." His eyes were tired. I didn't blame him.

"I know you didn't." I took his hands in mine. "And I believe you saw exactly what you say you did. And what Sébastien and I saw was also real."

"Jaya is enjoying her lecture a little too much," Sébastien said to Lane.

"I need you to hear me out," I said, returning to my lecturing position. "What I'm about to say is the only thing that makes any sense."

"Remove the impossible," Sébastien said, "and the only thing that remains, however improbable, is the truth."

"Exactly." I took a deep breath. "Marc strangled himself."

I watched for their reactions.

"He wouldn't have killed himself," Lane said. "Plus that doesn't explain his scream or why I found him at the bottom of the stairs with his neck at an unnatural angle."

"I didn't say he killed himself. I said he *strangled* himself. What you saw through the glass library doors—Marc was faking being strangled, just like Lane was tonight."

"Of course!" Sébastien said. "Misdirection. He wanted it to appear he was being strangled, but in reality, he wasn't. Not with any kind of force. He was putting on an act. It was for show. You'd already gotten him inside. He wanted you to run away."

Lane swore. "But I didn't. I couldn't just leave him there."

"You said you didn't actually see him falling down the stairs," I said.

Lane shook his head. "No. I heard his scream, heard the *thunks* as he fell, and found him lying at the base of the stairs. There was no other explanation for what happened."

"There's always another explanation," Sébastien murmured.

"Marc planned to steal the statue and other valuable items like Lane thought," I said, "but not for his family. Only for himself. He'd been divorced since Becca was little. She grew up with her mother, and although spending holidays here meant a lot to Becca, how do we know what Marc really felt? You yourself said Marc Durant was miserable. He faked his own death and disappeared."

I watched Lane's face as he struggled with the truth. The realization that he'd been traumatized by watching a man die—when that man had never died.

"We've been looking for the wrong killer," I said. "Marc isn't dead, and he killed the man who was about to prove it."

"The family's reluctance to come forward," Sébastien said. "You think it wasn't only that they thought the ghost killed him, but that his body disappeared?"

"I don't know exactly what happened yet," I said. "There are many ways he could have dealt with the issue of the body, some more gruesome than others. Lane, think back on what you saw in the library. Does my explanation fit with what you saw?"

He closed his eyes. "I knew there was something wrong at the time. Something *off* in what I was seeing. But I thought it was because of the oppressive atmosphere in that house. The ghost story. The painting. The whole history of that house."

"That house was made for a grand illusion," Sébastien said.

"Marc was miserable," Lane said, "but I can't believe he'd leave his daughter. The way he talked about her, he adored her."

"He probably cared more than he thought he did at the time. After all, he followed what she'd been up to. That's how Marc knew what she was doing—and how he found Rick."

"Rick," Sébastien said, "who figured out that the statue Marc stole led to a larger treasure in Cambodia. One that he was obsessed with finding."

"And now Marc knows that too," I said. "He's already lost everything and has nothing more to lose. He's going after the bigger treasure Rick discovered. Rick's meticulous research was his own downfall."

"But Cambodia is a big place," Lane said, "and has a long history with France. It's not like we'd get anywhere by waltzing into Raffles in Phnom Penh and asking, 'Do you happen to have seen a Frenchman in his forties?'"

"No," I said, "but we're forgetting something. Rick was giving me clues in the manuscript. He *wanted me* to find the treasure. We know the subject of the treasure, that it's the Serpent King's daughter and her prince. It was something Rick wasn't able to find seven years ago, so he was enticing me with the mystery."

"But he wasn't able to finish sending the book to you. And we know from Becca that she didn't believe in or care about that part of the mystery."

"I've been thinking about that. We now believe Rick was in Cambodia for his six missing weeks, right? We also know he'd previously done a lot of historical research on Cambodia."

"For *Empire of Glass.*"

"Right. The reason that's my favorite of his books is because the treasure wasn't a worldly possession, but *knowledge*."

"You think he was looking for that lost city he made up in *Empire of Glass*?" Lane asked.

I blinked at him. "You've read it?"

"Of course. It's a classic."

I kissed him.

Sébastien cleared his throat. Lane pulled away with a smile on his face.

"They've been excavating Cambodia for decades," I said, "even after the land mines from Pol Pot's regime and American bombs got in the way. From what we've pieced together from real history, Rick's hints, and what Becca knew, the missing snake sculpture was meant to hold the prince and princess. That's what we know. Beyond that, we've each been blinded by our weaknesses."

"So was Rick," Lane said. "He wouldn't ask for help. It nearly killed him once, and *did* kill him a second time."

"Marc never knew what he had when he stole the Serpent King. He thought it was one of his family's valuable works of art, nothing more. But Rick figured it out."

"You think that's why the author had to die?" Sébastien asked.

Lane's hair fell into his face as he shook his head. "I still can't imagine Marc as a killer."

"You're biased," I insisted. "Having a bad father doesn't excuse what he did, but it made you empathize with him and not see him for what he really was."

"I'm not saying he had a heart of gold," Lane said. "I mean the exact opposite. He was weak. He dropped out of his business and medical school programs, he never stood up to his father, he didn't fight for his family when they left for the United States."

"You barely knew the man," I insisted. "There's a good chance Marc is in Cambodia right now to find the treasure Rick was unable to find seven years ago because he didn't have the necessary information."

"It appears that you two," Sébastien said, "are going to Cambodia."

CHAPTER 37

"Fourteen hours." I groaned. "Fourteen hours to get to Siem Reap, Cambodia."

Sébastien was headed home to Nantes to resume his life with Fitz and the creations he worked on at the *Machines de L'île*. Lane and I were preparing for our trip to Cambodia. If not for Gabriela Glass's invitation to meet her in Siem Reap, we would have gone to the capital, Phnom Penh, to begin to seek out experts to consult. But Siem Reap was the natural starting point if we were heading straight to the temples.

"Count your blessings," Lane said. "It's nineteen from San Francisco. And might I point out, you're not complaining about where the money comes from to get last-minute tickets."

"We never finished that conversation we started at the house in Berkeley, did we."

"We've got a long flight ahead of us."

"I'm not having that conversation on an airplane."

"It's okay if you're not ready—"

"I didn't say I didn't want to talk. We've got five hours before heading to the airport, right? I've got a few emails to send, then we'll get the photos we'll need for our visas. After that I'm all yours."

"I think you've got that order wrong, don't you?" He linked his fingers with mine.

"Mr. Peters, are you trying to distract me?"

"It's one of my many skills."

"I'm aware."

An hour later, Lane stepped out of the shower while I was finishing my emails.

"You're not telling people where we're off to, are you?" he asked. "I thought we agreed—"

"We did. I was emailing my student Wesley. I wanted to ask him for more details about the letter Becca had taken from her family and planted. I also thought I'd see if I could find someone who knows about historical *naga* artwork in Siem Reap. Not an academic colleague who might talk to mutual acquaintances."

"It's probably an unnecessary precaution, but thanks for humoring me."

"It worked out fine. I don't know anyone personally there, but the Angkor National Museum has a large collection of *naga* art and history, so I emailed a curator there. Her bio shows an American education, so I know she'll speak English."

"I suppose it's time for that talk now."

"Yes, I—" My phone dinged. Wesley had already emailed me back. "Doesn't that kid sleep?" I was glad he didn't. "His authenticator x-rayed the letter! The squiggly lines. Becca's ancestor didn't only draw his map on the base of the sculpture. He drew his map on the letter."

Wesley emailed me the results, including the high-resolution photo of the letter he'd found planted in Becca's library book. I'd taken a photo with my own phone, but the x-ray version he sent me was different. It contained a sketch with hand-drawn lines, just like Gabriela had described. I wouldn't have thought it was a map if it hadn't been for the hint in Rick's manuscript. It was just a few overlapping lines. They were straight, like a grid, but with squiggly swirls where they met.

Wesley had dismissed them as well, which is why he hadn't mentioned them when I'd initially emailed about the letter.

"But we still have no frame of reference for what the lines and squiggles mean," Lane said.

"Which makes sense, because he wouldn't have given away

everything in the contents of a letter he sent to his son. There's no starting point for a frame of reference."

"Assuming it's a map leading to one of the temples that was covered by jungle when the French came as colonizers," Lane said, "even with a starting point, things have changed. There are probably a hundred times more roads than there were more than a century ago when this was drawn."

"What if it's not a map of roads. What if it's *rivers*. That could be why the lines have this added squiggly element."

Lane shook his head. "Rick would have found enough evidence with all his research."

"He needed my help with something. Otherwise he wouldn't have gone along with Becca's plan. And just like roads, rivers change too. The Angkorian Empire flourished because of the river tributaries from the Mekong as well as their own irrigation systems."

"I don't know." He scrunched his face as he looked at the image. "It doesn't look like either roads or rivers."

"It's a stretch, I know." I sighed. "But there's something not fitting together quite right for this to be the map to a temple."

"What are you thinking, Jones?"

"You're not going to like it. This is a snake treasure. What if it's protected by a snake as well? Have you heard of a Cobra Lock?"

"A lock that needs to be unlocked with a mantra, not a key."

I'd been thinking about *naga bandham* Cobra Locks, like the one Wesley had mentioned, and come to the realization that a lock isn't always something you unlock with a regular key. In the hypothetical example of the *naga bandham* tonal lock, it's the right frequency that unlocks something.

"What if it's the faded lines that tell us something about a tonal mantra?" Jaya asked.

"Even if you're right, we need some kind of map to get us there before we can know where to look for the lock."

I glared at him. "I'm trying to save your neck. You could at least appreciate that I'm thinking creatively."

*   *   *

I downloaded more Cambodian history to read on the plane, as well as a copy of *Empire of Glass*, the Rick Coronado novel set in Cambodia.

I didn't get far. I fell asleep an hour into the flight, hoping my own subconscious would tell me where I was going and what I was doing.

Instead, I dreamt of Gabriela Glass riding on the back of a motorcycle under the stone gates of Angkor Thom, clinging to the back of an unknown man, which morphed into me riding on the back of a motorcycle in India with my arms wrapped around Lane as we sped south from Kochi to Trivandrum. When we'd been on that trip in search of the Heart of India, we'd had a plan. I didn't usually run blind into a dangerous situation, but now, the need to protect Lane made me act in spite of my better judgment.

The dream shifted again. I was still with Lane, but had fallen into Gabriela Glass's Cambodian setting of *Empire of Glass* when Gabriela finds not the valuable, shiny treasure that she usually rescued from impenetrable lairs or evil masterminds, but *a lost city*. This wasn't a city filled with riches, but the remains of what had once been a thriving metropolis before the waterways of Cambodia shifted over time.

Critics had been divided about the book, as were fans. I was in the camp that loved it. Which probably explained why I'd fallen into it so vividly in my dream. I splashed into a vast lake at the base of a cliff. I lost sight of Lane, but caught sight of a serpent rising out of the water.

The story of the lost city in *Empire of Glass* mirrored the origin story of Indian prince Kaundinya, Khmer princess Soma, and Soma's snake king father. Using symbolism, as Rick Coronado loved to do, the lost city was literally a mirror of the cliff-top temple. In *Empire of Glass*, instead of sitting high on a mountain, Gabriela's lost city was found at the bottom of the cliff in a spot that had once been the *naga* king's watery kingdom. The spot where the cobra king drank up the water to present a gift to his precious daughter and her worthy husband.

Rick's fictional lost Angkorian era city was based on the real life Preah Vihear Temple that sits high on a cliff on the border between Cambodia and Thailand. It's still a disputed site. The French drew new maps of Cambodia when it was a French protectorate, and one such map included Preah Vihear as part of Cambodia. Yet the only entrance to the temple perched on that steep cliff is through Thailand, even though courts have ruled it belongs to Cambodia. As with many historical sites that existed before modern boundaries were drawn, there's no easy answer.

The treasure in *Empire of Glass* was knowledge, not physical objects like in *The Glass Thief*. But I'd forgotten something. Rick's editor had told me about a plot line that was cut.

My eyes popped open.

I pulled Lane's headphones off. "Preah Vihear."

"You think that's where Marc is going?"

"Rick's fictional city in *Empire of Glass* is based on it. It was the city itself that was the treasure in the book, but what if there's more there?"

"I hope you're wrong."

"I know. Because if I'm right, this just got a lot more complicated."

I grumpily accepted a glass of wine from the flight attendant as Lane put his headphones back on.

I eyed the wine before taking a sip. In Rick's novel, Gabriela was drugged by her nemesis. While delirious, she had a vision that princess Soma had sapphire blue eyes made of the gemstones, and her father, the *naga* king, had vibrant red eyes made of ruby gems, showing their true selves as semi-divine *nagas*.

Empire of Glass left it ambiguous as to whether Gabriela had really had a vision, or if it was a drug-induced dream. I thought it was pretty clear it had been the poison. It was her own subconscious that had put together the facts she needed to find the location of the lost city. I finished the wine and got back to sleep, but this time I didn't dream.

I woke up in the airplane seat with my head on Lane's shoulder, as an announcement told us we were getting ready to land in Hong Kong, where we had our layover.

I stretched my shoulders and ankles. "Why didn't you wake me?"

"You needed sleep. I saved you food."

He knew I would have murdered him if he hadn't. I accepted the foil-wrapped sandwich. "I needed to read—"

"I couldn't sleep, so I read for a few hours before getting a couple of hours rest myself. I have a feeling we're going to need our energy for what we'll find there."

"Why?" My grogginess dissipated as I looked at his worried face. "What did you find?"

"It's what I didn't find. We still don't know what we're getting ourselves into. I made that mistake seven years ago."

"Before you had me, remember?" My lips cracked from the dry plane air as I smiled.

"I won't blame you if you want to turn back. Are you sure you want to get on the next flight?"

CHAPTER 38

We arrived in Siem Reap shortly after eight o'clock in the morning.

The heat here was similar to Goa, but less oppressive. At least at this time of year. December was high season for tourism in Cambodia, with no monsoon rains and the most temperate climate of the year. It was barely seventy-five degrees as we walked from the plane to the airport terminal.

I checked my email while we were waiting to go through customs, and found an email from Dr. Sophea Kim, the Angkor National Museum curator I'd contacted. She was sorry to say she wasn't available after all that day, but her colleague Tina Chap could meet me. The message said Tina's cousin Leap was a tuk-tuk driver who gave tours, and she'd given him our flight information so he could meet us at the airport. I wasn't sure how we'd find him, but it turned out to be easier than I thought—and also far worse.

Lane swore. I followed his gaze as he pointed toward a skinny teenager holding a sign that read JAYA JONES.

"So much for anonymity," I murmured.

"Mr. Leap?" I said as we reached the young man holding the sign that broadcast our arrival.

Mr. Leap's face came to life as he smiled, and I realized he was older than I'd first assumed. He wasn't a teenager, but was closer to my age. "Please, *Oum* Leap."

"Uncle," I said, smiling as I remembered the term of respect.

He led us to his tuk-tuk. The tuk-tuk is an open-air form of transportation that's a cross between a car and motorcycle. The

Cambodian style tuk-tuk is a motorcycle with a built-in seating area behind it, with wide cushioned seats and a roof, but no outer doors or seatbelts. As we piled into the seats with our limited luggage, our guide noticed me looking at his dual shirt collars. He grinned and explained he didn't own a jacket, so since it hadn't yet reached eighty degrees that morning—chilly, from his point of view—he'd dressed in a second white dress shirt over the first for warmth.

We rode to the hotel passing through the main drag of hotels. Christmas decorations lined the street, from lights strung to form the shape of Christmas trees to reindeer made of wire. I'd never been there around Christmas, and even though Buddhism coexisted peacefully with all religions, I was surprised. When we came to a stop in traffic, I asked about it. Mr. Leap told us he was hoping to buy a Christmas gift for his fiancé. He hadn't figured out what to get her yet.

We talked with Mr. Leap while idling in traffic, and I was reminded how the best of humanity could be seen here. In spite of civil war, foreign invasion, mass murder, and family separation, the people of Cambodia I'd met were some of the kindest and most generous I'd encountered. It would be a simplification to say they were resilient and didn't bear the scars of the past that was still fresh in their minds. But smiles greeted me everywhere, even when I opened my mouth and was obviously American. Plus, I loved how spicy Cambodian food was, even though everyone I'd mentioned this to in Cambodia had always pointed out it was their neighbors who liked really spicy food.

Dr. Chap was available to meet us that afternoon, so we had time to go to our hotel first. Mr. Leap dropped us off at the hotel we'd booked, and it took me some time to convince him to accept our money. It wasn't that it wasn't the right currency—American dollars were used here, and we'd taken out extra ten-dollar and one-dollar bills in Paris—but that he was doing a favor for his cousin Tina. He said we could pay him if we used his services later during our stay. When Lane spoke a few words of Khmer, he finally accepted.

"If I've just stepped into a Gabriela Glass novel," I said to Lane as he lifted our bags from the tuk-tuk, "I'm going to scream. Don't tell me you speak yet another language. Really?"

His arms were full, but he tilted his head toward a wrinkled guidebook sticking out of the side of his travel bag. "While you were sleeping on the flight, I learned some helpful phrases."

Presumably using those phrases, Lane attempted to ask Mr. Leap to pick us up after lunch to meet Tina at the museum. Watching the baffled expression on our poor guide's face, I stifled a laugh as I realized Lane had completely failed at getting across his question. Lane got the hint. He switched to English. At least the man was human.

I grinned to myself as I walked up the stairs leading to an indoor registration lobby. My gaze fell to a sweeping inner courtyard that reminded me of a French chateau. The French had left their mark in Cambodia. Flanking two Christmas trees decorated in gold ornaments were Buddhist statues.

When I'd almost reached the top of the stairs, I ran back down again. Mr. Leap's helmet was back on his head, and he was sitting on the seat of the motorbike in front of the tuk-tuk, waiting for an opening in traffic.

"Can you wait a few minutes for us to check in? We have time to see a temple before lunch."

Lane accepted the change of plans without protest as well. The resigned smile on his tired face, as he stood at the top of the stairs holding my luggage, told me he knew and accepted me for who I was.

Ten minutes later, we were sitting in the back of Mr. Leap's tuk-tuk on the road to the Angkor archaeological park. The road quickly turned bumpy, and the temperature was heating up as it approached midday, but I hardly noticed either as we sped out of the city on the narrow roads cut through forest to bring travelers to the ancient temples.

The most popular temple in the Angkor complex is Angkor Wat, the temple that's come to symbolize the whole area, followed by Ta Prohm, made famous by the film *Tomb Raider* because of the iconic trees growing through its ancient carvings. Angkor Wat, which translates to "city temple," is often thought of as the single temple photographed with its majestic sandstone towers reflected in the lake in front of it. But in reality, it's an area of seventy-seven square miles—a massive complex, especially in comparison to areas like San Francisco, which is only seven square miles. Suryavarman II built Angkor Wat early in the twelfth century, shortly before Jayavarman VII built the Bayon and many other temples. The suffix "varman" means protector, so it was added to the names of the Khmer kings.

We drove past a low wall with tree roots poking through the stone. Modern preservationists didn't remove the spung trees that had grown up pushing their way through the seams of the temple's stones, because the roots now held together the temple foundations. It was the strangler fig trees that posed a danger to the temples. The invasive strangler fig trees were deceptive in their beauty, wrapping their branches and roots around the spung trees, but strangling the host trees and eventually killing them.

I closed my eyes as I thought of the strangling seven years ago that had brought us here.

"I'll be okay," Lane whispered in my ear as Mr. Leap pulled off the road.

We had to buy passes before we could enter the archaeological park, so that was our first stop.

"Sorry you miss the best time for Angkor Wat," Mr. Leap said.

Angkor Wat was most popular at sunrise, when the rising sun cast dramatic shadows over the temple's three largest spires, and light and shadow worked an alchemical magic in the water's reflection. But tourists who went for the view would miss the most meaningful parts of the temple—not the shadows, but the splendor of the temple itself.

"That's okay. I want to see the Bayon today." It was my favorite temple, and it had the added advantage that it didn't have anything to do with the Serpent King. Before we could meet Tina Chap and get more information, this was a place that could inspire us before we faced whatever was waiting for us in Cambodia.

The Bayon was perhaps the most peaceful temple I'd ever visited. Not for the lack of tourists, since it got crowded as soon as tour buses began to arrive, but because of the dozens of towering stone faces looking serenely down at visitors. From a distance, the faces blend into the stone architecture and look like stone flowers or filigrees, but as you step closer to the temple, the mysterious half-smiles on the humongous stone faces catch you off guard. Long before I'd read Rick Coronado's description of Gabriela Glass's visit to the temple, I'd been drawn to Jayavarman VII's enigmatic creation.

Mr. Leap parked his tuk-tuk across from the temple. As I remembered, at first glance the temple façade looked like ornamental towers. But look more closely, and the stone reveals itself to be gigantic smiling faces perched high above the tiny people walking through the sacred city. The Bayon's original name, before the French changed it, was Jayagiri—Victory Mountain.

"You want see the temple on your own," he asked, "or with guide?"

Most of the younger generation I'd met in Cambodia would tell me their English wasn't good, but as soon as I spoke with them for a few minutes I'd learn they were nearly as fluent as I was. Sure, there were a few stylistic or grammatical mistakes, but there was no problem communicating. Which was a good thing, since I'd only spoken a few dozen words of Khmer a decade ago, and realized that I'd forgotten nearly all of them.

"If you'll be our guide, then yes," I said, walking toward the temple entrance. "Come with us."

Mr. Leap laughed. "If I'm your guide, we start here, not inside." He pointed at a wooden lever and hunk of stone next to the parking lot. "This shows how those temple stones were made. The levers lifted the stones onto sand and rubbed the stones together to make smooth and fit together."

"The stones were brought from far-off quarries on river boats, right?" I said. "Then sanded to fit together." The intricate carvings were made on site, once the blocks of stone had been assembled. It was one of the great feats of the Angkorian Empire, how seamlessly the sandstone rocks fit together to form complex temple structures made only of stone.

Mr. Leap grinned. "You know almost as much about history as me. I call you Indiana Jones, not Jaya Jones. OK?"

"Actually, I—"

"She'd love that," Lane said.

"Don't feel left out, Mr. Peters," he said to Lane. "Peter Pan, OK? You have young soul, I can tell."

"That's perfect," I said, and ascended the steps leading to the temple. "Are you coming, Peter Pan?"

Miles of bas-relief carvings on high walls outside the temple depicted all aspects of Khmer life. The panels told the stories of kings and wars, but also the daily lives of regular people, such as the women shopping for fish in the market and the men who labored building the temples.

The kings who'd commissioned temples followed different Hindu or Buddhist sects over the centuries, so here in this land the stories, deities, and their representations fit together like a stained-glass window: beautiful, and with distinct pieces that came together to form a picture that was greater than the sum of its parts. Rulers from the Angkor Empire were primarily Hindu, with the exception of Jayavarman VII. Now, the meticulously carved sandstone temples of Angkor Wat and beyond were both Hindu and Buddhist.

Aside from what was depicted in the bas-reliefs, much of Cambodia's recorded history had been written either by foreigners or written centuries later by scholars who recorded older oral histories. How much of the true knowledge of the past had been lost?

I was in my element here in the midst of history. I ran my fingertips across the warm, smooth stone. So much of Cambodia's history was a mystery still to be pieced together. Much of the earliest Angkorian records were from Zhou Daguan, the Chinese envoy to the Mongol empire who'd visited Angkor in the late thirteenth century. Cambodians themselves knew much of their history through oral tradition—and the stones. The stone carvings of the temples told stories more intricate than history books. If you knew how to read them.

If only I knew how to read Rick's manuscript. Were the pages Rick had sent me hiding more than I realized?

CHAPTER 39

Fueled by a spicy Khmer noodle soup lunch, I was ready for the challenges of the day when Mr. Leap dropped us off at the Angkor National Museum to see the curator. The new museum housed in the terracotta-colored building wasn't as famous as the National Museum in Phnom Penh, but it was brimming with history. We were directed to a cozy office strewn with papers. A poster-size black-and-white photograph of a temple I didn't recognize adorned the largest wall.

A woman with gray hair and a warm smile looked up from the desk. "Dr. Jones? Mr. Peters?"

"Please, call me Jaya."

"And I'm Lane."

"Tina. Sorry that Sophea had to tend to an emergency today. I hope I can be of assistance." She spoke with an American accent, which was quickly explained as she showed us around the museum.

"I was born here," she said, "but when I was young my family fled as refugees." She and her siblings and parents had settled in the U.S., but her parents had died several years ago and she'd gotten divorced, so she moved to Siem Reap as a curator at the museum after getting burned out working at The Met in New York City.

"I prefer everything about Siem Reap except for two things," she said. "The lack of funding for the museum, and the dearth of Mexican restaurants." She made do with exquisite French, Indian, and Cambodian food, and if it was a choice between monsoons and snowstorms, she chose the monsoons. Even the mosquito spray didn't bother her; she found the air in the New York subway system she rode every day far more noxious than the weekly toxic cloud that swept through the city and surrounding areas.

She stopped in a room filled with *nagas*. As we looked around I saw that they shared some similarities with the Durant sculpture, but when I walked around the backs of the glass enclosures, none had markings on their flat backs, and we couldn't see their base.

"So many temples have been looted." Tina shook her head sadly. "We're doing our best to keep the history safe here."

Lane followed Tina's gaze to a statue that showed stone feet but was missing the rest of its body. "You're thinking of the looting during the seventies, when the Khmer Rouge was in power."

She nodded. "The fragments that remain on this pedestal always remind me of a similar tenth-century sculpture that we lost a few years ago. Glaring red flags should have gone off when an auction house put the top of that sculpture up for sale a few years ago. Nobody wanted to take responsibility for that blunder."

"Safe for a thousand years," I said, "only to be stolen fifty years ago."

"You'd think I'd stop being surprised by how much people in my field will look the other way when they encounter questionable provenance, if it doesn't serve their desired outcome. And also how frequently it's a rich philanthropist who needs to step in to buy back a piece so that both sides can agree and not feel cheated."

I looked from Tina to Lane. His face was impassive, but I knew how much he wished he could have taken back some of his deeds.

"Is that enough *nagas*?" she asked. "Let me make sure I understand what else you're interested in beyond serpents," she said. "Historical patterns of waterways and...musical compositions recorded on stone? I don't know that I can help with the music. I love Cambodian pop music, but that's not here at the museum."

"Anything you can tell us would be much appreciated," Lane said.

"The Khmer hydraulic engineers were masterful," she said. "They harnessed the power of the monsoons to turn the Tonle Sap River from a tributary of the Mekong into its own powerhouse, even reversing its course. It allowed for rice to be harvested up to four times a year, even though the country is dry for half of that time. Water is a big deal here.

"Angkor is in a central area between the Tonle Sap—the Great Lake—in the south and hills in the north," she said. "Numerous tributaries of the Siem Reap River and Mekong River flow through the country.

"Stone inscriptions provide the primary recorded history," Tina continued, leading us into another room, "so these historical maps might be more fiction than reality. But you're welcome to take a look if it helps. I need to go to a meeting now—everywhere in the world, so many meetings!—but please come find me before you leave. Here's my cell phone number if you need help tracking me down."

We spent the next hour looking at maps, but we didn't see anything that looked like the markings on the Serpent King statue.

"We're still missing something," I said.

"Several million dollars worth of LIDAR equipment that could survey this large amount of land," Lane said.

"Over the course of years," I said. New technology that could survey the land from above through overgrowth and even through earth and stone was allowing archaeology to advance. But even if we'd had access to such equipment, we didn't have any way to narrow down the area, so it would have been in vain regardless. "What does Marc know that we don't?"

Tina came back to check on us once she was done with her meeting.

"Find anything helpful?"

"I don't think so," I said. "Has anyone else been at the museum recently asking similar questions?"

"I can check."

She disappeared from the room, and came back a few minutes

later, her eyes wide with disbelief.

"I didn't think the answer would be yes," she said, "but an American woman came this morning. Blonde. Devi didn't have more of a description."

"A blonde American woman?" Lane repeated, looking sharply at me.

Had Becca fooled me about her true end game? Was she in reality working with her father and in search of the treasure, not seeking revenge for a murder she knew had never taken place?

CHAPTER 40

I wasn't able to find a good photo of Becca online since her social media accounts were private, but a couple of her friends had posted photos of her. It was impossible to stay completely anonymous in this day and age.

Tina showed the photo to staff member Devi who'd helped our mystery woman. "She said maybe. That's the best she could do. What I'm more interested in is the fact that she asked about the same thing as you two. Rivers, in particular."

I caught Lane's eye.

Tina crossed her arms. "Clearly there's more going on here than historical research. Why are you and a mystery woman asking about this?"

"You're in the museum world," Lane said. "You know how competitive institutions can be."

"Usually those people know what it is they're being competitive about."

I hesitated. Lane didn't react either.

"I looked you up," Tina continued. "I don't think you're trying to loot anything. You save pieces of history in unconventional ways. Which is often necessary. I get that. But I know you're not telling me why you're really here. If you want my help, you need to tell me what's going on."

Lane shrugged almost imperceptibly. His eyes were on mine. He was leaving it up to me.

"We think someone," I said slowly, "or multiple people, believe there's a hidden work of art that tells the story of the origin of the Khmer Kingdom."

"Looters?"

"Maybe," I said. "That's the problem. There's something going on we don't understand." I stopped short of mentioning a murder and that I needed to clear the name of the man I loved.

"Rulers, empires, and battles are well documented already. If you hadn't noticed, we're surrounded by stones that tell our story. What makes this special?"

"I believe it's a jewel-encrusted statue that shows the legend of the founding of Cambodia."

Tina's eyes grew wide. "Kaundinya, Soma, and the *naga* king?"

"The prince and princess," I said.

"And the *naga* king guardian."

I shook my head. "We think the *naga* king is a separate statue that holds this smaller one. It's somewhere else."

"The sun and the moon," Tina said wistfully, "joining two kingdoms and illustrating how our water systems can be controlled for good." She paused to laugh. "I always hated the most popular version of that story. Why is it a good thing if the Indian prince shot an arrow at the serpent king's daughter, princess Soma, to convince her to marry him?"

"Exactly!"

Lane cleared his throat. "There's also the version where the prince proves himself worthy, and the arrow is just a metaphor to illustrate his bravery."

Tina looked between the two of us, a mischievous gleam in her eye. "What can I say? I'm old and jaded. But not too old to help you figure out what your mystery woman and her accomplice are up to. When the museum closes shortly, I'd like to show you something."

While we waited we did one more round of the museum, and I was again struck by how important the *naga* protector was here in Cambodia. There was even a video about the cobra's symbolism. Where was the Durant's missing stone serpent and the prince and princess he was protecting?

*   *   *

Tina took us on a walk through the night market, where we ate fried tarantula (which tasted like crunchy chicken), watched happy children playing hide and seek in the stalls of merchants selling souvenirs, and spotted a silver bracelet that I thought Mr. Leap's fiancé would like based on what he'd told me of her. I snapped a photo of it so I'd remember to show him, and that's when I caught sight of what would become my own purchase. A dark brown leather shadow puppet of the monkey king Hanuman in a scene from the Reamker, Cambodia's version of India's epic Ramayana, a grand allegory about good and evil. The artisan seller was a man with only one arm. Lane thanked him in Khmer, or I should say he attempted to. The man's face widened in horror. Tina laughed and corrected Lane's Khmer, then thanked the man properly.

"Finally," I said, "a language you can't immediately speak perfectly."

"What did I say?" Lane asked Tina.

"You don't want to know." She smiled and gave a few coins to a child in a wheelchair who was playing Cambodian pop music on an ancient CD player. "The Khmer Rouge was opposed to anyone educated or religious, and even entertainers to a large extent. Many of my favorite singers, who were blending traditional music with Western influence in the 1960s, wanted to stay in Phnom Penh. They thought they'd be safe. They were wrong." She shook her head and wiped a tear off her cheek. "Sorry. It's been a long time. But..."

"I understand." I was speaking to Tina and Lane had fallen behind. When I turned, I caught a glimpse of what Lane was up to. He'd handed several dollars to the small girl.

"Hungry for a proper dinner?" Tina asked.

"Only if we can go somewhere with spicy food," Lane said, reaching our side. "Jaya refuses to eat anywhere that doesn't meet that requirement."

"We'll stay clear of the tourist spots. Cambodians don't consider our food spicy compared to Thailand and Laos, but I think

I know just the spot."

She brought us to a hole-in-the-wall restaurant. Its name was written in the Khmer script, so I didn't know what it was called, but it smelled amazing. The sun had set hours ago, and we sat outside under two baby palm trees. We hadn't brought anti-malaria pills with us, but that wasn't a problem in the tourist center of Cambodia. There wasn't a mosquito in sight, since the region was sprayed with a mosquito-killing fog once a week.

We ordered drinks (no ice) and an appetizer of green mango salad to start. The scents of coconut milk and lemongrass filled the air as a waiter appeared with our main course: fish amok, a coconut milk fish curry cooked inside single serving bowls made of banana leaves, steamed rice that had been grown in the water as it had been in the region for a thousand years, and several vegetable side dishes with edible water lilies and bright red chilies on top.

"I hope you meant what you said about spicy food," Tina said. "I requested extra bird chilies."

My lips and tongue tingled as I took a bite. Memories of eating similar flavors the last time I'd been in this region of the world washed over me, and for a moment I was transported back to a time when my only worries were avoiding stomach bugs when evaluating the freshness of the food sold by street vendors and figuring out what I wanted to do with my life.

"Jaya's in another world," I heard Tina say to Lane.

"Hmm?" I asked through a mouthful.

"I was telling Tina about our motorcycle ride along the west coast of India," Lane said. "You remember the place you insisted on stopping to eat?"

"Of course. I was going to pass out from hunger. Which is definitely not a danger here."

After we'd happily eaten most of the meal, and Tina's expression shifted, I felt like we'd passed a test.

Tina rested her elbows on the table. After a moment's hesitation, she leaned closer. "I know where the mystery woman is going."

I gaped at her. "How? And you know who she is? Is that what you were doing for that last hour?"

Lane put a protective hand on my arm. He'd taken the seat at the table that had the best view of the entrance and exit, as was his habit, but until that moment, I hadn't thought he'd done it as more than an unconscious habit. He couldn't possibly think Tina was involved, could he?

The lines around her dark brown eyes crinkled as she gave a wary smile. "You have to understand, I've dealt with all sorts of people over my long career, both in the States and Cambodia. When Americans start sniffing around a Cambodian treasure, I'm going to be wary. So yes, I held back information. I needed to do more research into you both. And since I'm old enough to know what's true on paper isn't always true in real life, I needed to spend some time with you."

"And now that you have?" I asked.

Tina nodded. "The American woman who Devi couldn't positively identify. The woman was extremely interested in the temple of Banteay Chhmar. You know of it?"

"The last great temple built during the Angkorian Empire."

CHAPTER 41

"We lost too much time," I said to Lane as we weaved through the narrow lanes of the night market on foot. Tina had gone home, still looking unsure if she'd made the right decision confiding in us. "It's too far away to go by tuk-tuk, but we can rent a car—"

"It's too late tonight."

I stopped next to a stall selling brightly colored shawls and patterned dresses. Lane nearly crashed into me. "If she'd told us this afternoon—"

"But she didn't. Which is good, because now we have time to figure out our next steps."

"There aren't any good ones," I snarled. "Our mystery woman—Becca or whoever it is—has the map and it told her to go to Banteay Chhmar. She's a whole day ahead of us. She could already have found the second treasure and have left the country."

"I doubt it." An 'Angkor Night Market' sign shone in neon colored lights above us, casting blue and yellow fluorescent light onto Lane's face. "It's either difficult to find, or looters are a century ahead of us and beat us all to it. There might be nothing left to find."

"I know," I said, lowering my voice. "We might all be on a fool's errand to try to find the treasure. Haven't you realized why I have to see this through? The person who's after the treasure is the person who can give us the answers to clear you."

*　*　*

The next morning, Mr. Leap was waiting for us with his tuk-tuk in front of the hotel.

"I'm sorry," I said. "I should have told you we have different plans out of town today. We're renting a car."

He grinned. "A car big enough for your guide?"

"This could be dangerous," I said as Lane tried unsuccessfully to dissuade him. "There's, um, a bad person who might try to hurt me."

"Or multiple people who might try to harm all of us," Lane added.

Mr. Leap was the same age as many of my students, but the look he gave us told me he'd seen more than most if not all of them. "I'm not afraid. Many of my family have been killed."

"That doesn't mean you have to choose to walk into danger if you can help it."

"Indiana Jones and Peter Pan need guide, yes?"

Tuk-tuks, motorcycles, bicycles, and cars kicked up dust in the road around us as we left Siem Reap. I insisted on driving. Sébastien hadn't let me drive his Porsche in Paris, but a Mercedes on the open road in Cambodia came close.

The temple complex of Banteay Chhmar was over a hundred miles away in a remote location near the Thai border. So many things worried me about this location our mystery woman was interested in, but I couldn't let that stop me.

Only once we'd driven an hour did Mr. Leap tell us we'd need to find a local guide in Banteay Chhmar as well.

"Why didn't you tell us that in Siem Reap?" I asked.

"I wanted to go." He grinned. "I've never been to Banteay Chhmar. And I can help."

Mr. Leap was sitting in the front seat to help me read the signs along the road, and Lane was in back.

"This is where the snake bite me." Mr. Leap showed Lane a scar on his forearm.

I took my eyes off the road for a moment to glance nervously at him in the passenger seat. "How did you get a snake bite?" I pressed the brake as I drove around a pot hole. Even in my sturdy boots, I was wildly unprepared for snakes.

"One of my cousins thought he could tame it. He was mistaken."

Lane covered his mouth, but one glance in the rearview mirror told me he was trying not to laugh.

I saw something else in the rearview mirror. "Does that car look like it's following us? Stop that! Don't turn around all at once!"

Mr. Leap shrugged.

"Try drive slowly," Mr. Leap suggested. "When the car passes, no problem."

"I don't think Jaya is physically capable of driving slowly."

"I'm totally capable of it. I just don't think it's especially safe to do so on the highway here. Besides, it's Becca we're following, not the opposite."

"Unless there are many people out to get you," Mr. Leap said.

I scowled at him. "I'm going to pull off the side of the road to get a cold drink."

I pulled the Mercedes into the shade of some jackfruit trees at the side of the road, letting the car pass. The suspicious car kept going, so we relaxed a little. We shouldn't have, but at the time it seemed like the sensible decision. With cold sodas in hand, we got back on the road for the rest of the drive to the temple.

When we arrived at Banteay Chhmar, there were no other cars in the dirt lot next to the temple's main entrance gates. I parked the car and turned off the engine. The heat hit me as soon as I cracked the door open. The sound of birds chirping filled the air, but I didn't hear any voices.

"Wait here under the trees," Mr. Leap said.

I was happy to do so, since the temperature had gone up at least twenty degrees since sunrise. I enjoyed the shade as Mr. Leap walked down the road to find us a local guide at the nearby NGO that trained locals to be guides.

"Come on," I said as soon as he was out of sight.

"I was wondering if that's what you had in mind," Lane said.

"You even had to wonder? Of course I'm not endangering the lives of two innocent guides. We'll ask for their help after we make sure nobody else is here."

As soon as we stepped through the stone entrance gates into the sprawling temple remains, I saw how difficult that would be to determine. Rocks taller than me were strewn around the grounds. Thick stone doorways with ornate carvings stood at awkward angles, seeming to defy gravity. Gnarled tree roots strangled stones and stretched to the sky.

Most western tourists didn't go to this Angkorian-era temple not only because it was a long drive from Siem Reap, but also because it was still being excavated and hadn't yet been prepared with walkways and stairs that made exploring easy. The only way to walk through the ruins was to leave ourselves exposed, jumping from one fallen rock to the next.

"I don't like this," Lane whispered as we stepped through a crooked doorway that led from one outdoor room to another.

I barely heard him as my gaze locked onto the oversize stone eyes in front of me. This was one of the few sites outside of Angkor that had the enigmatic faces carved out of multiple pieces of sandstone on high towers.

The temple complex was built under Jayavarman VII, so that wasn't surprising. Well-preserved bas-reliefs showing the history of the Khmers covered massive stone walls that surrounded the temple, but what made it most interesting historically was that after Jayavarman VII's ambitious reign, the empire began to collapse. Scholars have never agreed on why this happened, and theories ranged from climactic changes combined with poor oversight of irrigation systems, to different religions weakening power structures and allowing foreign invaders to gain ground.

I was pulled back to the present when a movement caught my

eye. We weren't alone. A person stood under the giant enigmatic face. It wasn't Becca Courtland. Nor was it her father, Marc Durant.

Standing before us, under the sprawling spung trees and amidst the crumbled stones, was another supposedly dead man: Rick Coronado.

CHAPTER 42

"But you're dead!" I said.

Rick Coronado, in all his rugged glory from the fedora that shielded his face from the harsh sun down to well-worn hiking boots, stood on a fallen slab of stone next to a bas-relief of dancing apsaras.

"I know I skipped out on you," a very alive Rick Coronado said, "but that's harsh."

"They fished your body out of the San Francisco Bay."

"Clearly the rumors of my death have been exaggerated." He gave a boyish grin. "I didn't even know there were rumors, but I suppose it's flattering. But listen, both of you—Lane Peters? I'd say it was nice to meet you, but you're in over your heads here. You should go home."

"You..." I stepped forward, but Lane saw the look in my eye and held me back. "You're the one who left that note for me in my office. Trying to scare me off."

Rick scratched the back of his neck. "I really am sorry for everything."

"You're the one who asked for her help," Lane pointed out in what I felt was an overly generous tone.

"Not like this. You're far from civilization. This isn't like your 'roughing it' on a Scottish dig or French amusement park. There's no mosquito repellant sprayed for the tourists here, so I hope you're both slathered in Deet."

This wasn't how I imagined meeting my literary hero. And how dare he leave out our motorcycle ride down the western coast of India? Though to be fair, I didn't tell the press the full story there.

Unlike the photos of Rick when he'd been found after his missing six weeks, scrawny, sunburned, and covered in bug bites, now he was fit and dressed in appropriate light clothing for the climate.

"Your jacket..." I said. Rick wasn't wearing his signature jacket here. "Oh no. Where's Vincent?"

"My brother? He's not into this kind of exploration."

"Have you talked with him since you got here?"

Rick's easy smile faded. "Why are you talking about my brother? I don't need him—"

"Did you travel with him to San Francisco? Did you give him your jacket to take back home since you wouldn't need it here?"

He looked away and pretended to adjust the brim of his hat. "Fine. Yeah, he came with me. I hadn't flown in such a long time. I won't exactly say it had become a phobia." He cleared his throat. "So yeah, Vince came with me so I wouldn't freak out on the flight, then went home."

"I don't think he did," I said softly.

With weak cell phone reception, the article I pulled up about the dead man in the Bay didn't load, so I couldn't show him the images of the jacket that had been posted. And because the body hadn't yet been identified, probably because the police were trying to find Rick at his home in New York, I wasn't sure how to get Rick to believe me.

"You're smart, Jaya. That's why I wanted to get your help in the first place. But I can see you're manipulating me just like I did you."

"I've already spoken with Becca," I seethed. "I know her connection to you. What I need to know now is why you're back here in Cambodia."

"You came all the way here. You're all in, I'll give you that."

"You," I said, trying not to yell, "are the one who asked for my help in the first place."

"It's complicated."

"Now that we're all here together," Lane began diplomatically, "why don't we pool resources and find out the truth."

"No offense," Rick said, "but I don't make deals with killers."

"He didn't kill Marc Durant," I said. Though now that we knew it was Rick, not Marc, threatening me, and he was here in Cambodia...I swore. "Where's your partner?"

"Becca?"

"Yes."

"San Francisco—no, I expect she'd be in France by now for Christmas with her grandparents."

"I know she's here in Cambodia. I meant, where is she *right now*? Is she somewhere on the temple grounds?" I glanced around the tumbled stones that excavators were slowly working to put back together. Several towers with enigmatic faces like those in the Bayon rose above this temple complex. They would be a great place for someone to hide.

"No way," Rick scoffed. "She's not here."

"We might not have much time."

Rick looked between us, and whatever he saw on our faces convinced him it was time to stop fooling around.

"All right." He held his hands up. "You win. Let's pool our ideas. Even though I contributed more."

I narrowed my eyes at Rick, annoyed with myself for once idolizing this man.

"I was working on *Empire of Glass*," he said. "I did so much historical research for the novel that I knew exactly what I was looking at when I heard about the Durant family's tragedy. I was the only one who saw the connection. You know my cobra symbolism in the Gabriela Glass novels."

Of course I knew. His intrepid heroine killed one with her bare hands in the first novel. I remembered the scene vividly. "It's not a unique discovery to realize the *naga* originated in India but took on a life of its own in Cambodia."

"But nobody else noticed it here. I study the significance of snakes in the different cultures I write about, so I'm the only one who saw what the Durants really had. The sculpture in the Durant family's collection had never been shown publicly or examined by art historians in person, since they didn't wish to sell it, so there was no issue with provenance. Nobody in the family would tell me all the details, but someone had stolen the sculpture from that house. Marc's father didn't want it reported, and I thought I knew why. Aristide Durant had looted the statue when he was in Cambodia during the time of the French Protectorate. He'd realized there was an even greater hoard to be had, so he wrote to his son. But he drew a map instead of writing the location in case the wrong person read it."

"The letter Becca had," I murmured.

"That kid is something, isn't she?"

I glared at him. "She's certainly something."

"Everyone missed the clues for years, but when she filled in the blanks for me, she must have told someone else about the treasure as well, because they're after it too." He eyed Lane suspiciously. "Probably the man who killed her father."

"We don't know who killed Marc," I said before the men could come to blows. "We don't even know for certain he's dead. I'm sure I'm right that Marc faked his own death at the mansion."

"Marc Durant is dead, Professor Jones."

"He put on an act for his friend, strangling himself, so that he could disappear when everyone thought he was dead."

"You should be a writer," Rick said, "because that's a great solution. It would be perfect if it wasn't for the fact that the statue really did disappear from that house. There's got to be a killer who smuggled it out." He again glanced suspiciously at Lane.

"Let's back up," I said. "Why do you think the prince and princess statue is here?"

"It turned out the kid was holding out on me so I'd keep writing. The family knew the location all along. Becca knew her great-great grandfather had found the Serpent King statues here at Banteay Chhmar. Only they didn't realize the significance. I told her what I knew, but the kid didn't care. How could she not care? It's a *real-life* treasure that shows the true history from which the legend of Cambodia sprang. It's where the *naga* king drank the water and gave it to his daughter and her Indian prince, and that's where I'll find the gemstone statue."

Which of course Aristide Durant had wanted to claim for himself. No wonder the family was cursed.

Rick said he thought he had enough information to go to Cambodia seven years ago. He was obsessed and wanted this to be his own real-world discovery. Something that mattered. People didn't take him seriously because of his Gabriela Glass plots. *Empire of Glass* was the closest he'd come to critical acclaim, because the treasure was knowledge. But he wanted more. His editor Abby had convinced him not to kill off Gabriela and write a literary novel, but he could do something else. He'd seen something others had missed. Everyone except for himself and Marc's killer. Only they understood that on the back of the stone was the map that gave them directions for finding the treasure, or, more precisely, for where to look inside the temple where it was concealed. He was only missing the detail that told him *which* temple, and Becca had finally told him in San Francisco.

"Wait," I said. "How did you learn about the tragedy of Marc Durant in the first place, seven years ago? I mean, I know Becca told you details this year. But none of the missing sculpture details were reported publicly."

He blinked at me. "You said you knew."

"No. I said I knew how you got your facts for your manuscript this year."

"Then isn't it obvious? You're not living up to your reputation, Professor Jones."

"Why don't you enlighten us," Lane said. His voice was calm on the surface, but I could tell he was about to strangle Rick, dead brother or not.

"From Abby, of course."

Sweat dripped into my eyes, but I couldn't move. "Your editor?

How on earth would she know?"

"Because she's Becca's mom."

I stared at him. "No, Becca's mom is named Gail." I thought back to the photograph. *Marc, Gail, and Rebecca.* I groaned. The name Abigail can be abbreviated to Abby or Gail. "Abby who I've been talking to? Abby Wu?"

"Yeah, her maiden name is Abby Courtland. She married Marc young, they had Becca and split soon after, and she married Alston Wu. She and I would have been great together, if only we hadn't been so young when we met. They didn't last long, but she kept his name because that's when her star was taking off as an editor."

I swore. Publishers didn't usually include photos of their editors on their websites, so I'd foolishly assumed a woman named Abby Wu would be of Chinese descent, not a blonde woman.

"It never occurred to you that *she* could be the one who killed Marc?"

"No way. Abby would never do that."

I looked at the man I'd once believed to be brilliant. He'd created a character I would always love, but Rick Coronado had many weaknesses. When it came to love, he was as foolish as any of us.

"You're still in love with her," I said.

He laughed ruefully. "I thought if I could prove myself worthy, I could win her affections. That's why I went after the treasure seven years ago. It seemed like it would be so easy! It was like a plot from one of my novels. Only in fiction, malaria is no big deal and it's easy to kill a snake. And the most important distinction is that I was wrong. There was no bad guy on my heels. No adventure. Only tedium, sickness, and the loneliness of working alone. And by choosing not to get help, I got lost and contracted malaria. And I never found the treasure. It broke me. I came home humiliated. I couldn't write another word.

"I gave up—until earlier this year. That's when Becca came to me. She had a crazy story. Said she'd figured out who'd killed her father. Becca wanted the world to believe the truth about her father's death. I wanted details to find the treasure, and that was something Abby never wanted to talk about. I didn't think I'd be hurting you, Jaya. You must believe that. Becca didn't tell me it was your boyfriend she suspected. She proposed it as a way to help us *both*—said she was your student and knew how great you were. That you could both solve the murder and lead me and Gabriela to the treasure.

"But the more she told me, the more I suspected there was something else going on. She insisted that Tristan shouldn't be sympathetic—which totally misunderstands the narrative craft. And after you figured out the Cambodia connection, Becca was angry, saying I was focusing too much on the treasure. She let it slip that Tristan was Lane.

"I had to see her. I was complicit in creating a monster, and it had to stop. I hadn't been on a plane since they flew me back from Thailand for my recovery, so Vincent came with me. Becca convinced me not to tell you anything else yet. It was partly mercenary, I admit; she said she wouldn't tell me more unless I upheld the agreement. Then I left, and Vincent went..." He pulled out his cell phone, but couldn't get a signal. His face went pale. He was finally starting to realize that I wasn't lying to him and accept my theory about the dead man in San Francisco. "You don't really think he's..."

"I'm sorry."

It wasn't me who spoke, though I echoed the sentiment. Rick had manipulated me, and his brother was decidedly a jerk, but that didn't mean Vincent deserved to die or that Rick deserved to be left alone, his last connection to the world taken from him.

"Abby?" Rick croaked. "What on earth are you doing here?"

Abby stepped out from behind a strangler fig tree We were all too in shock to move quickly enough as she wrapped one arm around Rick's neck. She pressed a knife to his side.

"For God's sake, Abby—" Rick began. He tried to pull away, but she tightened her stranglehold and pressed the knife further into his side. He cried out as a small trickle of blood ran down his shirt.

"It's only a matter of time before they identify Vincent and figure out what happened," Abby said. "I need to disappear. I need to find the treasure. Where is it, Rick?"

CHAPTER 43

Rick's chest heaved in disbelief. "You killed Vincent? And you're the one who killed Marc? That's why you shut down when you saw that I was interested in what had happened to him?"

"He wanted to steal our daughter!" Abby shrieked. "I couldn't let him do that. She idolized him. She would have chosen to live with him, even if it was in hiding in some God-forsaken country. He'd already accused me of stealing her because I moved back to the U.S. when we'd gotten divorced. My father was in California. It was good for Becca. Marc was going to fake his death, get rich selling the family heirlooms that he believed were worth a fortune, and become the artist he wanted to be in some ex-pat commune in a third world country. But don't distract me. The treasure. Where is it?" She pressed the knife more firmly against his side.

"I know where it is," I said.

Rick gaped at me. "You do?"

"It's not here. You were wrong about those lines being a map to get here. But I know what they are."

"I don't think so."

"I can tell you. But first, Abby, you need to let him go."

"That's not happening."

"It appears we have a stalemate," Rick said. "What would Gabriela Glass do?"

"Don't get cute."

Rick shrugged. "I can't help it." I was close enough to see his shoulders quiver. He wasn't as nonchalant as he was acting.

"I see what you're doing. Don't move! None of you. You don't understand."

"Help us understand," Rick said. "If you help me understand, I'll tell you where the treasure is."

"Jaya just said you were wrong and you don't know how to find it." Abby whipped her head back and forth, looking at each of us.

"But I know," I said. "And I'll tell you. After you fill in the blanks and let us out of here safely."

I was balanced precariously on a jagged stone, but I didn't dare try and move. One slip of Abby's knife could be the end of Rick—his second death the real one, just like Marc.

"Where. Is. It." Her eyes blazed at me. The knife pressed more firmly into Rick's side.

"In a minute," I said as calmly as I could. "I don't want the treasure. All I want is to have the truth. Am I right that your husband staged his own strangling?"

Abby nodded. Slowly at first, then vigorously, as if she'd made up her mind. As soon as she began speaking, the words poured out of her. She confirmed I was right that Marc's supposed strangling was an act he put on for the man she thought was his university friend. He'd locked the glass doors so Lane couldn't get in, then made it look like the ghost killed him. He knew that Lane would either flee, in which case he'd make his escape with the sculpture, or call for an ambulance. His partners were nearby waiting to get him and the sculpture out of there.

"But how did you know?" I asked.

"I'd taken Becca to France for the holidays, arriving earlier than planned because I thought it would be a nice surprise for everyone, because I wanted my daughter to know both sides of her family. Even though Marc and I had a terrible breakup and I took her far away, that didn't mean he should be able to steal my daughter away from me."

"Steal her?"

A tear escaped and rolled down her cheek. "I overheard him

talking on the phone with his accomplice. I figured out what he was up to. He was going to disappear. I knew he was going to take her with him. She's always adored him, put him on a pedestal. Even now. All of this is about him!"

"That can't be right," I said. Lane wouldn't have had conversations on the phone about the theft, plus he hadn't known Marc was going to fake his own death. Someone else had to be involved.

"It was an awful plan thought up by a cruel man, but yes, that's what happened."

"You're lying," I said, receiving a sharp glance from Lane. "The thief wasn't in on the plan for Marc to fake his death. If we accept your deal to trade the treasure for our lives and the truth, you need to tell us what really happened."

"I'm not lying," Abby said. "I never said it was the thief he was talking to. The thief was a patsy. I overheard Marc speaking on the phone to his other accomplice."

Other accomplice?

Lane tensed next to me. I could tell he wanted to ask so much more, but didn't want to reveal anything about his past, since Abby seemed unaware that he was the "thief." Instead, he said, "What about the ghost?"

"The ghost? That's a secret that's been passed down to the women of the family for generations. Durant men are notorious, it's a wonder any of us marry them in the first place...but they have a certain charm. And money. Pots of money. Daphne killed her husband Beaumont. Not for herself, mind you. He was essentially murdering poor workers on a daily basis and making life impossible for his family.

"Before she killed her husband, Daphne Durant had already hidden an important piece of paper—a letter Aristide wrote to his son that included the name of the Cambodian temple where he'd found half of an important sculpture. This was back before anyone called the removal of artifacts stealing or looting. Aristide told his son that the ship he meant to take home to France had sunk, so he had to stay in Cambodia longer than expected. There was a thriving French community there, so he lived well there—until he caught a fever and died. His possessions were eventually shipped back to the family.

"Daphne's husband Beaumont had told her in confidence, during one of his moments of marital weakness, that he hoped to visit Cambodia to become an adventurer like his ancestor before him. He wanted to find the treasure in Banteay Chhmar that he thought was rightfully his—a fragile jewel-encrusted piece that had been lost to history—but he was worried about who would look after his workers and the business. Their children weren't yet old enough. Their children—that's what made Daphne snap. It's completely understandable, the need to protect our children. It's natural."

Abby's knuckles were turning white as she clutched the knife. Her hand was sweating.

"He was going to mold their son into a version of himself, and she couldn't stand for that. One night after he'd berated the children and slapped her, she saw him standing at the top of the stairs. She pushed."

Abby paused. Was she remembering how she had pushed her own husband down the stairs in that same house?

"The rest of the people in the house heard the commotion and rushed out," she continued. "Daphne didn't make an attempt to flee. She stood there, in shock. He was dead, and they all remained silent. But Daphne was a good person. The knowledge that she had killed her own husband drove her mad. She'd been a painter and performer before marrying into the family, so she had the skills and dexterity to alter the painting. She wanted her sins to look at her. But it was too much. She could no longer bear it. A year after she killed him, she threw herself down the stairs. That's when the ghost story truly took hold.

"She revealed everything in her journal. That's how I learned the truth. The dusty old book had been lost in that rambling house until I found it. It explained so much about that family, and how I was a victim too. That's how I got the idea of altering the painting to make it look as if the ghost had struck again. I'm not a painter by training, but Marc and I had painted side by side for the first year of our relationship, before everything went wrong. So I knew no one would suspect me. And it worked. For seven years. Until Rick decided to write again."

"What did you do with the snake sculpture?" I asked.

"What? I didn't take it."

"Of course it was you."

"How could I have gotten it out? It was impossible."

"You got it out with the ambulance workers," I said, and watched her face pale. I knew I was right. Why was she denying it?

"Don't you think I'd have sent Becca to private school and moved into something better than my tiny walk-up in New York if I had that Durant family treasure?"

"I know that was Marc's plan," I insisted, the pieces falling into place as I spoke. "That's how he planned to get out with it in the first place. *Two* sets of ambulances arrived. Everyone said that. Nobody paid attention to that fact, because there are multiple ambulance companies in France, so more than one might have showed up to such a high-profile location. But I also read that one of the paramedics was reported to have been afraid of seeing a ghost—now I know that wasn't because he was afraid of the ghost, but because he couldn't believe his accomplice was dead. Marc was supposed to get out of the house with the sculpture on the gurney with the help of his co-conspirator. But you were the one who ended up working with the criminals instead. That's how the sculpture got out without making tracks in the snow—because it *didn't* get out until the paramedics came into the house. You were already there hiding, lying in wait. You only needed to slip out with the gurney."

"You're wrong," Abby said. "Well, *half* wrong. The first two paramedics who showed up were his accomplices—men he'd met in medical school who'd also hated it. But by the time they arrived, the sculpture *had already vanished*. In the commotion, I was able to convince them they were already accomplices to murder, so they let me slip out underneath their gurney—using the harness that they'd planned on using to smuggle out the statue with a fake-dead Marc on top. But now, Marc was really dead, and the straps meant to hold the statue held me as they left the house."

I stared at Abby in disbelief. That meant it truly was impossible. I'd solved the mystery of Marc Durant's ghostly death, but the missing sculpture had indeed vanished.

CHAPTER 44

Abby's hands shook. More blood ran down Rick's side. "I never wanted the statue, or the long-lost treasure it was meant to be guarding. It's only now, when I need to flee—"

"Why, Abby?" Rick whispered.

"Why? Why were *you* writing this story after all this time? When you told me you were writing again, I didn't realize this was the story you were writing—until Jaya told me. I still don't know how you found out the details, since I couldn't very well tell you it was real."

Children watch and learn, I thought to myself. Nobody suspected Becca had seen and realized as much as she had. She knew the documented stories Lane and the ambulance staff had told the police, both of which were partial truths, but she didn't know the full truth.

"Becca," Rick said. "It was Becca who came to me and told me."

"Don't drag my innocent daughter into this."

"Innocent? She's the one who wanted revenge against the person who killed her father. This man. Don't you recognize him?"

Lane tried to remain as still as possible, poised on one of the fallen stones that surrounded us. This was a remote temple with hardly any visitors on this side, away from the excavations. What would Abby do if someone else arrived?

"You're trying to confuse me," Abby said. "Just like you've been doing as you evaded me."

In the near-silence of the remote temple I was keenly aware of the sound I made as I inhaled deeply. "You're the one who was following me to see what I knew."

"I need the prince and princess to have the money to get away. I can't find it on my own. I need—Rick, why did you go in search of the treasure in the first place?" Her bravado was faltering. I didn't know if that was a good or bad thing. "Why? You have so much money. Why did you care so much about living out the fantasy of being in one of your novels?"

"I've been blind, but so have you." Rick spat out the words. "Don't you know the answer to that? I wanted to prove myself worthy to *you*, Abby. I was in love with you. For so many years. But you...You killed your husband and my brother?"

"Vincent said he knew! He was going to blackmail me. Your royalties were drying up after so many years without a new book. He was great at growing your empire, but even he couldn't work miracles. He needed money for his lavish lifestyle."

"He knew nothing." Rick's voice cracked. "You know Vince. You *should have* known. He was all talk. If he saw weakness, he'd take advantage of it. You killed him for nothing."

"No, I..." She loosened her grip, and Rick slipped out of her grasp.

"No!" Abby screamed, raising the knife above her head.

"Stop," I said, holding up my phone, "or your daughter will hear you commit murder. She now knows what you've done. Don't make it any worse."

While Abby was distracted by Rick, I had called Becca. I wanted her to hear the truth. I raised the volume so we could hear Becca.

"Mom!" Becca screamed through the crackling phone. "Don't!"

When Abby realized Becca was really on the line, her face contorted. I thought she was going to crumple onto the stones beneath her feet, but I was wrong. She ran forward toward me, the knife in her outstretched hand.

Lane jumped in front of me. The knife sliced into his chest.

CHAPTER 45

Someone screamed. I'm pretty sure it was me.

While I rushed forward to grab Lane before he fell to the jagged stones beneath his feet, two new figures appeared from behind a stone arch.

Mr. Leap and another man, who was carrying a large fishing net. They dropped the net over Abby.

"Let go!" she cried, as Rick and the two men subdued her.

"Sorry we late," the Banteay Chhmar guide said. "We needed to find a net to hold the bad lady."

"Police will be here soon," Mr. Leap said as he wrestled to gain control of the net along with Rick and the guide. He shook his head. "Indiana Jones, you were supposed to wait for me to go inside the temple."

"An ambulance," I said. "Call for an ambulance."

I knelt next to Lane on the uneven rocks. I cradled his head in my hands. Blood seeped from his chest.

"No ambulance come here, miss," the local guide said.

I called out for one of the men to give me their shirts to press to Lane's wound.

Mr. Leap made sure the other men had a firm grip on Abby beneath the net, then ran to my side. His shirt was off by the time he reached me. The way he applied the right amount of pressure to the wound told me this wasn't the first time he'd done so. At least one of us was calm.

"Stay with me," I whispered to Lane.

"I'm sorry, Jones," he whispered back. His eyes fluttered shut.

CHAPTER 46

The next day, Abby was sitting in jail, and Lane was recuperating in our Siem Reap hotel courtyard. He'd been treated in Thailand overnight and insisted on coming back.

Abby's knife had gone through his clavicle and hadn't punctured a lung. He'd stayed the night under a doctor's care at a local facility but hadn't needed to be evacuated to a larger hospital.

Mr. Leap had accepted our large tip of thanks and would now be able to buy his fiancé a bracelet in the night market, though he picked out a different one.

I made sure Lane was comfortable in the lounge chair with pillows, snacks, coffee, water, and several distracting novels, but he didn't look too happy when I stood to leave.

"Be careful," he said.

"Abby is in jail. All I'm doing is finishing this quest."

Rick said he wanted to see things through before he went home to bury his brother, so we were heading back to Banteay Chhmar to follow the map.

I knew why the lines of the map were both squiggly and grid-like—they were a map not *to* a temple, but a map *within* the temple's sprawling complex. The grid was the outer layout, how all temples in the Angkorian style were built with grid-like architecture of concentric walls, and the squiggles reflected the ornate stone carvings that were reference points to follow within the temple grounds. Tina and Leap were coming, too. They were already in the car when I came through the lobby.

"I'm sorry, Jaya," Mr. Leap said, nodding toward Rick in the backseat. "He is looking more like Indiana Jones than you."

"That's all right, *Oum* Leap," I said. I expected Rick to jump in with a quip like "damn straight," but he only acknowledged the remark with a polite nod of his head. The death of his brother was finally sinking in.

"You don't have to come," I said to him.

"The truth is, I couldn't get a flight home until tonight without paying an arm and a leg. Abby wasn't kidding that I need to write a new book."

"I'm not sure how long this will take," Tina said. "We might not make it back until after your flight leaves. You'd better stay behind."

He didn't put up a fight, so I knew he was in bad shape.

Tina was driving us in her car, a tiny model I wasn't familiar with. She turned onto a road going a different direction.

"I think you turned the wrong way," I said.

"We're not going to the temple."

I looked nervously out the window. "What's going on?"

"I'm really sorry about yesterday. I'm so glad your boyfriend is going to be all right."

I began to sweat in spite of the rattling but highly functional air conditioning in the car. I tried to gauge how quickly we were going. Could I jump out and survive?

"We're going to my house," Tina added. "I have something to show you. I'll explain everything there."

"You were supposed to wait for me yesterday," Mr. Leap said.

"You too?" I croaked. "You're in on this?" I closed my eyes. Of course. Tina hadn't been the curator I'd contacted. I remembered that curator Sophea Kim, who I'd contacted first, had an "emergency" the day before, so I was told Tina would be the one to meet with me. And Leap was Tina's cousin.

"Oh no!" Tina said. "Jaya, you have the wrong impression. Leap and I don't have anything to do with that murderer. What we do have is the answer to the riddle you've been trying to solve."

"You sent your cousin to spy on us." I tried to catch Leap's eye, but he took a sudden interest in his fingernails.

"I've been so careful all these years, I couldn't let a good first impression affect my better judgment. I had to know for certain that I could trust you." She pulled off the road and parked in front of a modest house.

She ushered us into the house and offered tea. I was going to decline except my throat was so constricted I could barely speak. Leap and I made the most awkward small-talk imaginable while we waited for Tina to return.

She came back ten minutes later with a gorgeous French tea set, including a tea cozy resting over the teapot.

"I'm starving, Leap," she said. "Could you take my car and get us some lunch?"

Leap felt bad about what had happened the day before, so he made sure he knew exactly what I wanted before leaving.

"You're not hungry," I said once he left.

"No. But it's not a good idea for him to see what I'm about to show you." She removed the tea cozy, and it wasn't a tea pot beneath. Like a *naga* guardian, the fabric was protecting something: a carving of prince Kaundinya with inlaid ruby eyes and a sapphire-eyed *nagini* princess Soma.

The sandstone carving was more detailed than those at temples, because it wasn't a bas-relief carved only on one side of the stone. The prince and princess stood on a small boat, bow and arrows in each of their hands, looking fondly at each other.

My own eyes grew as wide as the gemstone eyes of the prince and princess. "Is this what I think it is?"

She nodded. "They've been waiting all these years for the *naga* king guardian to be returned to them."

CHAPTER 47

"You're familiar with the world of museum curation and art antiquity authentication?" Tina asked.

"A bit."

"This treasure came across my path many years ago in New York. Not through public channels, but through people who know of my interest in Cambodian treasures. It didn't have proper provenance, since I'm pretty sure it was looted from Banteay Chhmar during the rule of the Khmer Rouge, so the owner couldn't put it up for a legal auction. But I knew—I knew it was real and that it needed to be returned to Cambodia. I didn't want it for myself. I wanted it for a Cambodian museum. But with the sketchy credentials of the seller, I knew it would be a bureaucratic nightmare."

I coughed. "I might know a thing or two about those."

She smiled. "I know you do. Remember, I looked you up. As soon as Sophea told me what you were interested in, I got nervous and looked into you. This was the day before you arrived, near the end of our workday. Based on who you were, I wondered...So I told Sophea about a possible acquisition for the museum. I made it sound far more enticing than it really was, so she'd feel the need to look into it right away, and I could offer to speak with you instead. I needed to find out what you knew about this treasure that had both blessed and wrecked my life."

"How did you get it?" I asked, my eyes drawn again to the smiling princess with sapphire eyes.

"I didn't leave the Met for the reason I told you. Not exactly. I really did get divorced and was sick of New York. But both came about because I spent my last dime on buying the prince and princess from the seller, privately. My husband was furious. He didn't understand. We got divorced. I would have had to start from scratch in one of the world's most expensive cities, plus keep the treasure safe when it had no legal provenance."

"Siem Reap is a lot less expensive and more beautiful," I said.

She smiled. "When I met with you and learned you knew about the protector *naga* that's supposed to hold the prince and princess, I was going to tell you. But when Devi said there was another person looking for the royal couple, I didn't know what to do."

"So you kept an eye on me, and then asked Mr. Leap to do so too."

"We didn't know there was a killer." She shook her head and closed her eyes. "I'm so sorry about what happened to Lane. We thought you were being protective of your discovery when you said dangerous people might be after it."

"It was never my discovery," I said. Just as Frenchman Henri Mouhut hadn't "discovered" Angkor, I hadn't discovered this bejeweled Cambodian treasure.

"But you know where the *naga* king statue that holds the prince and princess is," Tina said. "Leap said you knew about the family who'd looted it. You can reunite the treasure?"

I looked at her hopeful expression. The woman who'd sacrificed so much for this.

"I think I know where it is," I said, "but it'll take me several hours to make sure I'm right." With everything I'd heard and figured out the previous day, I thought I knew where the *naga* king was. But I'd been wrong about so much lately, I had to be certain.

"A few hours is nothing," she said. "But when you find it, I have a favor to ask. I don't care about the money I spent buying this under the table. I have a good life here. I don't need money. But I want to return the treasure to Cambodia and my museum."

"I'm already there with you." I squeezed her hand. "We'll

reunite the *naga* king with the prince and princess before we present them to your museum publicly. The family who possessed the snake sculpture never reported it stolen, since they knew it was looted. So if I'm right—"

"You'll be right."

"If I'm right, we can suggest the looted items were found together. With nobody disputing it or claiming it. It'll be Cambodia's property."

The missing *naga* king that had vanished from the Durant mansion in Paris. I now had all the information I needed to know where it was. And I knew who could help me figure out if I was right about this as well—if I wasn't too late this time.

Sébastien pretended he didn't mind being awakened in the middle of the night. But I could tell he wasn't lying when he said he'd be more than happy to drive one of his Porsches back to Paris (the Panamera again, since we told him he'd need room in the trunk). This time he took Fitz. I wasn't sure about that, but if the man would be sticking with Sébastien, he should know his true nature. If he didn't know about Sébastien's spirit of adventure yet, it was time he learned.

That night, Tina and I paced around the hotel room that Lane and I shared, driving Lane crazy, while we awaited Sébastien's phone call.

"You were right," he said when he called that night. "It was tricky to get past the security system that had been fixed, but together we were able to do it. We found the Serpent King at the bottom of the grandfather clock."

The clock that was one of the pieces of French furniture he'd had custom made when he was living in Cambodia. The clock had stopped working just a few minutes past the time when Lane watched Marc die the first time, while Lane went up into the attic to look for the person who'd supposedly killed his friend.

Marc moved the statue into the clock that his own ancestor

Aristide had used to get the Naga King out of Cambodia. That's how the serpent had made its way to France after Aristide's death from a fever in Cambodia.

I figured it out because if there was no logical way for the statue to have left the house, then the only explanation was that it hadn't left. The oversize clock with the pendulum was at the bottom of the stairs. Since the statue was heavy, Marc must have decided it would be easier to transfer it to the ground floor for quick transfer to the gurney. So after Lane had gone to the attic he moved the statue to the clock, as an intermediate spot before his accomplices arrived. When Marc went back upstairs to lie down and pretend to be dead, Abby snuck out of her hiding spot (which could have been any number of closets since she knew the house well) and pushed him down the stairs. She hadn't seen him putting the statue inside the clock. But because the pendulum had been moved, the clock stopped working.

There were no secret panels that Sébastien had missed. Bas-relief carvings have flat backs. The statue was hiding in plain sight as a simple weighted stone base of the large clock, as it had hidden in plain sight on its sea voyage to France.

The Durant family moved out of the house in haste, so nobody cared that the clock had stopped, and the statue was never found. When we'd searched the house, we were looking for evidence of how someone could have faked a ghost and gotten away with the crime. Instead, the supposedly haunted house that pushed Lane Peters to move on from his past life of crime was again giving us an unexpected gift.

CHAPTER 48

Sébastien and Fitz decided they wanted to come to Cambodia for New Year's. If an eccentric retired magician wanted to bring a trunk full of his old magic acts with him to Cambodia, so be it, the customs officials thought. I cringed when I learned the *naga* king would be dressed in a vampire cape as a disguise, but that meant he'd soon be reunited with the treasure he was meant to be guarding. The *naga* statue and its daughter and son-in-law with gemstone eyes would be reunited and displayed in the Angkor National Museum. With no bureaucracy to speak of.

Lane wasn't yet fit to travel home, or to visit his mom in Europe, so he and I celebrated Christmas in Cambodia. Beyond the Christmas decorations at hotels and the marketing aimed at persuading the younger generation to buy each other gifts, the Christmas festivities in the primarily Buddhist country were low-key. Which was perfect. All I wanted to do was sleep for days.

For a man recovering from a heroic knife wound (Lane) and now-humbled woman who'd kinda sorta found a treasure (me), our low-key Christmas meant sitting on the hotel's shaded patio in the moderate warmth, listening to a live band of musicians playing a combination of traditional Khmer music and Western Christmas songs, and eating sour mango salad with green bell peppers and plenty of spicy, bright red bird chilies. Back at the room, red stockings filled with mini mince pies inside were waiting on our pillows.

"I'm sorry I didn't know we'd be here for Christmas or I'd have bought you something," Lane said.

"You did. You jumped in front of a knife for me." If that sacrifice didn't represent the spirit of Christmas, I didn't know what would. His heroic deed was especially meaningful across the world from home, in this land where legend had it that a magical kingdom was created when a foreigner had proved his worth to the woman he loved.

"I was also thinking," I added, "that I haven't opened that envelope you gave me yet. I think I'll do that now."

He raised an eyebrow. "You're ready?"

"Just this week, I've been threatened and manipulated by one of my idols, chased through the jungle and watched you nearly die, and had my ego put in check by failing to find what I was after because it had already been found. I'm ready for anything."

I popped the mini mince pie in my mouth and opened the envelope. Inside were three printouts, each with a hand-written note scrawled in the margin.

The first was a copy of a living trust, specifying the huge sum of money Lancelot Caravaggio Peters could receive beginning on his twenty-first birthday. My throat went dry as I looked at the number of zeros.

The note in the margin read, *I haven't touched this yet because it's from my father, but it's there if we need it or if we want to use it for the house.*

I stared at him. "Why didn't you tell me?"

He started to shrug, but the pain in his shoulder made him wince. "It feels less legitimate to me than what I made on my own. Legal, but unethical."

The second was two stapled sheets of paper, the top one being a bank statement with identifying information redacted. It wasn't as big as the trust, but it was big enough that I stopped feeling guilty that Lane had gotten us first class tickets to Siem Reap. Stapled behind the statement was a news article from ten years before about a corrupt London financier who had been arrested based on information the authorities found when they were called in to investigate the theft of millions of dollars' worth of jewels at his home. The scrawled note next to the article read, *No regrets.*

The third item in the envelope was a list of charities I thought highly of. The note read, *Your choice. Robin H.*

I glanced up. "Embracing your inner Robin Hood?"

"You missed one last thing."

Behind the last printout was indeed a small sheet of paper I'd overlooked. It was a skillfully drawn sketch of a pack of cigarettes with an X through it. The handwritten text stated, *I might fail, but I'm trying.*

"I don't want you to change for me," I said, and I realized I meant it completely.

"I'm not. Smoking is a bad habit. As for everything else, I don't regret what I've done. But after our fight, you got me thinking about how I've never touched my father's money. It could be better used by some of those charities than sitting untouched in a bank."

"And you're paying for the Berkeley house with the payments from your own exploits."

"That's me, Jones."

"I know."

"I'll also be putting up the Paris apartment for sale to cover the cost."

"Don't," I said.

"Don't?"

"I don't want to change you. I also don't want you to do this on your own. I've gotten enough money from finder's fees and rewards the past couple of years that I want to be your partner with this house. When we move in together, I want it to be a place that's truly both of ours."

"You said 'when,' not 'if.'"

"I suppose I did."

CHAPTER 49

Two weeks later

The new semester would be starting soon.

I was finished with my grading. Becca's research had been stellar, aside from the real letter she'd used falsely, which wasn't included in her final paper. But I learned she would also be taking a leave of absence for the spring semester, no doubt to process what she'd learned about her mother. She'd been seeking revenge for seven years against the wrong person.

The dean of faculty called me to a meeting in his office, so I walked the six blocks to where I'd parked my car and drove to campus.

I didn't think I'd gotten any bad publicity for my latest discovery, which wasn't even my discovery. Vincent Coronado had now been identified as the body in the bay, though I could hardly be blamed for that. And if anyone took issue with my being a fan of Rick Coronado novels, that was their problem, not mine. I was no longer going to hide the spines of my favorite fiction. Rick's books were displayed proudly next to my academic books.

I'd forgiven Rick. Sort of. I still loved his books, though I wished I hadn't met him under these circumstances. I'd learned I wanted to be friends with Gabriela Glass, not Rick Coronado.

Rick had lost two of the people closest to him. He mourned the loss of his brother. Even though Rick knew Vincent was a sleazy guy in many ways, he blamed himself because of his own early success that Vincent could never attain. Personally I didn't think sibling rivalry should justify Vincent's actions, but Rick had accepted his brother for who he was.

Harder to wrap his head around was Abby's betrayal. Rick had grown up with her in the strange world of publishing for more than half his life, and he'd been in love with her for much of that time. She'd been the reason he wanted to find the Cambodian treasure he believed existed.

But from the news reports that showed his Ithaca neighbor who was now watching his dog Clifford, a tiny woman who masterfully managed the huge mastiff, I thought he'd be just fine in time. As for whether he'd write again, that future remained uncertain.

As was mine.

I knocked on the dean's door.

"Jaya! Good, good. Thanks for meeting with me. In person is best for some things, don't you think?" He offered me a seat on the stiff gray couch across from his desk. It was not meant to inspire prolonged visits with the busy man.

"Sure. Why did you want to see me?" I tried to get comfortable on the unfriendly cushions.

"I'd like you to submit your tenure paperwork this week before the new semester begins."

"I don't have all my requirements together yet. But thank you for suggesting it. I know Naveen applied. He told me himself."

"I appreciate your speaking up on his behalf about that false accusation. That plagiarizing student will not be returning to the program in the spring."

"Glad to help."

"Not everyone would have done that, you know. I know you and Naveen think there's only enough funding for one of you to get tenure."

"Isn't that the case?"

The dean sat back in his leather desk chair. "Yes. Yes it was. Until last week. It appears you've impressed some important people."

I sighed. "I can't take responsibility for finding the Kambuja statue. And the stone *naga* protector statue I found wasn't a historical find, it was simply a missing object." I didn't add that it was only possible for me to solve the crime of the disappearing statue because of things I'd learned from Gabriela Glass novels, not from academia.

"This has nothing to do with how you spent your winter break in France and Cambodia."

"It doesn't?"

"Nice work cultivating Wesley Oh to study history."

Cultivating? That was an odd word choice for the dean. "He's really enthusiastic and smart," I said. "I don't know if he'll major in history, though." Although Wesley did tell me he had ideas for how he might locate specific sunken ships under San Francisco. I could hardly wait to see what he'd find.

"He declared his major when he registered for spring semester," the dean said. "It's history. His mother is incredibly happy that he's finally fallen in love with school. Apparently Wesley almost dropped out a couple of times. You're the reason he didn't. You know who Wesley's mother is, don't you?"

I shook my head.

The dean looked taken aback. "Really? That's not why you helped him?"

"I hope I help all my students." This conversation was getting stranger and stranger.

"Wonderful. Wonderful! I'm glad you're the person I thought you were."

The dean explained that Wesley Oh wasn't exactly the starving college student I'd assumed him to be. His mother was a tech billionaire in the Silicon Valley, just south of San Francisco. Someone with so much money that of course she'd donate some of it to the university department and the professor who'd helped her son.

The dean sent me on my way so he could get other work done,

leaving me to get the rest of the details from Wesley himself. Who luckily was on his cell phone every waking hour of the day, and probably while he was sleeping as well.

Wesley's mom, Nina Oh, was a woman with brilliant ideas and some questionable business practices that Wesley wanted nothing to do with. Wesley accepted tuition money from his family but wouldn't take anything beyond that. But since he'd never held a job before college, he was terrible at keeping one, so he was constantly broke. Wesley had grown up around computer engineers, which is where he'd gotten the *naga bandham* Cobra Lock idea for the project Naveen had rejected.

When Wesley told his mom about me, Nina Oh decided to donate money to the university to create a chair for real world historians—history professors who didn't confine themselves to the halls of academia. After I submitted my tenure paperwork, I would become the first endowed chair. The deal was that I had to teach at least one advanced course per year to help the university attract top-notch students, but beyond that I wasn't confined to a specific classroom schedule and was free to explore and see where history took me.

Now all I had to do was submit my tenure paperwork as a formality, and I'd be Associate Professor Jaya Anand Jones, Oh Chair of Real World History.

CHAPTER 50

I was dreading telling Nadia that I'd decided to move out. I knew she'd easily find another renter in spite of the not-quite-legal status of the apartment. The reason I didn't want to have the conversation is that we'd become good friends. I wasn't leaving an apartment. I was putting in motion the end of an era. Nadia had been there for me in tough times, and we'd solved a historical mystery together.

"Come on," Sanjay said for the fifth time. He'd been trying to get me off the couch since he'd arrived for moral support.

"It's not only Nadia I'm abandoning," I said, "but the neighborhood."

"You curse the parking situation on a daily basis."

"True, but will I find another barista who doesn't raise a pierced eyebrow when I order my favorite off-menu sandwich?"

"That gross peanut butter and egg thing? You need to move on from *that*."

"Miles and Tamarind are only together because Miles lives down the street and they met through me."

Sanjay flipped his bowler hat onto his head and pulled me up from my spot on the sofa. "Meaning your job here is done."

"Fair enough." I looped my hand around Sanjay's elbow, and we headed downstairs.

"Come in!" Nadia called after Sanjay's hearty rap on the door knocker.

When we stepped inside, she wasn't alone.

"Jack!" I ran up to Nadia's paramour and embraced him. The

edges of his bushy mustache scratched my cheek. "I haven't seen you around in ages."

"Because you're always jetting off somewhere new."

I let go of him and laughed. "I believe that's what's known as the pot calling the kettle black. It's good to see you."

"You too, kiddo." The lines around Jack's eyes crinkled as his smile lit up.

Jack Dalton had been Nadia's on-again off-again significant other for as long as I'd known her. I couldn't remotely guess their ages—they could have been anywhere from their late fifties to their eighties. Their stories (which I wasn't entirely sure were true, but I wouldn't put it past them) led me to believe they were on the older side, but their joy for life kept them young. Sometimes I felt like Jack was younger than me.

"This Sanjay?" Jack asked. "You look like your posters."

"Nice to meet you." Sanjay shook Jack's hand warmly. "I was beginning to think you were a Snuffleupagus."

Nadia frowned. "Jack is much more handsome than a Snuffleupagus."

"Nadia asked me to come over since I'm manly and brave." He looked at her with mischievous eyes. "I'm selling my old plane and retiring. We were thinking it might be nice to move in together."

"That's wonderful," I said.

"Almost," Nadia said. "Almost wonderful. Jack needs a studio space for all the items he now keeps in an airplane hanger, but there is no room in this house."

"You're selling it?" Sanjay asked. "A Victorian in this part of the city will make you a wealthy wom—"

"You can't sell it," I cut in. "You've put so much love into this place since you bought it decades ago. I know how much you love this place. You can't—"

"She's not selling," Jack said. "She refused to be a bad guy either. We were hoping we might help you find a bigger place to live. That way Nadia and I can have the attic apartment as part of our house. Just the two of us here together."

Sanjay burst out laughing.

"It is funny that Jaya will be homeless?" Nadia asked. Her Russian accent became thicker when she was agitated. Her eyes narrowed as she spoke, and she put a protective arm around my shoulders.

"Actually," I said, "I already have a place in mind for myself. It's perfect for you and Jack to have the house to yourselves."

Sanjay lifted his bowler hat from his head and pulled a full bouquet of fresh roses from within. Don't ask me how he does it. I still have no idea. "We wish you both all the happiness in the world."

Sanjay and I took our leave. On the front porch, he stopped me and gave me a hug.

"What was that for?" I asked.

"Because I don't have another bouquet of flowers in my hat, but I wish you all the happiness in the world as well. Both of you. Now isn't there somewhere you're supposed to be?"

There was.

Normally Sanjay and I would be playing at the Tandoori Palace that night, but Raj had finally decided to retire. We'd had a last-minute big celebration on New Year's Eve at the restaurant that was also a bon voyage retirement party for Raj.

Head chef Juan was the natural person to take over, and that's why Raj had decided the restaurant would be in good hands and he could enjoy retirement. Juan was toying with changing the name from Tandoori Palace to "Odisha to Oxaca," to emphasize how he'd be incorporating more fusion dishes that combined Indian and Mexican flavors. Sanjay and I weren't sure the name was quite right, even though the word "dish" inside the spelling of the Indian state of Odisha and Juan's graphic designer girlfriend made a cool logo that highlighted "dish." Juan was still playing with ideas before the grand opening that would take place in a couple of months.

Since the restaurant was closed in the meantime, I had other evening plans.

* * *

I met Lane at the Berkeley house. The stresses of the world slipped away as I walked through the ivy-wrapped arch and walked up the winding path to the Tudor house.

Lane had only recently gotten back to California. He'd stayed longer in Cambodia than I had because he needed more recuperation in the warmth and I needed to get back to my university responsibilities.

I found him in the backyard, watching the sunset over the San Francisco skyline and the Golden Gate Bridge. A light wind was blowing, but the ghostly fog from December had been replaced by a crisp, clear January.

I snuck up behind him and wrapped my arms around his waist. Gently, because of his injury, but not too gently. I'm only human. He turned around and kissed me. Electricity shot through my body whenever he kissed me, distracting me from the world around me. I was only vaguely aware of something wrapping around my wrist.

When I opened my eyes I saw what it was. "You can't—"

"It's glass," Lane said. "The ruby is a glass replica of the Rajasthan Ruby bracelet you saw. As for the real one, it's going to a museum. One of your choosing. It'll be anonymously donated, of course."

"Of course." The scent of sandalwood washed over me as I kissed him.

When we pulled apart and I opened my eyes, the orange sky had nearly turned indigo. A light on the back porch cast light over most of the backyard. A canopy of trees flanked the two sides of the yard that adjoined neighboring properties, and a small patio sat directly behind the house, but most of the yard wasn't landscaped.

"This space has so much potential," I said. Not that I knew how to plant anything.

"I know. I was thinking this back patio would be the perfect place for the wedding."

I turned from the twilight sky to face him. "Whose wedding?"

"Ours." His chameleon hazel eyes were hopeful.

"Mr. Peters, are you proposing?"

"I need to tell you…I wasn't completely forthcoming when I said I was going to stay in Cambodia recuperating that whole time. On my way home, I had stops to make in Goa and London."

"What's in Goa and London?"

"Not what. Who. Our parents. Your dad is still in Goa, and I had to make up the Christmas trip to see my mom. They both give their blessing."

Lane got down on one knee. He opened a small velvet box, revealing the solitary Rajasthan Ruby, the one that had been freestanding. It was now set in a custom ring.

"Is that what I think it is?" I whispered.

He nodded. "This one isn't glass. It was the only gem all on its own in the dirt on that archaeological dig. It needed a good home. I think I found the perfect one. If you agree. Jones, would you do me the honor of making me the happiest man on earth?"

It might not have been the best day of my life, but it came close.

Author's Note

As is the case with all of my Jaya Jones Treasure Hunt Mysteries, the treasure in *The Glass Thief* is fictional, but it's based in real historical facts, and the settings are described as I experienced them. Therefore, something like these treasures *could* exist and be waiting to be discovered.

A few key details about the history and places in the book are below. Information on these subjects could easily fill multiple books on their own, so I've compiled additional information, suggested reading, and photos on my website, gigipandian.com.

French colonialists traveled to both India and Cambodia, as described in *The Glass Thief*. In 1860, French explorer Henri Mouhot came upon Angkor Wat; he didn't "discover" it, as it hadn't been lost to the Khmer people. Mouhot died of malaria not long afterward, but through his writings, the Western world learned about the temples of Angkor.

Naga is the Sanskrit word for serpent. The semi-divine beings are prominent in the art of India and Cambodia. The *naga* are associated with waterways, and are known to be the guardians of treasure. History and myth are intertwined in the many differing versions of the legend of Brahmin prince Kaundinya and the *nagini* princess Soma, whose union created the kingdom of Kambuja, which became Cambodia. The legends in the novel are but a few of many.

Sadly, historical sculptures have often been looted from Cambodian temples. One high profile example from 2012 saw a sandstone sculpture of a Khmer warrior (listed at a prominent U.S. auction house with an estimate of $2-3 million), which some experts believed was looted during the reign of the Khmer Rouge. There are no easy answers for how to resolve such situations, but wealthy philanthropists have been known to step in to buy back historical treasures to repatriate them to their country of origin.

The Cambodian cities of Siem Reap and Phnom Penh, and the temple ruins of Ankgor Wat, the Bayon, and Banteay Chhmar, are all places well worth visiting. I wrote my locked-room mystery short story "The Cambodian Curse" (available in *The Cambodian Curse & Other Stories*), about a Cambodian sculpture disappearing from a San Francisco museum, at a café in Phnom Penh, after breaking my ankle while exploring Banteay Chhmar.

In India, the *naga bandham* "Cobra Lock" is a real mystery that exists at the Padmanabhaswamy Temple in the Indian state of Kerala. In 2011, a vast treasure was unearthed in the temple—but only a portion of the temple was searched. Untold riches remain hidden in Vault B, which is locked with an iron door that bears the image of a cobra.

In San Francisco, you can follow the Barbary Coast trail and walk above many of the abandoned Gold Rush ships that make up part of the landfill that expanded the city. A detailed map created by the San Francisco Maritime National Historical Park shows the location of nineteenth century sunken ships.

Jaya learned first-hand about the sunken ships under San Francisco in *Pirate Vishnu*, the second Jaya Jones Treasure Hunt Mystery, when she discovered the secrets of her great grand uncle, the first of the Indian side of her family to travel to the United States shortly before San Francisco's Great Earthquake of 1906.

There's so much fascinating world history that remains a mystery. Historian Jaya Jones has plenty to keep her occupied for the foreseeable future.

GIGI PANDIAN

USA Today bestselling and multi-award-winning author Gigi Pandian is the child of cultural anthropologists from New Mexico and the southern tip of India. She spent her childhood traveling around the world on their research trips, and now lives outside San Francisco with her husband and a gargoyle who watches over the garden. Gigi writes the Jaya Jones Treasure Hunt mysteries, the Accidental Alchemist mysteries, and locked-room mystery short stories. Her debut novel, *Artifact*, was awarded a Malice Domestic Grant and named a Best of 2012 Debut by Suspense Magazine, and her mysteries have also been awarded the Agatha, Rose, Lefty, and Derringer awards. Learn more and receive a free novella by signing up for Gigi's email newsletter at gigipandian.com/newsletter.

**The Jaya Jones Treasure Hunt Mystery Series
by Gigi Pandian**

<u>Novels</u>

ARTIFACT (#1)
PIRATE VISHNU (#2)
QUICKSAND (#3)
MICHELANGELO'S GHOST (#4)
THE NINJA'S ILLUSION (#5)
THE GLASS THIEF (#6)

<u>Short Stories</u>

THE LIBRARY GHOST OF TANGLEWOOD INN
THE CAMBODIAN CURSE & OTHER STORIES

Henery Press Mystery Books

And finally, before you go...
Here are a few other mysteries
you might enjoy:

STAGING IS MURDER

Grace Topping

A Laura Bishop Mystery (#1)

Laura Bishop just nabbed her first decorating commission—staging a 19th-century mansion that hasn't been updated for decades. But when a body falls from a laundry chute and lands at Laura's feet, replacing flowered wallpaper becomes the least of her duties.

To clear her assistant of the murder and save her fledgling business, Laura's determined to find the killer. Turns out it's not as easy as renovating a manor home, especially with two handsome men complicating her mission: the police detective on the case and the real estate agent trying to save the manse from foreclosure.

Worse still, the meddling of a horoscope-guided friend, a determined grandmother, and the local funeral director could get them all killed before Laura props the first pillow.

Available at booksellers nationwide and online

Visit www.henerypress.com for details

THE HOUSE ON HALLOWED GROUND

Nancy Cole Silverman

A Misty Dawn Mystery (#1)

When Misty Dawn, a former Hollywood Psychic to the Stars, moves into an old craftsman house, she encounters the former owner, the recently deceased Hollywood set designer, Wilson Thorne. Wilson is unaware of his circumstances, and when Misty explains the particulars of his limbo state, and how he might help himself if he helps her, he's not at all happy. That is until young actress Zoey Chamberlain comes to Misty's door for help.

Zoey has recently purchased The Pink Mansion and thinks it's haunted. But when Misty searches the house, it's not a ghost she finds, but a dead body. The police suspect Zoey, but Zoey fears the death may have been a result of the ghost...and a family curse. Together Misty and Wilson must untangle the secrets of The Pink Mansion or submit to the powers of the family curse.

Available at booksellers nationwide and online

Visit www.henerypress.com for details

FATAL BRUSHSTROKE

Sybil Johnson

An Aurora Anderson Mystery (#1)

A dead body in her garden and a homicide detective on her doorstep...Computer programmer and tole-painting enthusiast Aurora (Rory) Anderson doesn't envision finding either when she steps outside to investigate the frenzied yipping coming from her own back yard. After all, she lives in a quiet California beach community where violent crime is rare and murder even rarer.

Suspicion falls on Rory when the body buried in her flowerbed turns out to be someone she knows—her tole-painting teacher, Hester Bouquet. Just two weeks before, Rory attended one of Hester's weekend seminars, an unpleasant experience she vowed never to repeat. As evidence piles up against Rory, she embarks on a quest to identify the killer and clear her name. Can Rory unearth the truth before she encounters her own brush with death?

Available at booksellers nationwide and online

Visit www.henerypress.com for details

I SCREAM, YOU SCREAM

Wendy Lyn Watson

A Mystery A-la-mode (#1)

Tallulah Jones's whole world is melting. Her ice cream parlor, Remember the A-la-mode, is struggling, and she's stooped to catering a party for her sleezeball ex-husband Wayne and his arm candy girlfriend Brittany. Worst of all? Her dreamy high school sweetheart shows up on her front porch, swirling up feelings Tally doesn't have time to deal with.

Things go from ugly to plain old awful when Brittany turns up dead and all eyes turn to Tally as the murderer. With the help of her hell-raising cousin Bree, her precocious niece Alice, and her long-lost-super-confusing love Finn, Tally has to dip into the heart of Dalliance, Texas's most scandalous secrets to catch a murderer before someone puts Tally and her dreams on ice for good.

Available at booksellers nationwide and online

Visit www.henerypress.com for details

3 1901 06188 1654

CPSIA information can be obtained
at www.ICGtesting.com
Printed in the USA
LVHW020330121119
636966LV00015B/50/P